A
TREE
OR A
PERSON
OR A
WALL

[STORIES]

ALSO BY MATT BELL

In the House upon the Dirt between the Lake and the Woods

Scrapper

A
TREE
OR A
PERSON
OR A
WALL

[STORIES]

Matt Bell

Published by
Soho Press, Inc.
853 Broadway
New York, NY 10003

Library of Congress Cataloging-in-Publication Data
is available upon request.

ISBN 978-1-61695-523-6
eISBN 978-1-61695-524-3

Interior design by Janine Agro, Soho Press, Inc.

Printed in the United States of America

10 9 8 7 6 5 4 3 2 1

To Michael Czyzniejewski,
with gratitude and friendship

Why does tragedy exist? Because you are full of rage. Why are you full of rage? Because you are full of grief.

— Anne Carson, Grief Lessons

CONTENTS

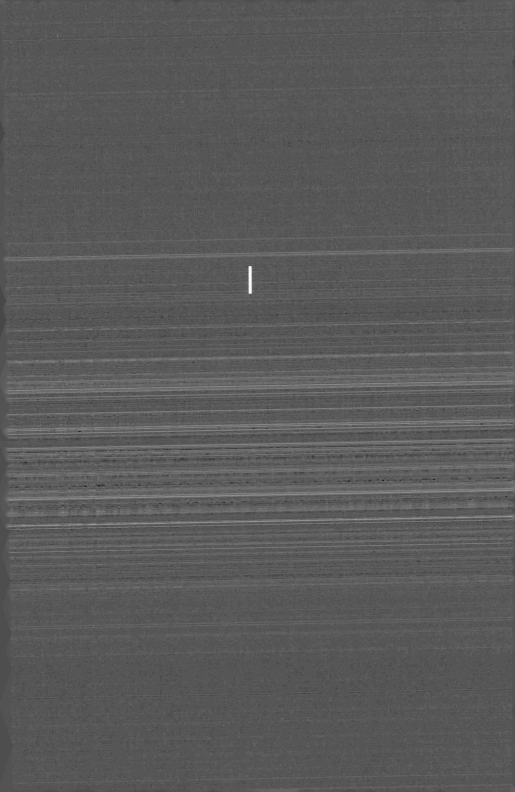

A Tree or a Person or a Wall

E VEN BEFORE THE MAN WITH rough hands brought the boy to the locked room, even then there was always already the albino ape sitting on the chair beside the nightstand, waiting for the man and the boy to come.

Once inside the room, the man with rough hands carried the boy across the musty carpet and laid him upon the bed, where he told the boy he was not allowed to leave, that if he tried there would be consequences.

The man said, I do not want to restrain you, but I do have a number of restraints available.

He said, I do not want to hurt you, and then he pointed to the ape.

The ape picked a melon from a bowl on the nightstand and wrenched the fruit's rind open with its white-furred fists. While it licked the juice from its pale fingers, the man with rough hands said again, I do not wish to hurt you, and then he left the locked room for the hallway beyond its door.

After a while, the boy sat up on the bed. He tucked his scraped knees under his chin, wrapped his bruised arms around his legs, and then he stared at the ape.

He stared at the ape, and the ape stared back.

———

True to his word, the man with rough hands did not further hurt the boy, not in any of the ways the boy was afraid the man might.

Everything the man with rough hands meant to do to the boy was done before they arrived in the locked room, and so when the man with rough hands did come, it was only to feed the boy and the albino ape, and then to watch.

For the boy, the man with rough hands made cheese sandwiches and tomato soup.

For the ape, he brought bowlfuls of melons or else walnuts, both of which the ape devoured as if starving, as if it had been a long time since he had been fed.

After the boy ate, he watched the ape and watched the ape and watched and watched the ape.

The boy watched the ape because it was better than watching the man with rough hands, who himself stood in the corner and scratched his arms and legs and watched the boy eat, then watched the boy sit on the bed beside his plate, then watched the boy watching the ape.

In this way, he was not just the man with rough hands but also the man who watches.

The boy saw that the man was both of these people, but still thought of him as the man with rough hands, because it was the man's hands that had brought him to the locked room, that had done whatever had been done to his head, which ached and also buzzed.

The man watching didn't mean anything else to the boy. He was just watching, and what could that hurt? It was a nothing, an action shaped like a void, and so the man with rough hands never became the man who watches, even though there would be much more watching than there had ever been rough handling.

There was something wrong with the boy's head that made him unable to remember as well as he wanted. After the bruises on his arms and the scrapes on his legs healed, he realized he no longer knew if there were other people outside the locked room who would miss him, or if it had always been him and the man with rough hands and the albino ape, always he and he and it.

Sometimes, when the man with rough hands fed the boy very late in the day, after the setting of the sun, then the boy was surprised to see the man, because he had forgotten him too.

The boy knew it was after dark because when the door to the locked room was opened the boy could see the hallway past the door, and in that hallway there was a window through which it was sometimes light and sometimes not.

Outside that window was something else, something seen from too far away and for too short a time for the boy to be sure of what it was.

The boy did not know exactly, but he thought it was either a tree or a person or a wall, and although it could be all three it was probably only one.

The boy's bed was broken, bent inward on its frame so that the mattress sagged in the middle, leaving his back aching most mornings.

What the boy could not be sure of was whether he had broken the bed or whether it had already been broken.

He thought that if he broke the bed, then he would remember doing so, but perhaps not, considering the buzzing in his ears and the screeching of the albino ape.

Whenever the man with rough hands was gone, the boy lay back on the bed and ran his fingers through his hair, looking for the dent or crease or crack that might account for the buzzing, for the lack the buzzing attended.

Sitting on the bed, the boy ran his fingers through his hair, while in its chair the albino ape cracked open its melons, the motions of ape and boy so synchronized that sometimes the boy thought they were the same, that the noise of the rinds giving way was the sound of his own fingers nearing the crevice in his skull into which he or his memories had fallen and would continue to fall, unless he found the crack and stopped up its slow leak.

At first, the boy did not talk to the albino ape, but sometimes the ape talked to him. What the ape said, it was not words or sentences, or not just words and sentences.

What the ape said, it sounded like EEEEECHHHHH-SCRAAAAA.

The albino ape made this sound whenever it wanted the boy to watch it, which was whenever the man with rough hands was not with them in the locked room.

Sometimes the ape wanted to show the boy how it cleaned itself, picking loose the fleas from its fur and flicking them to the carpet, where they stayed only until they could climb onto the boy's bed, where they left his legs pocked with red bites or else scratches from his own too-long nails.

Sometimes the ape wanted to show the boy how it nearly used the litter box, spraying its urine all over the box, the wall behind the box.

Sometimes the ape wanted him to watch it split another melon rind, to crack another nutshell, as if the boy hadn't already seen those a thousand times.

Sometimes the ape wanted him to watch it masturbate, and this the boy would not, no matter how many times the ape said, EEEEECHHHHHSCRAAAAA.

To distract himself while the ape relieved itself or opened melons or masturbated, the boy tried to remember the shapes of the words he'd once spoken outside the room.

Once, he was sure he'd made words like --- or --- or ------ or -------.

Words like t-k--.

Or like s--e --.

Or h---.

He remembered the amount of air it took to make the word-sounds without remembering the sounds themselves, and so when he made the mouth-shapes the sounds used to come from, nothing came out, or rather nothing he wanted.

More and more, whatever came out of his mouth sounded like EEEEECHHHHHSCRAAAAA and nothing besides.

The buzzing, the ape, and his mouth, all of them were EEEEECHHHHHSCRAAAAA, and the boy was afraid that soon this sound would be all that remained.

He was afraid of this but welcomed it too, because if there was nothing of him but a sound, then how could the man with rough hands keep him trapped any longer?

The man might trap a boy, might lock him in the room with an ape, but could he do the same to a sound, even a sound shaped like a boy?

The man with rough hands would open the door, and then the sound-boy would slip out, into the hallway and through the window in the hallway, where he would use the tree or person or wall to get away.

When the boy could not stand to be alone in his head anymore — trapped inside this cracked skull trapped inside the locked room — then he sat up in the bed and turned toward the ape and made the only sound that still seemed sure.

EEEEECHHHHHSCRAAAAA, the boy said.

EEEEECHHHHHSCRAAAAA, the ape said back.

Now the boy heard words inside the sounds that came from the albino ape's mouth and from his own mouth and from the crack in his head, which he still could not find, and he knew that this was how he could talk to the ape.

The boy said, EEEEECHHHHHSCRAAAAA, and asked the ape its name, using the words his mouth could make only after first making this other, louder sound.

The ape said, EEEEECHHHHHSCRAAAAA, and replied, Sixes.

My name is Sixes, the ape said, and the boy nodded because that was the ape's right name.

I don't have a name, said the boy, but the ape shook his head and said, EEEEECHHHHHSCRAAAAA.

Yes, you do, said the ape named Sixes. You have a name and the man with rough hands knows it.

The ape said, One of the ways the man hurt you was the keeping of your name, the making of you to forget.

He has your name, but a name is not all you have, and its absence is not all that hurts you.

Whatever you do, don't also forget the window, as you have forgotten so much else. If he takes the window from you, then we will both be lost.

The ape named Sixes said, EEEEECHHHHHSCRAAAAA, and then they were both quiet while the boy practiced remembering giving his name to the man with rough hands.

It hadn't happened in the locked room, of that he was sure. Where had it happened then? Through the window? On the other side of that smear of glass, where the tree or person or wall was?

Somewhere in the boy's voided memory, the man with rough hands had asked him his name, and the boy had whispered it back, had whispered because he was afraid.

The man with rough hands had smiled, said, It's the right name.

The name I was looking for, he said, and then he said nothing else, only —

Only what? Only EEEEECHHHHHSCRAAAAA?

Only whatever words had been needed to bring the boy to the locked room, where the ape named Sixes and the broken bed and the empty bowl for melons and walnuts had waited.

There was more to what had happened, but what it was

lay on the other side of the window now, and the boy could not reach it with his cracked mind.

The window: that which the ape named Sixes said the boy must not forget.

The boy focused on the window's square shape, on its width slightly greater than the width of his own shoulders.

He focused on its nature, on how it was something that could be seen through, and how on the other side of it there was a tree or a person or a wall.

He focused on how it might be opened, and how once opened he might be able to crawl through it, if only he could get past the man with rough hands.

So he would not forget it again, the boy named the window Escape, and then there were at least two things for which he knew the names.

Inside the locked room, there was an albino ape named Sixes, and in the hallway outside the locked room there was a window named Escape.

In both places there was a man called the man with rough hands, but the boy thought that was not a name, except when, at other times, he thought it was exactly what a name meant.

Also there was himself, who was just the boy, because the man with rough hands had taken his right name away.

The man with rough hands had taken his name, and the boy wondered if the ape named Sixes would help him take it back.

No, said Sixes. I am a prisoner here too, because the man

with rough hands has some power over me too, even as I have some power over him.

The ape named Sixes said this, but when the boy asked him to explain, the ape said only, EEEEECHHH-HHSCRAAAAA, and then returned to its melons and its walnuts.

Knowing the ape was named Sixes did not make the boy less afraid of the ape. It did not give the boy over the ape what the man with rough hands had over the boy, and the boy did not know why.

That night, the boy ate his sandwich and drank his soup and he watched the ape watch the man with rough hands watch him.

He knew it was night because, when the man opened the door to the locked room, the window named Escape was dark.

The tree or person or wall, it was on the other side of that darkness, and the boy could not see it.

Inside the locked room, the boy had never before talked to the man with rough hands, but now he tried.

He said, I want to go home.

He said, I don't want to eat any more sandwiches or drink any more soup.

He said, I don't want to be in this locked room, and I don't want you to watch me either.

The man with rough hands said nothing for a long time, only rubbed the small of his back. Then he walked over to the ape named Sixes and took the ape's right ear in his fingers.

The man with rough hands twisted the ear of the ape named Sixes until the ape screamed EEEEECHHHHH-SCRAAAAA.

The boy screamed too, the normal scream of a small boy.

I take it back, the boy said.

I want to stay.

I'm sorry.

Please don't hurt it again.

And then the boy knew that knowing the name Sixes would not give him any power.

Knowing the name Sixes was only another trap, because while he might have suffered the albino ape to hurt, he would not let the ape named Sixes do the same.

What the boy never forgot: The ape named Sixes. The window named Escape. One because it was always present, and one because it was the only chance of leaving the locked room or, rather, the hallway outside the locked room.

What the boy did forget, and often: the man with rough hands.

The boy always forgot him every night, so that by the time the man came to feed him the next day the man would already again be a surprise, again be something new set to happen twice a day.

The first time was when the window named Escape showed the boy a tree or a person or a wall.

The second time was when it showed him nothing but darkness.

Those were the two times of the day when the boy had

to know about the man with rough hands, but he did not have to know him any other time.

Sometimes the boy could forget on his own, but other times, when the man with rough hands had watched him for too long, then the boy needed help.

When this happened, what the boy would do is lie on the crooked bed with his body straight.

What he would do next was take his hands from behind his back and put them over his eyes.

He would leave his eyes closed and his ears open, and then he would say, Please.

To the ape named Sixes, he would say, Please, sing to me, and then Sixes would put down his melons and sing the EEEEECHHIIHHSCRAAAAA until the boy forgot the man with rough hands and the locked room and his aching back and the fleabites on his arms and legs and everything else besides, everything except for the ape named Sixes and the window named Escape.

With his eyes closed, the EEEEECHHHHHSCRAAAAA sounded like a void so wide the boy could crawl inside, and so that is what the boy did.

He crawled inside the void, but not by leaving the bed, because he was not allowed to leave the bed, not even now.

Inside the void of the sound, there was always only the boy and the ape named Sixes, and nothing else but a floating darkness, the quiet centered inside a song or else a scream, a series of syllables that approximated one or the other.

In the floating darkness, the boy always asked Sixes, How long have I been here?

And Sixes always said, You have always been here.

And the boy always said, That does not seem true.

Oh, the truth, said Sixes.

You did not ask for the truth, said Sixes, always.

And then always the boy was quiet, and then always the boy said, What else would I want?

Comfort, said Sixes. Acceptance. Forgiveness. Succor.

And also, always: EEEEECHHHHHSCRAAAAA.

In the locked room, the man with rough hands had left a bucket for the boy beside the bed, into which the boy was expected to urinate and also to defecate. The boy was careful when he used it not to tumble off the bed, because he thought the ape would not tolerate that, not even now that the boy knew its name.

This was not so hard when the boy only had to urinate, but if he needed to do anything else, he had to hang his rear over the edge of the bed or else risk bringing the sloshing bucket up onto the bed with him, where if he spilled it he would have to live with the mess, because the man with rough hands had not changed the linens once since bringing the boy there.

Changing the linens would mean letting the boy off of the bed, and that, the boy knew, the man with rough hands would not do.

What the boy did not know was whether the ape would not let the man, or if it was the man with the rough hands who ordered the ape.

Once the boy had thought he'd known, but now he thought he did not, because when the man with rough hands was in the room, the ape named Sixes never spoke.

Perhaps the ape was not even named Sixes, then, because the man with rough hands did not seem to know.

And then the man with rough hands stopped coming. The boy did not notice at first, not until he had been hungry for a long time, not until his bucket was full to overflowing.

Not until the bowl of melons on the nightstand had dwindled, until the walnut shells on the floor fell into dust.

Whatever happened to the man with rough hands had happened outside the locked room, and so the boy would never know what word-shapes described the man's end, his capture or his death.

All the boy knew was what the ape named Sixes could tell him, by saying EEEEECHHHHHSCRAAAAA over and over: that the man with rough hands would not return, and that the locked room would stay locked, and also the boy's bucket would not get emptied and his sand-wiches and soup would not be brought, and Sixes would receive no more melons or walnuts.

Worst of all, it meant the boy would not twice a day see the window named Escape, or the tree or person or wall beyond that window.

The boy panicked and said, EEEEECHHHHH-SCRAAAAA, and then EEEEECHHHHHSCRAAAAA and then EEEEECHHHHHSCRAAAAA, which sounded like the hunger in his belly and then the aching in his back and then the itching of fleabites on his legs and his arms.

The ape named Sixes let the boy say EEEEECHHHHH-SCRAAAAA until he exhausted himself, and then it said EEEEECHHHHHSCRAAAAA back.

It said, EEEEECHHHHHSCRAAAAA, but not in the way it had always said it before.

What was different, the boy could not say, not even after the ape named Sixes had already said EEEEECHHHHH-SCRAAAAA many times.

When at last the boy was readied, the ape named Sixes said, The door is locked and can only be unlocked by the man with rough hands.

Or, rather, a man with rough hands.

It said, Once, there was another child in this room. A little boy, as different from you as he was similar.

There was another boy, and there was another man with rough hands.

There was a boy and a man, and I was always here too.

I was here because wherever there is a boy kept in a locked room and a man with rough hands, then I am there.

Because the other is not coming back, I can tell you now that you can leave this place without going through the window you named Escape, but you cannot do so without becoming a man with rough hands, because you cannot open the door to the locked room without becoming such a thing.

You can escape without going through the window, but not without leaving me here to await your return.

One day you will come back, and on that day you will

bring with you a boy, a boy whose boyish hands will be held by your rougher ones.

You will bring me a boy, and I will watch him for you so that when your need is great you might watch him too, and in return you will give me all the melons and walnuts I desire, and then finally you will give me the boy as your man with rough hands has given me you, whether he wanted to or not.

The ape named Sixes said, EEEEECHHHHHSCR- AAAAA, and then he said, Now you know all there is to know, but knowing alone changes nothing else, so if you try to step off the bed as a boy, then I will kill you and you will never see the other side of the door that leads to the hallway that leads to the window.

The boy laid his body down on the broken bed for a long time.

There were no more sandwiches or soup, but after a while the boy did not miss either.

There was no one to empty his bucket, but without food or drink eventually the boy stopped needing to use it anyway.

The boy knew he was supposed to be growing bigger but also that he wasn't, and maybe as long as he didn't try to grow he wouldn't again need to eat or drink or defecate.

Lying in the caved-in rut of the mattress, the boy fit himself into the space left there by the boy the ape named Sixes claimed had been there before, whose own laps around the edges or jumps from the center might have been the ones to break the box springs, crooking the frame boards that bounded them.

The boy thought about this other boy, and he wondered what he looked like.

He held his own hands in front of his face in the dimness of the nightstand lamp, wondered what he himself looked like too.

It had been so long since he'd seen his own face, if he'd ever seen it.

If he'd ever seen it, it had happened outside the locked room, and so he did not remember.

What the boy thought was: What was the name of the thing a boy could look in to see himself?

A window? Was that it?

Was that what it was called?

And if not that, then what?

To the ape named Sixes, the boy said, I cannot remember everything you told me to remember.

He said, There is something wrong with my head and I cannot find it, no matter how many times I feel with my fingers for the crack that lets in the buzzing.

The ape named Sixes bared its yellow teeth in a snarl or else a smile, and then it said EEEEECHHHHHSCRAAAAA, or, maybe, There is not much left to remember.

The ape named Sixes pointed at its white chest with a white finger: Remember that I am an ape named Sixes.

It pointed toward the locked door and said, That is a locked door you cannot reach, and while it is unreached and still locked, then this is the locked room, which you cannot leave.

The ape named Sixes dipped its pale fingers into its bowl

and took out one last melon, and then it cracked the fruit open. It said, Beyond the locked door there is a window, and the window has a name, a name which you gave it and that it never had before. I have named the window Hope, but that is not its right name. It is more like a joke. Do you remember the name you gave it?

The ape named Sixes said, If you have forgotten the window's name, then it is too late for you to be saved, and you will become a man with rough hands, and I will be your ape, and my name will be Sevens.

The ape still named Sixes, it said, What is the window's name?

It said, Boy, do you remember the window's name?

And then the boy thought.

He thought for a long time, and while he thought he searched the nest of his hair with his fingers, hoping to find the crack, to hold its leak shut so he could at last hear something else.

Boy, the ape said.

Boy.

What is the name of the window?

The boy said, The window's name is EEEEECHHH-HIISCRAAΛΛΛ, and before he was even done naming it the ape named Sixes had already begun to stomp and screech upon its chair. The ape flipped over the night-stand, destroying the lamp, their light, and also its own bowl and the half-chewed rinds of the melons, releasing the seep of their juices into the always damp murk of the carpet.

It was dark in the locked room, and in the dark the boy heard the EEEEECHHHHHSCRAAAAA but did not know if it came from his mouth or his head or the ape named Sixes and furthermore he did not know if it mattered which of them it was.

The boy followed the EEEEECHHHHHSCRAAAAA for a long time, first with his ears and then with his body. He followed it around and around his bed, and as he followed it he once again began to grow.

He grew not bigger but older, and he grew older by growing smaller, or at least that was how it felt in the dark.

He did not rest often from the following of the sound, but when he did, he still searched his skull with his fingers, until one day the skin on his face and scalp told him his hands were now rough where once they had been soft, and then the next time he reached for the crack he found a doorknob instead, and when he turned the doorknob he found a hallway with a window.

He walked down the hallway, but not before locking the door behind him, because inside the room was an albino ape that he did not wish to allow to leave.

How he locked the door was he put his mouth to the keyhole and then he said, EEEEECHHHHHSCRAAAAA.

After the door was locked, he again put his mouth to the door, and then he said the name Sixes.

He said, Sixes, I will be back, and I will bring you melons and walnuts.

He said, I promise, and the ape named Sixes said nothing back, because that was no longer its name.

Leaving the door behind, he walked down the hallway,

past the window, through which he had once seen a tree or a person or a wall. At last he knew which of the three it was, but it no longer seemed important. He named what he saw and then he kept walking.

The hallway brought him to another door, another hallway, and then another door, on which was written the many, many syllables needed to sound the word *escape*.

He was free now, he thought, even without going through the door.

He was free to do whatever he wanted, and so he touched his soft face with his rough hands and wondered what he looked like.

It had been so very long since he had seen, and he was sure he had changed very much. More than anything, he wanted to know who he had become, but for that he would need to see his new face. He had been in the locked room for a long time, and in that time he had forgotten the names of so many things. Now he couldn't remember: What was the thing you looked at to see yourself look back?

A window?

A door?

A tree or a person or a wall?

Or a boy named EEEEECHHHHHSCRAAAAA?

Doll Parts

THE YOUNGER SISTER—IF SHE COULD still be called that, since she was no longer anyone's sister, nor younger, lacking an older to be younger than—did not want a girl doll. What she wanted instead was a boy doll, one that could do all the things the brother had once done.

The sister said, The doll must have brown hair. And brown eyes.

It should look like it is the same age as me, and only we will know it's older.

It must have freckles, but not too many freckles.

There is a perfect number of freckles, and that is how many I want my doll to have.

And so the mother sewed—inexpertly but with great care—a boy doll as tall as the girl, with soft cloth limbs chubby with cotton stuffing. With a premade rubber head, on which the mother painted brown hair and brown eyes and not too many freckles, adding a few more when the sister objected to the count. The sister watched impatiently through the long days of the doll's construction, and when it was nearly ready she tore it from the mother's arms, squeezed it to her own small chest, hugging the doll so tight its stuffing pressed at its seams.

The mother said, It's not done yet.

She said, I haven't finished sewing its clothes.

The doll wore only a pair of plain white underpants, imperfectly sewn, unevenly concealing the flat crotch, the just-as-flat buttocks. But the sister didn't care that there was no shirt to cover the doll's chest, no shoes to cover its nearly webbed feet.

Mine? she whispered.

Yes, the mother said. On one condition.

The mother knelt in front of the girl, put her hand on the hard rubber hair of the doll. She said, The doll must never go outside. If you take the doll outside I will take it away and you will never get it back.

The sister squeezed the doll tighter, turned to put her body between the mother and the doll.

But why?

Never. The doll stays inside. You stay with the doll.

Before the brother died, they used to play outside all the time. They played in the front yard and in the backyard and even, sometimes, in the woods that stretched far behind the house, to where the brother said there was another road.

The brother had never taken the sister to see this second, far-off road.

He had wanted to, but she was too afraid to follow.

She was not afraid of the road, although she was not supposed to go near roads either, but of the woods.

Inside the fence was safe. Inside the fence was home.

Outside the fence was everywhere else. Outside the fence was the woods and the road and then whatever was past the woods and the road.

What happened to the brother was that one day the sister had been too sick to play. She had been too sick even to climb out of bed, and so the brother had gone outside to play alone.

The sister did not see him at lunch that day, or at dinner, or at bedtime.

At bedtime, she did not see the father either, only the mother.

Normally, she saw the brother and the father and the mother all together, gathered for a bedtime story selected from a book of tales the brother and sister loved, but tonight there was only the younger sister, only the mother.

When the younger sister asked where the brother was, the mother said the father had gone to find him.

But when the father came back in the morning, he did not have the brother. And now the younger sister wasn't allowed to play outside, the only place the brother might yet be found.

The sister did not say any of this to the mother.

To the mother, what the sister said was, The doll will protect me. It is big and strong and handsome, like brother was. And it is not afraid.

The mother shook her head. The mother said, The doll is so frightened that if you take it outside, then it will stop loving you. The doll will stop loving you, and then I will take it away.

The sister thought about how much the doll looked like the brother, just as she had wanted, and how the brother had not been safe outside either. Once she started thinking about the brother, she could not stop thinking about him, or about his kisses, about how he used to leave his bed and crawl into hers so that he could kiss her cheeks and her lips and her nose. So he could kiss the palms of her hands, the tips of her fingers.

She could not stop thinking about how he had loved her so very much, and how he had told her so every single night while he lay beside her in her bed, even though he was supposed to be in his own bed on the other side of the room. Even though mother said he was too old to sleep with her anymore, that she was too old to let him.

But to the sister, they had not seemed old at all.

The sister thought about the brother, and about how much the brother loved her, and then she decided this was how much she would love the doll.

The mother asked again, Will you keep the doll inside?

The sister told the mother yes, and then for a long time she did not speak to her or anyone else. Not to anyone but the doll.

The doll was hard to carry, with its body heavied with stuffing and its heavier rubber head. If the sister set the doll down in a chair, its head lolled forward onto its chest, or else backward, impossibly, as if the doll's neck had been broken.

The doll was not beautiful, but the sister knew that you

could make an ugly thing beautiful if only you loved it enough, and so she loved the doll very much.

What the girl was trying to do was to learn to love the doll for what it was, as the brother had loved her.

The brother had loved her even though she was the ugly twin, born with her umbilical cord wrapped around her neck, five breathless minutes after the brother.

The brother had loved her even though one of her eyes was slightly lower than the other, even though her voice was not beautiful like his.

Her voice was not something anyone wanted to hear too much of, the mother had once told her, in a moment of exasperation.

Children were better seen but not heard, the mother had said, but the sister knew she was not much good for looking at either.

The brother had loved her even with her straw hair, which she could not help twisting from her head strand by strand by strand, which she could not help swallowing afterward, always three strands at a time.

The girl thought perhaps the brother had been taken away because he was too beautiful, but what she really wondered was whether or not it was because he was too beautiful for her.

When the sister had first asked the mother where the brother had gone, the mother said that the brother was never coming back, which was not at all what the sister had asked.

The mother said that the brother lived inside the

sister now, in her heart, but the sister did not believe this either. If the brother lived within her, she would feel him, would be able to talk to him, to tell him how much she missed him.

The sister didn't ask who had taken the brother, but the mother said that it was God, that he had taken the brother home to heaven. But the sister wasn't stupid. She knew better than that.

It wasn't God that had taken her brother, but a man. Or else God wore a red raincoat with big wooden buttons.

The mother and the father talked about the brother only when they believed the sister was asleep. But sometimes she would leave her bed to sneak into the hallway, where she could listen at the mother and father's bedroom door, because often they talked about the sister instead. That was how the sister knew that the mother and the father thought she rarely talked because the brother was gone. But that was not the only reason.

The other reason was because, home sick on the morning that the brother disappeared, she had seen the man who took the brother at the edge of their backyard, standing just inside the tree line—but also just outside the fence line—and although the sight of him in his red raincoat had made her shake, she said nothing.

She saw the man standing in the few feet of grass between the trees and the fence.

She saw his red raincoat, slick with rain.

She saw the wooden buttons attached to the cords on his hood.

She saw the cords pulled tight, so that the hood was drawn close to the man's head, so that his face could not be seen.

She saw him raise his naked wrist, as if he was checking his watch. The man tapped the space where his watch would have been, as if trying to make a stalled hand move. Then he lowered his watchless arm and walked back into the woods, the woods where the brother had gone to play alone.

Where the man still was, the sister thought.

Where maybe he would always be, she told the doll, the only person she still spoke to, always in whispers. Perhaps the man was still there, only deeper in the woods now, so deep she couldn't see him, so deep no one would ever find him, like they never found the brother.

Although the sister no longer spoke loud enough for the mother or father to hear, she did often whisper to the doll, putting her soft lips to his rubber ear, making the smallest sound she could. She told the doll a great many secrets, almost always having to do with the brother.

The very first secret she told the doll was how she—and only she—knew where the brother was.

How she knew was because she had gone looking for him, after the brother disappeared, but before the mother made the doll.

This was the day the mother wore her black dress and black shoes and black hat. This was the day the father wore a black suit and black tie. Before they left, the father told the sister that she was to stay in the house no matter what, that they would be gone for ninety minutes and then they would come back.

Before they left, the father took a timer from a drawer, wound it, and set it on the table.

He said, Before that timer rings, we'll be back.

He said, Stay inside. Don't answer the door or the telephone. Don't go near the windows. All the doors are locked, but maybe it would be best if you stayed in your room and played quiet.

But when the sister was sure they were gone — when ten minutes had passed, according to the timer — she put on her long red coat and her winter boots, then shoved the timer into the coat's big pocket and went outside.

The sister didn't know where the mother and the father had gone, but she knew that if they were trying to find the brother, they were looking in the wrong place.

The brother wasn't anywhere you could drive to.

The brother was in the woods, with the man.

She hoped she would find the brother waiting alone, so she would not have to see the man again.

She already saw him enough, every time she closed her eyes.

Thinking of his red raincoat meant the sister had to stop in the foyer and pull three strands of hair out of her head, one at a time, swallowing each one in succession until her heart rate returned to normal, until she was able to open the door, able to climb down the steps of the porch and into the front yard.

From the front yard, she walked around the house and into the backyard.

From the close edge of the backyard, she walked to the tree line, the last grassy patch between the yard and the pine straw of the woods.

One, two, three more strands of hair, and then she crossed the tree line.

One, two, three, and then she was able to walk farther into the woods, where there was no path, until, when she turned around, she could not see her house anymore.

The sister took the timer out from her pocket and held it in her hands, close to her mouth, so close her breath fogged its plastic face, so close she could hear the whir of its mechanism. The whir was the sound of time passing, and the sister held it so that she would know how much time she had left, and also so she would have something from home — something that her father and mother had touched, less than an hour ago — to keep her safe.

She knew the straight line she was walking in — a line that, if she turned around upon it, would lead back to her own yard — was probably not the best way to find a person. And so she was not surprised she did not find the brother, only his checkered shirt buried beneath a blanket of snow where no one but she would find it, its buttons torn free of their stitches, its flannel covered in mud and leaves and something else the sister told herself was also mud and leaves.

One, two, three strands of hair, and she was able to pick it up.

One, two, three more, and she was able to press it against her face, to smell the brother's last smell.

Three more hairs and she was able to turn around, to put her back to the place where she had found his shirt.

Her throat itched. She wanted to cough, to vomit the hair ball she felt caught there. She picked another strand. She curled it around her fingers. She pulled, and when the follicle ripped free of her sore scalp, she jumped, not from the pain but from the buzz of the timer, which was going off in her other hand, telling her that now her mother and her father were supposed to be home and that she was supposed to be there waiting for them.

With the timer in one hand and the brother's muddy maybe muddy shirt in the other, the sister ran home in a line exactly as straight as the one she had taken to this place.

She ran until she crossed the tree line, then hurried from the backyard to the front yard, up the porch stairs and into the house.

She yelled, I found his shirt!

I know where he is!

He needs us to go find him!

But the mother and father were not home, even though the timer had gone off, even though the father had promised they would be, and when they came home only a moment later the sister did not forgive them. By then she had already locked the front door and stowed her boots and her coat. By then she had hidden the shirt at the bottom of her toy box, beneath all the other dolls, dolls that did not look like the brother and that she would never touch again, except to move them out of the way whenever she wanted to hold his shirt to her face, hoping to smell something other than the dried mud and dead leaves obscuring all the brother's better scents, missing still.

The sister loved the doll, loved it almost as much as she had once loved the brother, lugging the heavy doll from one room to the next, sitting it in all the brother's favorite spots.

She put the doll in the brother's rocking chair, the one the father had made for him when he was still too small to sit in it, and then she sat in her own identical chair.

She sat the doll at the dinner table, in the seat beside her, and on the couch, where she held its hand while she watched the television.

At night, the sister laid the doll in the brother's bed, pulling the blankets up to its neck, then tucked the blankets under the doll's body. In the morning, she took the doll into the bathroom with her, where the mother drew the line at her taking it into the bathtub. So she sat the doll on the closed toilet seat while she soaked in the tub, and she watched it from the water.

The doll's head fell onto its chest, threatening to pull it forward off the toilet, but usually it stayed where it was.

If it did fall, the sister immediately got out of the tub and righted it, not caring if she dripped across the bathroom's already musty carpet.

The doll was the right size to dress in the brother's clothes, and when the girl changed her own clothes she also changed the doll's. The doll would never grow out of the shirts and pants and shoes the brother had left behind, although the sister was already getting bigger, stretching the dresses she'd worn when the brother was alive.

The doll, she thought, was exactly the size she wanted it to be.

More than anything, she wished she could stay the same

too, that she could somehow stop herself from growing even one inch taller than the doll she loved so much, than the brother the doll had come to replace.

At night, the sister sometimes dreamed about the man in the red raincoat.

In the dreams, she was able to slow down her memories, to see each detail individually, to memorize them as discrete pieces of a whole. She saw that his raincoat had been buttoned all the way to his throat, and that the buttons had not been buttons at all, but wooden toggles painted red and threaded through loops of thick black cord. She saw that the raincoat had a hood, but the man had not pulled the hood up over his head. And yet still she could not remember his face, which she must have seen.

She often woke gasping from these dreams, desperate to reach her head, only to discover her hand already working on its own, shoving strands of her hair into her throat, her fingers choking her before the hair could do the same.

The mother grew used to the sister's silences and her hair pulling and her dragging of the awkward, ugly doll — which she often regretted making — but the father did not. The father accused the mother of encouraging the sister, of making her sicker, but the sister did not know what this meant. The sister did not feel sick, had not been sick since the day the brother was taken. Whenever she heard her parents fighting, she hid the doll under her bed — always her own, never the brother's — and then she climbed in after it, holding the doll in the cramped dark and telling it that she would keep it safe, no matter what, because the parents were incapable of keeping anyone safe. Because they had failed the brother, and because they had not come home the day the timer went off while she was still in the woods, the same woods where the man in the rain-coat lived.

It was during the silence after one of the parents' fights that the sister heard the knock on the house's front door.

She listened intently from the stairs as the policeman told her father and mother what had been found: one part of the brother but not the brother himself.

After the policeman left, the mother collapsed to the liv-ing room floor in tears, while the sister dragged the doll upstairs and laid it upon the brother's bed.

First, she tried removing its right arm with her own hands. When the seams refused to rip, she crept back down the stairs and into the den where the mother kept her craft supplies, her sewing machine with its pedals and spindles. To reach the den, the sister had to sneak by the mother, now crying on the couch, and then again past the father, clinking ice into a glass in the kitchen.

Without the doll dragging behind her, banging into everything she passed, the sister was mostly invisible.

Returning with the sharp scissors in her hands, she was still something no one was trying to see.

Back in the bedroom, it was easy enough to cut through the cloth, easy to remove the doll's arm. Inside the split cloth, cotton stuffing fluffed forward into the opening, waiting to be touched, to be pulled from within.

The sister had never considered this, had never thought to imagine what was inside the doll.

The sister took the arm and placed it at the bottom of the toy box, where she wrapped it in the brother's shirt, then covered them both with all her unwanted toys.

After crawling into the brother's bed, the sister soothed the doll, pressing her fingers against the wound she had created. And the next time she felt the need to pull out her hair, she reached her hands into the doll's wound instead, taking a small bit of its stuffing in her palms, worrying the patch of stuffing between her fingers for days, until it became moist with sweat and filth, until the stuffing fell apart, until she had to go back for more.

Later she understood that with enough stuffing she might not need the doll at all, but still she carried him everywhere she went.

At night, in their bedroom, the mother told the father that healing was complicated, but surely the sister was getting better, that although she still rarely talked she was beginning to move on from the brother's death, from the difficulties she'd had even before his disappearance.

The father did not agree. He panicked at the first sight of the one-armed doll and did not stop panicking even after the mother pointed out that the sister now smiled occasionally, whenever she held a particularly large bit of stuffing, rolling it between her fingers.

After a few attempts to stitch shut the hole, the mother

realized that the sister wanted it open and could easily tear the resewn seams herself, now that the doll's body had been compromised. Instead the mother bought extra bags of cotton stuffing, so that whenever the doll began to look deflated she could take it away from the sister and refill it behind the now-locked door of the den.

Earlier that evening, the father stood in the hall, holding back the sister as she wailed and banged on the door for the mother to give her back her doll, to give her back her doll right now.

Right fucking now, the sister yelled, and then the father hit the sister across the face, his palm open and his chest pounding.

Immediately the girl stopped crying, but now her not crying was even worse.

Why, the father asked the mother, did she cry over a doll, but not cry when she was slapped?

When later the father left and did not come back, the sister asked the mother where he'd gone, and the mother said that the father loved her very much, that he hadn't left because of anything the sister had done wrong.

The sister had not even thought of this. The idea had not even once occurred to her until the mother tried to convince her that it was not true.

Back in her bedroom, the sister tried to ask the doll many questions, but the doll did not answer.

Why had the father left, if not because of her?

She wondered, When the brother came home, would the doll share a bed with the brother, or would it sleep with her?

Better yet, the doll could have the brother's bed, and

the brother could share hers. Then she would never lose him again. Then he could once again give her his floating kisses, his whispered words.

The brother had always told her she was beautiful.

The doll never had, no matter how hard the sister tried to make it love her.

The sister pulled the doll closer, then shoved her hand in through the doll's shoulder hole, plunged her arm in past the elbow, as far as it would fit.

The sister gathered with her fingers, until she had a whole handful of stuffing from the very center of the doll.

She closed her hand around the stuffing, massaging it where it lay, slowly crushing the fluffy fibers until they were the size of a boy's fist, until they were the shape of a particular human heart she'd once known.

Now that the father was gone too, the mother sat the sister down at the kitchen table and said, Mommy's going to have to go back to work.

She said, Until your father starts paying child support, I can't afford a babysitter either, and then she started to cry.

The sister said, What's a babysitter?

A babysitter is someone who looks after you, so that you don't get hurt when I'm not around.

The sister nodded. I'm the doll's babysitter.

Yes, you are, said the mother, wiping her face. But now the doll has to be your babysitter too. The doll has to make sure that you are safe while I'm working.

The doll has to make sure that you do not use the oven, because you might burn yourself or start a fire.

The doll has to make sure that you do not run up and down the stairs, because you might fall and get hurt.

Most important, the doll has to make sure that you do not go outside. It has to make sure that you keep the doors locked and that you stay away from the windows.

The mother looked at the daughter for a long while, and then she said, Can the doll do that? Can it babysit you?

The sister had never considered that just as she kept the doll safe, it might do the same for her. That perhaps it had been doing so all along.

It had been almost a year now since the last time she went outside to play. It had been almost a year now since the brother had gone, and it was the doll who kept her from thinking about his loss too often, from feeling it as acutely as she had before the doll was made.

Yes, the sister said.

Yes, the doll and I will be fine together.

It was only an hour the sister was ever alone with only the doll to watch over her. The hour went from the end of the school day when the bus dropped her off — she was the first one on the bus in the morning and the last one off — to when the mother arrived home from work, looking exhausted and tense.

This hour passed very quickly most days, because the sister had gone without the doll and so all she wanted was to be with it, to hold it in her arms, to rock with it in her bed.

At school, she was not allowed to have the doll, but she did not need the whole doll. Just enough of it, some mass of stuffing that she could carry with her, that she could finger in the pocket of her jumper whenever someone made her nervous, whenever some boy looked at her too long or a teacher asked her a question she didn't want to answer.

The sister did not know the answers to many questions. She had trouble concentrating, had trouble paying attention to her lessons, spoke only in inaudible whispers. All her mind was on the doll, on the little piece of its harried insides she'd brought with her.

When she got home, she would run to the porch, where she would use her key to open the front door, then step inside, close the door, and relock it from the inside. Then she would put the key in the small ceramic dish beside the door. The entire process of getting in the house took a moment, but she wanted only to be upstairs in her room, in her brother's bed with the doll between her legs, clenched tight in her arms.

Every day after school, it was exactly this sequence that happened: Off the bus, to the door, key in the lock, open the door, step through, close behind. Lock the door. Put the key in the dish. Run upstairs. Hold the doll until the mother came home.

Every day, this lasted one hour. This was a routine. This was a method to get from one part of the day to another.

The sister liked routines, needed them like she had needed the hair-swallowing game, like she needed the fistfuls of stuffing that had replaced it.

Or, rather, the stuffing had nearly replaced the hair swallowing, because even with routine there was still the chance of making a mistake, of forgetting a step or reverting to a previous plan. How sometimes she kept the key in her pocket instead of putting it in the dish, how another time she forgot to lock the door altogether. How once she left the key still in the door, hanging from the lock until the mother found it, and then there was a whole evening of yelling, of crying, of the mother saying if the sister left the key in the door, then anyone might come in.

Anyone might come in, and then it would be the sister and the doll and the stranger, and what then?

What then? asked the mother. Then what?

The sister did not know, and when she asked the mother — when she repeated the mother's questions in her low voice — the mother stood up and left the room.

All the sister knew was that she would try harder to focus on the steps of the routine, to be sure that she completed each one before moving on to the next.

She would try, but it was difficult, because at the end of the routine was the doll.

Turning the key in the lock, feeling the tumblers flip over and release the bolt, it was all she could do not to run right then, up the stairs and into her room, where the doll was waiting.

When it was spring again, the sister started looking out the windows once more, because after months of snow and ice there was finally something new to see.

From her bedroom window, she watched the grass turn green, the backyard trees bud with leaves. She watched the birds come back after a winter away, red birds and blue birds and yellow birds, and she wondered what kinds of birds they were.

The brother would have known, but of course the doll did not.

As she watched the birds through her window, she wondered if her brother would return now too, or if the man in the raincoat would keep him another season, in the woods or on the road beyond or in the places the road could go.

Every day she thought about this, while she watched the yard renew its splendor.

At the end of the yard there was still the fence, and beyond it the evergreen dark of the woods, unchanged by the now-past winter, no longer snow choked but as imposing as before.

She thought about her brother, lost to those woods, and she thought about herself, stuck inside the house, safe with the doll.

She thought about how her brother probably didn't look like the doll anymore, even though the brother and the doll were both missing an arm. The sister was now a whole head taller than the doll was, and the brother had always been taller than she.

Thinking about how the doll and the brother were probably no longer the same, it made her love the doll a little less.

Loving the doll a little less made it easier to think about leaving it inside so that she could go and look for her brother in the woods or else, she thought, beyond them, somewhere down the road the brother said lay on their other side.

With both fists full of the doll's stuffing, this is what the sister saw —

through the window: only the yard, the fence, the woods, the space between the fence and the yard.

in her dreams: Only the man in the red raincoat. Only the wooden toggles threaded through their loops. Only the hood, which was raised or not raised. Only the rain or the not rain.

in her arms: the doll, or what was inside the doll, because they were now the same thing.

on her head: a full thicket of hair, the patch she'd once picked bare finally healed.

At the door, she paused.

With the doll held around its waist, she reached for the door with the other hand.

She reached for the door handle and then she stopped.

She lowered the doll to the floor, then sat down to slide her hand inside the doll, through the torn seam of its shoulder.

Fistful after fistful, she emptied the doll's body of its stuffing, tearing the stuffing from its body and then pushing the fibery mass into her mouth. Then chewing this mass until it was soaked with saliva, wet enough to choke down, to store inside her stomach.

When what was inside the doll was inside her, when she was so full she thought she was crying, she left the shell

of its skin upon the floor, its clothes half shirked, unable
to hang on to its formless body. Only its rubber head was
still the shape it once was, and for a moment the younger
sister considered twisting the head from off its seam. It was
too big for the pocket of her red coat, but she could carry
it in her hands, could use its eyes to help her search for the
older brother.

She picked the deflated doll up by the head to look
into its painted-on eyes, as empty and flat as they had
always been, as they were even when the body was full.
The head was not what she wanted. It was not the body
but what was inside the body that would sustain her.
She dropped the doll to the ground, steadied herself
against the thump of rubber hitting wood.

The younger sister jerked on her red coat, then reached
into the coat's pocket for the timer, still there those seasons
after she last watched its turning dial.

She turned the dial as far to the right as it would go, then
set it beside the doll's head.

Listening to its unwinding hum, the sister said, Before
that timer runs out, I will return.

She gagged back the cotton in her throat, trapped and
sodden and trying to rise. She said, If I do not return before
the timer goes off, do not be afraid, because all of you that
matters goes with me, and in me I will keep you safe.

A startling new warmth flooded through the opened
door, the first hot day of spring. By the time the younger
sister crossed the tree line she was sweating under her red
coat, her stomach cramped and bulged and burning. If
she could not find her older brother—if she could not find

the man in the raincoat—then she would walk until she reached the far-off road, the road beyond the woods where they both must have gone. Her throat ached, but the heat made her want to speak. Once under the trees she opened her mouth, and in the loudest voice she could muster she began to call out her brother's name, not caring who else might hear it and come running to find her, hollow for what she contained, as long as at last someone came who wanted her.

But if no one came, she thought, now she could live with that too.

Dredge

THE DROWNED GIRL DRIPS EVERYWHERE, soaking the Ford's backseat. Punter stares at her from the front of the car, first taking in her long blonde hair, wrecked by the pond's amphibian sheen, then her lips, blue where the lipstick's been washed away, flaky red where it has not. He looks into her glassy green eyes, her pupils so dilated the irises are slivered halos, the right eye further polluted with burst blood vessels. She wears a lace-frilled gold tank top, a pair of acid-washed jeans with grass stains on the knees and the ankles. A silver bracelet around her wrist sparkles in the window-filtered moonlight, throws off the same glimmer he saw through the lake's dark mirror that made him drop his fishing pole and wade out, then dive in after her. Her feet are bare except for a silver ring on her left pinkie toe, suggesting the absence of sandals, flip-flops, something lost in a struggle. Suggesting too many things for Punter to process all at once.

Punter turns and faces forward. He lights a cigarette, then flicks it out the window after two drags. Smoking with the drowned girl in the car reminds him of when he worked at the plastics factory, the taste of melted plastic in every puff of smoke. How a cigarette there hurt his lungs, left him gasping, his tongue coated with the taste of polyvinyl chloride, of adipates and phthalates. How that taste would leave his throat sore, his stomach aching every weekend.

The idea that some part of the dead girl might end up inside him—her wet smell or sloughing skin or dumb luck—he doesn't need a cigarette that bad.

Punter crawls halfway into the backseat and positions the girl while he still can. He's hunted enough deer and rabbits and squirrels to know she's going to stiffen soon. He arranges her arms and legs until she appears asleep, then brushes her hair out of her face before he climbs back into his own seat.

Looking in the rearview, Punter smiles at the drowned girl.

He waits for her to smile back.

He starts the engine. Drives her home.

Punter lives fifteen minutes from the pond, but tonight he keeps the Ford five miles per hour under the speed limit, stops longer at every stop sign. He thinks about calling the police, about how he should have already done so, instead of dragging the girl onto the shore and into his car.

The cops, they'll call this disturbing the scene of a crime. Obstructing justice. Tampering with evidence.

What the cops will say about what he's done, Punter already knows all about it.

At the house, he leaves the girl in the car while he goes inside and shits, his stool as black and bloody as it has been for weeks. Afterward he sits at the kitchen table and smokes a cigarette. The phone is only a few feet away, hanging on the wall. Even though the service was disconnected a month ago, he's pretty sure he could still call 911, if he wanted to.

In the garage, he lifts the lid of the chest freezer that sits against the far wall. He stares at the open space above the paper-wrapped bundles of venison, then stacks the meat on the floor until he's sure there's enough room. He goes out to the car and opens the back door. He lifts the girl, grunting as he gathers her into his arms like a child. She's heavier than she looks, with all the water filling her. He's careful as he lays her in the freezer, as he brushes the hair out of her eyes again, as he holds her eyelids closed until he's sure they'll stay that way. Even through her tank top he can see the way the water bloats her belly like she's pregnant.

Punter wakes in the middle of the night and puts his boots on in a panic. In the freezer, the girl's covered in a thin layer of frost, and he realizes he shouldn't have put her away wet. He considers thawing her and toweling her off, but it's too risky. One thing Punter knows about himself is that he is not always good at saying when.

He closes the freezer lid, goes back to the house, back to bed but not to sleep. He pictures the curve of her neck, the interrupting line of her collarbones intersecting the thin straps of her tank top. He reaches under his pajama bottoms, past the elastic of his underwear, then squeezes himself until the pain takes the erection away.

On the news the next morning, there's a story about the drowned girl. The anchorman calls her missing, but then says the words *her name was*. The girl is younger than Punter had guessed, a high school senior at the all-girls school across town. Her car was found yesterday, parked behind a nearby gas station, somewhere Punter occasionally fills up his car, buys cigarettes and candy bars.

The anchorman says the police are currently investigating but haven't released any leads to the public. The anchorman looks straight into the camera and says it's too early to presume the worst, that the girl could still show up at any time.

Punter shuts off the television, stubs out his cigarette. He takes a shower, shaves, combs his black hair straight back. Dresses himself in the same outfit he wears every day, a white t-shirt and blue jeans and black motorcycle boots. On the way to his car, he stops by the garage and opens the freezer. Her body is obscured behind ice like frosted glass. He puts a finger to her lips, but all he feels is cold.

The gas station is on a wooded stretch of gravel road between Punter's house and the outskirts of town. Punter's never seen it so crowded. While he waits in line he realizes these people are here for the same reason he is, to be near the site of the tragedy, the last place the girl was seen.

The checkout line crawls while the clerk runs his mouth, ruining his future testimony by telling his story over and over, transforming his eyewitness account into another harmless story.

The clerk says, I was the only one working that night. Of course I remember her.

The clerk says, Long blonde hair, tight-ass jeans, all that tan skin—I'm not saying she brought it on herself, but you can be sure she knew people would be looking.

In juvie, the therapists had called this narrative therapy, constructing a preferred reality. The clerk has black glasses and halitosis and fingernails chewed to keratin pulp. Teeth stained with cigarettes or chewing tobacco or coffee. Or all of the above. He reminds Punter of himself, and he wonders if the clerk feels the same, if there is a mutual recognition.

When it's Punter's turn, the clerk says, I didn't see who took her, but I wish I had.

Punter looks away, reads the clerk's name tag. OSWALD. The clerk says, If I knew who took that girl, I'd kill him myself.

Punter shivers as he slides his bills across the counter, as he takes his carton of cigarettes and his candy bar, as he flees the air-conditioned store for the heat of his sun-struck car.

The therapists had told Punter that what he'd done was a mistake, that there was nothing wrong with him. They made him repeat their words, to absolve himself of the guilt they were so sure he was feeling.

The therapists had said, You were a kid. You didn't know what you were doing.

Punter said the words they wanted but never felt the

guilt. Even now, he has only the remembered accusations of cops and judges to convince him that what he did was wrong.

Punter cooks two venison steaks in a frying pan with salt and butter. He sits down to eat, cuts big mouthfuls, then chews and chews, the meat tough from overcooking. He eats past the point of satiation on into discomfort, until his stomach presses against the tight skin of his abdomen. He never knows how much food to cook. He always clears his plate.

When he's done eating, he smokes and thinks about the girl in the freezer. How she had threatened to slip from his arms and back into the water. How he'd held on, carrying her up and out into the starlight. He hadn't saved her — couldn't have — but he had preserved her, kept her safe from decay, from the mouths of fish and worse.

He knows the freezer is better than the refrigerator, that the dry cold of meat and ice is better than the slow rot of lettuce and leftovers and ancient crust-rimmed condiments. Knows that, even after death, there is a safety in the preservation of a body.

Punter hasn't been to the bar near the factory since he got fired, but tonight he needs a drink. By eight, he's already been out to the garage four times, unable to keep from opening the freezer lid. If he doesn't stop, the constant thawing and refreezing will destroy her, skin first.

It's midshift at the factory, so the bar is empty except for the bartender and two men sitting at the rail, watching the ball game on the television mounted above the liquor shelves. Punter takes a stool at the opposite end, orders a beer, and lights a cigarette. He looks at the two men, tries to decide if he knows them from the plant. He's bad with names, bad at faces. One of the men catches him looking and glares back. Punter knows that he stares too long at people, that it makes them uncomfortable. He moves his eyes to his hands to his glass to the television, but he doesn't linger on the game. Sports move too fast, are full of rules and behaviors he finds incomprehensible. During commercials, the station plugs its own late-night newscast, including the latest about the missing girl. Punter stares at a picture of her, his tongue growing thick and dry for the five seconds the image is displayed. One of the other men drains the last gulp of his beer and shakes his head, says, I hope they find the fucker that killed her and cut his balls off.

So you think she's dead then?

Of course she's dead. You don't go missing like that and not end up dead.

The men motion for another round as the baseball game comes back from the break. Punter realizes he's been holding his breath, lets it go in a loud, hacking gasp. The bartender and the two men turn to look, so he holds a hand up, trying to signal he doesn't need any help, then puts it down when he realizes they're not offering. He pays his tab and gets up to leave.

He hasn't thought much about how the girl got into the pond or who put her there. He too assumed murder, but the who or why or when is not something he's previously considered.

In juvie, the counselors told him nothing he did or didn't do would have kept his mother alive, which Punter understood fine. Of course he hadn't killed his mother. That wasn't why he was there. It was what he'd done afterward that had locked him away, put him behind bars until he was eighteen.

This time, he will do better. He won't sit around for months while the police slowly solve the case, while they decide that what he's done is just as bad. This time, Punter will find the murderer himself.

He remembers: Missing her. Not knowing where she was, not understanding, wishing she'd come back. Not believing his father, who told him that she'd left them, that she was gone forever.

He remembers looking for her all day while his father worked, wandering the road, the fields, the rooms of their small house.

He remembers descending into the basement, finding the light switch, waiting for the fluorescent tubes to warm up. Stepping off the wooden stairs, his bare feet aching at the cold of the concrete floor.

He remembers nothing out of the ordinary, everything in its place, the hum of the olive-green refrigerator and the hum of the lights the only two sounds in the world.

He remembers walking across the concrete and opening the refrigerator door.

More than anything else, he remembers opening his mouth to scream and not being able to. He remembers the scream trapped in his chest, never to emerge.

—

When the eleven o'clock news comes on, Punter is watching, ready with his small spiral-bound notebook and his golf pencil stolen from the keno caddy at the bar. He writes down the sparse information added to the girl's story. The reporter recounts what Punter already knows—her name, the school, the abandoned car—then plays a clip of the local sheriff, who leans into the reporter's microphone and says, We're still investigating, but so far there's no proof for any of these theories. It's rare when someone gets out of their car and disappears on their own, but it does happen.

The sheriff pauses, listening to an inaudible question, then says, Whatever happened to her, it didn't happen inside the car. There's no sign of a struggle, no sign of sexual assault or worse.

Punter crosses his legs, then uncrosses them. He presses the pencil down harder onto the paper. The next clip is of the girl's father and mother, standing behind a podium at a press conference. They are both dressed in black, both stern and sad in serious clothes. The father speaks, saying, If anyone out there knows what happened—if you know where our daughter is—please come forward. We need to know where she is.

Punter writes down the word *father*, writes down the words *mother* and *daughter*. He looks at his useless telephone. He could tell these strangers what they wanted, but what good would it do them?

According to the shows on television, the first part of an investigation is always observation, the gathering of clues.

Punter opens the closet where he keeps his hunting gear and takes his binoculars out of their case. He hangs them around his neck and closes the closet door, then reopens it and retrieves his hunting knife off the top shelf. He doesn't need it, not yet, but he knows television detectives always carry a handgun to protect themselves. He only owns a rifle and a shotgun, both too long for this kind of work. The knife will be enough.

In the car, he puts the knife in the glove box and the binoculars on the seat. He takes the notebook out of his back pocket and reads the list of locations he's written down: the school, her parents' house, the pond, and the gas station.

He reads the time when the clerk said he saw her and then writes down another, the time he found her in the pond. The two times are separated by barely a day, so she couldn't have been in the pond for too long.

Whatever happened to her, it happened fast.

He thinks that whoever did this, they must be local to know about the pond. Punter has never actually seen anyone else there, only the occasional tire tracks, the left-behind beer bottles and cigarette butts from teenage parties. The condoms discarded farther off in the bushes, where Punter goes to piss.

He thinks about the girl, about how she would never consent to him touching her if she were still alive. About how she would never let him say the words he's said, the words he still wants to say. He wonders what he will do when he finds her killer, whether his investigation will end in vengeance or thanksgiving.

Punter has been to the girl's school once before, when the unemployment office sent him to interview for a janitorial position there. He hadn't been offered the job, couldn't have passed the background check if he had. His juvenile record was sealed, but there was enough there to warn people, and schools never took any chances.

He circles the parking lot twice, then parks down the sidewalk from the front entrance, where he'll be able to watch people coming in and out of the school. He resists the urge to use the binoculars, knows he must control himself in public, must keep from acting on every thought. This is why he has barely talked in months. Why he keeps to himself in his house, hunting and fishing, living off the too-small government disability checks the unemployment counselor helped him apply for.

The counselor hadn't wanted him to see what they wrote down for his disability, but seeing those words written in the counselor's neat script didn't make him angry, just relieved. He wasn't bad anymore. He was a person with a disorder, with a trauma. No one had ever believed him about this, especially not the therapist in juvie, who had urged Punter to open up, who had gotten angry when he couldn't. They didn't believe him when he said he'd already told them everything he had inside him.

Punter knows they were right to disbelieve him, that he did have feelings he didn't want to let out.

When Punter pictures the place where other people keep their feelings, all he sees is his own trapped scream, a devouring ball of sound, hungry and hot in his guts.

A bell rings. Soon the doors open, spilling girls out onto

the sidewalk and into the parking lot. Punter watches parents getting out of other cars, going to greet their children. One of these girls might be a friend of the drowned girl, and if he could talk to her, then he might be able to find out who the drowned girl was. Might be able to make a list of other people he needs to question so that he can solve her murder.

The increasing number of distinct voices overwhelms Punter. He stares, watching the girls go by in their uniforms. All of them are identically clothed, and so he focuses on their faces, on their hair, the blondes and brunettes and redheads waiting for their mothers to pull up.

He watches the breeze blow all that hair around all those made-up faces. He presses himself against the closed door of his Ford, holds himself still.

He closes his eyes and tries to picture the drowned girl here, wearing her own uniform, but she is separate now, distinct from these girls and the life they once shared. Punter's glad. These girls terrify him in a way the drowned girl does not.

A short burst of siren startles Punter, and he twists around in his seat to see a police cruiser idling its engine behind him, its driver's-side window rolled down. The cop inside is around Punter's age, his hair starting to gray at the temples, but the rest of him young and healthy looking. The cop yells something, hanging his left arm out the window, drumming his fingers against the side of the cruiser, but Punter can't hear him through the closed windows, not with all the other voices surrounding him.

Punter opens his mouth, then closes it without saying anything. He shakes his head, then locks his driver's-side door, suddenly afraid that the cop means to drag him from the car, to put hands on him as other officers did when he was a kid. He looks up from the lock to see the cop outside of his cruiser, walking toward Punter's own car.

The cop raps on Punter's window, waits for him to roll down the glass. He stares at Punter, who tries to look away, inadvertently letting his eyes fall on another group of girls.

The cop says, You need to move your car. This is a fire lane.

Punter tries to nod, finds himself shaking his head instead. He whispers that he'll leave, that he's leaving. The cop says, I can't hear you. What did you say?

Punter turns the key, sighs when the engine turns over. He says, I'm going. He says it as loud as he can, his vocal cords choked and rusty.

There are too many girls walking in front of him for Punter to pull forward, and so he has to wait as the cop gets back in his own car. Eventually the cop puts the cruiser in reverse, lets him pass. Punter drives slowly out of the parking lot and onto the city streets, keeping the car slow, keeping it straight between the lines.

Afraid that the cop might follow him, Punter sticks to the main roads, other well-populated areas. These aren't places he goes. A half hour passes, then another. Punter's throat is raw from smoking. His eyes ache from staring into the rearview mirror, and his hands tremble so long he fears they might never stop.

At home, Punter finds the girl's parents in the phone book, writes down their address. He knows he has to be more careful, that if he isn't, then someone will come looking for him too. He lies down on the couch to wait for dark, falls asleep with the television tuned to daytime dramas and court shows. He dreams about finding the murderer, about hauling him into the police station in chains. He sees himself avenging the girl with a smoking pistol, emptying round after round into this faceless person, unknown but certainly out there, surely as marked by his crime as Punter was.

When he wakes up, the television is still on, broadcasting game shows full of questions Punter isn't prepared to answer. He gets up and goes into the bathroom, the pain in his guts doubling him over on the toilet. When he's finished, he takes a long, gulping drink from the faucet, then goes out into the living room to gather his notebook, his binoculars, his knife.

In the garage, he tries to lift the girl's tank top, but the fabric is frozen to her flesh. He can't tell if the sound of his efforts is the ripping of ice or of skin. He tries touching her through her clothes, but she's too far gone, distant with cold. He shuts the freezer door and leaves her again in the dark, but not before he explains what he's doing for her. Not before he promises to find the person who hurt her, to hurt this person himself.

Her parents' house is outside of town, at the end of a long tree-lined driveway. Punter drives past, then leaves his car parked down the road and walks back with the binoculars around his neck. He knows the names of the midwestern trees he moves among, identifies them as easily as the animals he knows they shelter, oaks and pines and birches hiding raccoon and owls and white-tailed deer. Moving through the shadows, he finds a spot a hundred yards from the house, then scans the lit windows for movement until he finds the three figures sitting in the living room. He recognizes her parents from the television, sees that the third person is a boy around the same age as the drowned girl. Punter watches him the closest, tries to decide if this is the girl's boyfriend. The boy is all movement, his hands gesturing with every word he speaks. He could be laughing or crying or screaming, and from this distance Punter wouldn't be able to tell the difference. He watches as the parents embrace the boy, then hurries back through the woods as soon as he sees the headlights come on in front of the house.

He makes it to his own car as the boy's convertible pulls out onto the road. Punter starts the engine and follows the convertible through town, past the gas station and the downtown strip malls, then into another neighborhood where the houses are smaller. He's never been here before, but he knows the plastics plant is close, that many of his old coworkers live nearby. He watches the boy park in front of a dirty white house, its windows barred and its door locked behind an iron gate. He watches through the binoculars as the boy climbs the steps to the porch, as he rings the doorbell. The door opens and obscures Punter's view, but the boy doesn't go all the way inside. Whatever happens only takes a few minutes, and then the boy is back in his car. He sits on the side of the road for a long time, smoking. Punter smokes too. He imagines getting out of the car and going up to the boy, imagines questioning him about the night of the murder. He knows he should, knows being a detective means taking risks, but he can't move. When the boy leaves, Punter lets him go, then drives past the white house with his foot off the gas pedal, idling at a crawl. He doesn't see anything he understands. This is not exactly new.

Back at the pond, his tire tracks are the only ones backing up to the pond, his footprints the only marks along the shore. Whoever else was there has been given an alibi by Punter's own clumsiness. He finds a long branch with its leaves intact and uses it to rake out the sand, erasing the worst of his tracks. When he's done, he stares out over the dark water, trying to remember how it felt to hold her in his arms, to feel her body soft and pliable before surrendering her to the freezer.

He wonders if it was a mistake to take her from beneath the water. Maybe he should have done the opposite, should have stayed under the waves with her until his own lungs filled with the same watery weight, until he was trapped beside her. Their bodies would not have lasted. The fish would have dismantled their shells, and then Punter could have shown her the good person he's always believed himself to be, trapped underneath all this sticky rot.

For dinner he cooks two more steaks. All the venison the girl displaced is going bad in his aged refrigerator, and already the steaks are browned and bruised. To be safe, he fries them hard as leather. He has to chew the venison until his jaws ache and his teeth feel loose, but he finishes every bite. Watching the late-night news, Punter can tell that without any new evidence the story is losing steam. The girl gets only a minute of coverage, the reporter reiterating facts Punter's known for days. He stares at her picture again, at how her smile once brought her whole face to life. He doesn't have much time. He crawls toward the television, puts his hand on her image as it fades away. He turns around, sits with his back against the television screen. Behind him there is satellite footage of a tornado or a hurricane or a flood. Of destruction seen from afar.

Punter wakes up choking in the dark, his throat closed off with something, phlegm or pus or he doesn't know what. He grabs a handkerchief from his nightstand and spits until he clears away the worst of it. He gets up to flip the light switch, but the light doesn't turn on. He tries it again. He realizes how quiet the house is, how without the steady clacking of his wall clock the only sound in his bedroom is his own thudding heart.

In the kitchen, the oven's digital display stares blankly; the refrigerator waits silent and still. He runs out of the house in his underwear, his big bare feet slapping at the cold driveway. Inside the garage, the freezer is silent too. He lifts the lid, letting out a blast of frozen air, then slams it shut again after realizing he's wasted several degrees of chill to confirm what he already knows.

He dresses hurriedly, then scavenges his house for loose change, for crumpled dollar bills left in discarded jeans. At the grocery down the road, he buys what little ice he can afford, his cash reserves exhausted. Back in the garage, he works fast, cracking the blocks of ice on the cement floor and dumping them over the girl's body. He manages to cover her completely, suppressing the pang he feels once he's unable to see her face through the ice. For a second, he considers crawling inside the freezer himself, sweeping away the ice between them. Letting his body heat hers, letting her thaw into his arms.

What he wonders is, Would it be better to have one day with her than a forever separated by ice?

He goes back into the house and sits down at the kitchen table. Lights a cigarette, then digs through the envelopes on the table until he finds the unopened bill from the power company. He opens it, reads the impossible number, shoves the bill back into the envelope. He tries to calculate how long the ice will buy him, but he never could do figures, can't begin to solve the cold math.

He remembers: the basement refrigerator had always smelled bad, like leaking coolant and stale air. It wasn't used much, had been kept out of his father's refusal to throw anything away more than out of any sense of utility. By the time Punter found his mother there, she was already bloated around the belly and the cheeks, her skin slick with something that glistened like petroleum jelly.

Unsure what he should do, he'd slammed the refrigerator door and ran back upstairs to hide in his bedroom. By the time his father came home, Punter was terrified his father would know he'd seen, that he'd kill him too. That what would start as a beating would end as a murder.

Only his father never said anything, never gave any sign the mother was dead. He stuck to his story, telling Punter over and over how his mother had run away and left them behind, until Punter's voice was too muted to ask.

Punter tried to forget, to believe his father's story, but he couldn't.

Punter tried to tell someone else, some adult, but he couldn't do that either. Not when he knew what would happen to his father. Not when he knew they would take her from him.

During the day, while his father worked, Punter went down to the basement and opened the refrigerator door.

At first, he only looked at her, at the open eyes and mouth, at how her body had been jammed into the too-small space. How her throat was slit the same way his father had once demonstrated on a deer that had fallen but not expired.

The first time he touched her, he was sure she was trying to speak to him, but it was only gas leaking out of her mouth, squeaking free of her lungs. Punter had rushed to pull her out of the refrigerator, convinced for a moment she was somehow alive, but when he wrapped his arms around her, all that gas rolled out of her mouth and nose and ears, sounding like a wet fart but smelling so much worse.

He hadn't meant to vomit on her, but he couldn't help himself.

Afterward, he took her upstairs and bathed her to get the puke off. He'd never seen another person naked, and so he tried not to look at his mother's veiny breasts, at the wet thatch of her pubic hair floating in the bathwater.

Scrubbing her with a bar of soap, he averted his eyes the best he could.

Rinsing the shampoo out of her hair, he whispered he was sorry.

It was hard to dress her, but eventually he managed, and then it was time to put her back in the refrigerator before his father came home.

Closing the door, he whispered, Goodbye, I love you, I'll see you tomorrow.

The old clothes, covered with blood and vomit, he took them out into the cornfield behind the house and buried them. Then came the waiting, all through the evening while his father occupied the living room, all through the night while he was supposed to be sleeping.

Day after day, he took her out and wrestled her up the stairs. He sat her on the couch or at the kitchen table, and then he spoke, his normal reticence somehow negated by her forever silence. He'd never talked to his mother this much while she was alive, but now he couldn't stop telling her everything he had ever felt, all his trapped words spilling out one after another.

Punter knows she wouldn't have lasted forever, even if they hadn't found her and taken her away. He had started finding little pieces of her left behind, waiting wet and squishy on the wooden basement steps, the kitchen floor, in between the cracks of the couch.

He tried to clean up after her, but sometimes his father would find one too. Then Punter would have to watch as his father held some doughy flake up to the light, rolling it between his fingers as if he could not recognize what it was or where it came from, before throwing it in the trash.

Day after day, Punter bathed his mother to get rid of the smell, which grew more pungent as her face began to droop, as the skin on her arms wrinkled and sagged. He searched her body for patches of mold to scrub them off, then held her hands in his, marveling at how, even weeks later, her fingernails continued to grow.

Punter sits on his front step, trying to make sense of the scribbles in his notebook. He doesn't have enough, isn't even close to solving the crime, but he knows he has to if he wants to keep the police away. If they figure the crime out before he does, if they question the killer, then they'll eventually end up at the pond, where they'll find Punter's attempts at covering his tracks.

Punter doesn't need to prove the killer guilty, at least not with a judge and a jury. All he has to do is find this person, then make sure he never tells anyone what he did with the body. After that, the girl can be his forever, for as long as he has enough ice.

Punter drives a circuit, circling the scenes of the crime: the gas station, the school, her parents' house, the pond. Even with the air-conditioning cranked he can't stop sweating, his face drenched and fevered, his stomach hard with meat. He's halfway between his house and the gas station when his gas gauge hits empty. He pulls over and sits for a moment, trying to decide, trying to wrap his slow thoughts around his investigation. He opens his notebook, flips through its barely filled pages. He has written down so few facts, so few suspects, and there is so little time left.

In his notebook, he crosses out *father, mother, boyfriend*. He has only one name left, one suspect he hasn't disqualified, one other person that Punter knows has seen the girl. He smokes, considers. He opens the door and stands beside the car. Home is in one direction, the gas station the other. Reaching back inside, he leaves the notebook and the binoculars but takes the hunting knife and shoves it into his waistband, untucking his t-shirt to cover the weapon.

What Punter decides, he knows it is only a guess, but he also believes that whenever a detective has a hunch, the best next move is to follow it to the end.

It's not a long walk, but Punter gets tired fast. He sits down to rest, then can't get back up. He curls into a ball off the weed-choked shoulder, sleeps fitfully as cars pass by, their tires throwing loose gravel over his body. It's dark out when he wakes. His body is covered with gray dust, and he can't remember where he is. He's never walked this road before, and in the dark it's as alien as a foreign land. He studies the meager footprints in the dust, tracking himself until he knows which way he needs to go.

There are two cars parked behind the gas station, where the drowned girl's car was before it was towed away. One is a small compact, the other a newer sports car. The sports car's windows are rolled down, its stereo blaring music Punter doesn't know or understand, the words too fast for him to hear. He takes a couple steps into the trees beside the road, slows his approach until his gasps for air grow quieter. Leaning against the station are two young men in t-shirts and blue jeans, nearly identical with their purposely mussed hair and scraggly stubble. With them are two girls — one redhead and one brunette — still wearing their school uniforms, looking even younger than Punter knows they are.

The brunette presses her hand against her man's chest, and the man's own hand clenches her hip. Punter can see how firmly he's holding her, how her skirt is bunched between his fingers, exposing several extra inches of thigh.

Punter thinks of his girl thawing at home, how soon he will have to decide how badly he wants to feel skin held close to his own. He thinks of the boyfriend he saw through the binoculars. Wonders if *boyfriend* is really the word he needs. The redhead, she takes something from the unoccupied man, puts it on her tongue. The man laughs, then motions to his friend, who releases his girl and lifts a twelve-pack of beer up off the cement. All four of them get into the sports car and drive off together in the direction of the pond, the town beyond. Punter stands still as they pass, knowing they won't see him, that he is already — has always been — a ghost to their world.

Once the decision is made, it's nothing to walk into the empty gas station, to push past the waist-high swinging door to get behind the counter. It's nothing to grab the gas station clerk and press the knife through his uniform, into the small of his back. Nothing to ignore the clerk's squeals as Punter pushes him out from behind the counter.

The clerk says, You don't have to do this.

He says, Anything you want, take it. I don't fucking care, man.

It's nothing to ignore him saying, Please don't hurt me.

It's nothing to ignore the words, to keep pushing the clerk toward the back of the gas station, to the hallway leading behind the coolers. Punter pushes the clerk down to his knees, feels his own feet slipping on the cool tile. He keeps one hand on the knife while the other grips the clerk's shoulder, his fingers digging into the hollows between muscle and bone.

The clerk says, Why are you doing this?

Punter lets go of the clerk's shoulder and smacks him across the face with the blunt edge of his hand. He chokes the words out.

The girl. I'm here about the girl.

What girl?

Punter smacks him again, and the clerk swallows hard, blood or teeth.

Punter says, You know. You saw her. You told me.

The clerk's lips split, begin to leak. He says, Her? I never did anything to that girl. I swear.

Punter thinks of the clerk's bragging, about how excited he was to be the center of attention. He growls, grabs a fistful of greasy hair, then yanks hard, exposing the clerk's stubbled throat, turning his face sideways until one eye faces Punter's.

The clerk's glasses fall off, clatter to the tile.

The clerk says, Punter.

He says, I know you. Your name is Punter. You come in here all the time.

The clerk's visible eye is wide, terrified with hope, and for one second Punter sees his mother's eyes, sees the girl's, sees his hand closing their eyelids for the last time.

OSWALD, Punter reads again, then shakes the name clear of his head.

The clerk says, I never hurt her, man. I was just the last person to see her alive.

Punter puts the knife to flesh. It's nothing. We're all the last person to see someone. He locks his wrist, pushes through. That's nothing either. Or, if it is something, it's nothing worse than all the rest.

And then dragging the body into the tiny freezer. And then shoving the body between stacks of hot dogs and soft pretzels. And then trying not to step in the cooling puddles of blood. And then picking up the knife and putting it back in its sheath, tucking it into his waistband again. And then the walk home with a bag of ice in each hand. And then realizing the ice doesn't matter, that it will never be enough. And then the walk turning into a run, his heart pounding and his lungs heaving. And then the feeling he might die. And then the not caring what happens next.

By the time Punter gets back to the garage, the ice is already melting, the girl's face jutting from between the cubes. Her eyelids are covered with frost, cheeks slick with thawing pond water. He reaches in and lifts, her face and breasts and thighs giving to his fingers but her back still frozen to the wrapped venison below. He pulls, trying to ignore the peeling sound her skin makes as it rips away from the butcher paper.

Punter speaks, his voice barely audible. He doesn't have to speak loud for her to hear him. They're so close. Something falls off, but he doesn't look, doesn't need to dissect the girl into parts, into flesh and bone, into brains and blood. He kisses her forehead, her skin scaly like a fish's, like a mermaid's.

He says, You're safe now.

He sits down with the girl in his arms and his back to the freezer. He rocks her as she continues to thaw all over him. He shivers, then puts his mouth to hers, breathes deep from the icy blast still frozen in her lungs, lets the air cool the burning in his own throat, the horror of his guts. When he's ready, he picks her up, cradles her close, and carries her into the house. Takes her into the bedroom and lays her upon the bed.

He lies beside her, and then, in a loud, clear voice, he speaks. He tries not to cough, tries to ignore the scratchy catch at the back of his throat. He knows what will happen next, but he also knows all this will be over by the time they break down his door, by the time they come in with guns drawn and voices raised. He talks until his voice disappears, until his trapped scream becomes a whisper. He talks until he gets all of it out of him and into her, where none of these people will ever be able to find it.

Wolf Parts

FTER RED CUT HER WAY out of the wolf's belly — after she wiped the gore off her hood and cape, her dress, her tights — she again found herself standing on the path that wound through the forest toward her grandmother's house. Along the way, she met with the wolf, with whom she had palavered the first time and every time since. Afterward, she went to her grandmother's, where she again discovered the wolf devouring the old woman, and where he waited to devour her too, as he had before. Once again she was lost, and once again, she cut herself out of his belly and back onto the stony path. Over and over, she did these things until in desperation she lay across the stones and, with the knife her mother had given her, gutted herself quickly, left to right, crying out in wonder at the bright worlds she found hidden within.

The first time she saw the wolf, she did not run but let him circle closer and closer, even as his querying yips turned to growls. With one hand, she reached to stroke his fur — full of wretched possibilities, thick and gray and softer than she expected — and with the other she reached into her basket. She dug beneath the jam and pie and paper-wrapped pound of butter for her knife, the only protection her mother had sent with her, as if all it took to keep her safe from the wolf were this tiny silver blade.

At the wolf's suggestion, she left the path to pick some flowers for her grandmother, who was sick and could not care for herself anymore. Tearing each blossom from its roots, she didn't notice the hour growing late, didn't understand the advantage she'd conceded by allowing the wolf to reach the cottage first.

In another version of this story, the flowers cried out warnings of the wolf's trickery, never realizing she could no longer hear their voices. In a previous form, she had lain among their petals and stalks, conversing with them for hours. She had lost this ability when her mother—just days before sending her to her grandmother's—said it was time for her to grow up, to stop acting like a child.

Only his head was that of a wolf. The rest of his body was that of a man and resembled in all ways that of the only other man she had ever seen without clothes. He had the same hands and arms and legs, the same chest with the same triangle of downy hair that pointed to another thicker thatch of fur below. Even with his wolf's head, the girl was able to recognize his expression, knew that the snarled lips and the exposed canines betrayed the same combination of hunger and apology that she had seen on her father's face years before, when he too had pushed her to the ground and climbed atop her, when he had filled her belly with the same blank stones that the wolf now offered: first gently, then, after she refused, not.

The wolf and Red had always shared the twin paths through the forest, but it wasn't until the girl started to bleed—not a wound, her mother said, but a secret blood nonetheless—that he began to follow her, began to sniff at the hem of her skirts and cape. She asked the wolf what he wanted from her, but he would not use his words, would not form the sounds that might have made clear what he expected her to offer. Instead he nudged her with his muzzle, away from the path of pine needles she had been instructed to walk, toward the other, thornier path he more often walked alone.

For three days, the grandmother waited in her bed, glued twitching to her sweaty sheets by a fever that choked and burned her, by a hunger that left her furious for foodstuffs, for cakes and butter and tea and wine. For bread that might soak up her fever, if only she were strong enough to get out of the bed to eat.

And then on the third day, a knock, and on the third knock, a voice.

Raise the latch, she cried, before she even fully heard, and certainly before she realized how deep the voice was, how terribly unlike a little girl's.

The wolf's breath smelled of chalk, and his paws were covered in flour. It wasn't enough to trick the girl, but she allowed herself to pretend to be fooled. She opened her cloak and invited him in, so that he might do what he came to do.

From inside the wolf's stomach, the grandmother could hear only every third or fourth word her granddaughter spoke, and only slightly more of the wolf's responses. She heard *teeth* and *eyes* and *grandmother*. She heard *better* and *my dear* and *come closer, come closer*. She heard *to eat you with* and then, with so little time left, she acted, placing her hands against the walls of her wet prison. She pressed and she pushed, stretching the wolf's stomach until it burst, and then she wrapped her hands around the bars of his ribs. When she could not pry her way out, she did not despair. Instead, she opened her mouth into a wide smile, which if seen earlier would have warned the wolf of her excellent sharp teeth. She bit down hard, first on lung and heart, then indiscriminately, casting about in a great gnashing, devouring all she could until the wolf she was inside was also inside her, until she was sure the grand-daughter was safe.

The girl dreamed often of the wolf and the grandmother, of the two together, as they were when she found them: the grandmother, with her gasping mouth and her skirts bunched tight in the clenched centers of her fists, and then the wolf, on top of the grandmother with his back arched and his head down, his nose pressed between her legs. In the dream, what captivated her was not the sight of the beast and the woman together, but the sound: the scratch of the wolf's tongue lapping at her grandmother's cleft, at the little red hood atop it. The wolf's tail wagged eagerly, distracting the girl for a second from seeing his engorged penis, the red weight of which she knew was destined for her grandmother's body, if she did nothing.

She had not done nothing.

By the power of his voice, the wolf stripped the girl nearly naked, commanding her to throw her shoes into the fire, then her skirt and bodice, until she wore only her red cape and hood, which she would not remove, no matter how urgently he pleaded.

After she knew the heat of the wolf would keep her warm, she allowed herself to be led outside, where, at his urging, she climbed onto his back. Her body shuddered as his muscles flexed between her legs, as the sharp knuckles of his spine pressed against her. The wolf howled, terrifying and thrilling her, and then they were off, the wolf bounding faster and faster, carrying her away from all the paths she had known, toward a part of the forest where the brambles were thickest, where without a guide it was possible to get lost forever.

When she would not love him as a boy, he went into the woods and became a wolf, the better to take from her what he wanted. If only he had waited until later, when he was a man and she a woman, their fates might have been different.

I say *wolf*, but of course there are various kinds of wolves.

Red cried out when she saw the grandmother dressed as a wolf, but calmed herself, breath by breath, until she was ready to listen and learn. After all, it was not the first time the grandmother had shown Red the shapes she herself might employ one day. When Red was a child, the grandmother had turned into a bird to show her flight, then into a turtle to show her safety. At the time of her first blood, the grandmother had become a boy her own age, and then a woman slightly older, to show her two kinds of physical love that she might one day choose between, and now, as the wolf, the grandmother wanted to show her something else. If Red did not quite understand what the lesson was, she trusted her grandmother, even though it hurt worse than anything that had come before.

The girl blamed the wolf for leading her off the path, for slowing her while it rushed ahead to devour her grandmother, to paint the lonely cottage with gore. Of course she blamed the wolf. Who would have forgiven her for dooming her grandmother if she blamed instead the singing birds, the babbling brook, the clustered glamour of a thousand bright forest flowers, ripe for the picking?

She was taken by surprise, despite knowing her sisters had always been jealous of her red chaperon, that dash of color against the dullness of their world. When she awoke, lashed to a tree deep within the forest, she cursed their names loudly and without pause, hoping her father would hear and come to her rescue. After the wolf came instead, her screams turned to stammering, then to pleading. She shut her tear-stung eyes, cried out anew as the wolf's hungry breath filled her nostrils. She reopened her eyes only when, instead of the teeth she expected, she felt his tongue rough against her cheeks, licking away her tears. Her fear fell away, was replaced with some other emotion she had not yet experienced, one like the affection she felt for her father but darker, more thickly warm and urgent.

Afterward, the wolf chewed through the ropes and freed her from the tree while she told him about her sisters' betrayal. The wolf howled and bid her to climb upon his back. His gait was impressive, and his strength even more so when he splintered open the door of their cottage, when he rent and devoured her sisters, as they themselves had hoped he might do to her.

Her father made the wolf's fur into a rug and laid it in front of the hearth. He said that it would serve as a reminder that his daughter was not to be touched or harmed in any way, that this was the penalty for such a transgression.

Whenever the girl was left alone in the house, she took off the red cape and the clothes beneath it, then sprawled naked upon the wolf's skin, setting her smooth back against his. There she touched herself, feeling again the friction of fur, the proximity of some new life she sensed the wolf would have bestowed upon her had they not been caught. When she howled, it was with her mouth against his unhearing ear, her lips close to his stretched and taxidermied jaws, full of the teeth she had just once felt so lovingly against her skin.

On four legs he could easily devour her, could take her in his jaws as fast as he could any deer or rabbit. But on two? On two she was often the one who mastered him.

The wolf tied the girl with silken thread and stashed her in the closet, unsure what to do with her. He was too full from the grandmother to eat, but little girls were rare this deep in the forest. When he heard her thrashing against the closet door, he emitted a low growl meant to frighten her. When the thrashing only intensified, he opened the closet to scare her again, with a flash of teeth or a swipe of paw.

There was no girl inside the closet, only a puddle of thread, cut and discarded.

The wolf did not see the girl again, not for many years. When she returned, grown stubborn and brave, he himself had declined, aged and weak. He was not sorry for what he'd done—he was a wolf, after all—but still he cried out for mercy. The lovely girl acted as if she couldn't hear him, scowling as she twisted her own ropes around his body, binding him still before setting to work on him in the same fashion he'd once intended for her—with sharp objects meant to cut, meant to tear, meant to render meat separate from bone.

With blade and trap, with fire and water, with drowning and crushing and boiling and slashing and cutting and stabbing: these are the ways she killed them, one after the other.

After the incident, Red became a great enemy of the wolves, vowing that never again would she wait for one of their kind to molest her upon the path. She took to the woods in her hooded cape, knowing the wolves would see her coming, but also that this warning would not be enough to save them. She tanned and sewed and dyed each of their hides, then gave away the fur-trimmed cloaks to the women of her village until the whole of the woods was filled with red hoods and red capes, each of them concealing a girl or a woman, a knife or an ax.

Given the opportunity, he chose once more to be a man instead of a wolf, and by doing so he gained certain abilities, lost others entirely. His man's face and courtier's clothes made it easier for him to lure his prey — not the deer and elk he had recently hunted, but the other, comelier prey he had long desired — and certainly he believed he had made the right choice, even if he no longer smelled as acutely, could no longer hear a doe approaching from miles away. This is how he failed to sense the women following him out of the village and into the woods, how he didn't notice until it was too late that each of them carried her own small knife, her own sharp stone. When they pinned him down in the thistles beside the path, he howled as each of them made a cut in a place of their choosing, then again as their tiny fingers shoved their stones through the openings they had made.

As commanded, she climbed into the bed naked, speaking in soft, mock-innocent syllables, pretending not to notice that the figure in the nightgown was not her grandmother, so that the great, hairy wolf would feel safe to reveal his true intentions. She waited, polite and acquiescent, but as the wolf forced himself inside her she sprung her trap, showing him that she too knew what it meant to consume someone whole.

An ax is a knife is a pair of sewing scissors: tools as weapons, weapons as tools. Ways to cut yourself out from inside a wolf or, in other circumstances, to cut your way back in.

Red and her grandmother had seen this trick before and so could not be taken by surprise. Red refused to leave the path, the grandmother declined to open the door, and when they each questioned the wolf through the bolted wood, they already knew the cheap answers he would offer. The only one surprised was the wolf, who knew not where these women had gotten their knives nor where they had learned the sharp skill with which they wielded them.

Every winter, the villagers sent one of their own girls into the forest as tribute. Although the wolf promised to return each girl by spring, it had been years since any had made her way home, as they once had. Even back then, they returned damaged, scarred, bereft, hardly the girls they had been before their time with the wolf. With few options remaining, the villagers had no choice but to send Red in place of the too-lovely girl they had previously chosen. At twelve, Red was almost too old for the wolf's tastes, but the villagers were sure that her radiant innocence would win him over, would please the ravener they all feared so much.

Before sending her down the path, they gave her a red riding hood, the better to see her when she emerged from the forest, and they gave her a knife, sharp as the wolf's own teeth, the better to saw her way from his belly when the time came.

For months the villagers fretted and worried. Then, when the sun was highest on the first day of spring, they saw Red appear at the tree line, her face grim and her forearm — still clutching the knife — covered in slick gore. In her other hand she held the hand of a child, and that child held another and then another and then another.

The villagers rejoiced and praised Red above all others, but she did not join them in celebration. She remained apart no matter how they pleaded for her company, her face a slab of pale skin and blank teeth. By the time she departed the following winter, the villagers were glad to see her go. Although they made great shows of protestation, they knew she was changed by what she had done, and while they would not say so aloud, each secretly feared the sight of her hood, of the knife she still carried whole seasons after she had last needed it.

In another telling, Red never returned, and in the following years there appeared more and more wolves in the woods around the forest, until the villagers felt afraid to walk the path leading to the city. Each of these new pups had thick red fur, and when they howled in unison at the moon, it was in one voice, less like that of a wolf and more like a woman screaming, like a girl who, if the rumors in the city were true, the villagers had knowingly sent to be raped

and tortured and, after she gave birth, torn limb from pale-
fleshed limb.

Or maybe Red returned not with a line of small girls but
with the wolf himself in tow, a rope turned cruel around
his neck and her knife wet with his protests. In this version, it wasn't until she reached the village center that
she slit the wolf from throat to tail. Too late, she retrieved
each and every child from the wolf's stomach, each one
bruised and bloodied and without breath. In anger, the
villagers filled the wolf's belly with stones while Red
held close his howling head, recounting for him the many
names of these dead children, the many pounds of shale
and limestone it would take to buy their penance.

If the wolf had always been the wolf, and the grandmother
always the grandmother, why did Red so often struggle
to tell them apart? Perhaps it was because, after pulling
her knife from the wolf's flesh, she frequently found wet
scraps of bloodied nightgown stuck to the blade, or else
how, while kissing her grandmother's pursed lips, she
so often tasted raw meat rotting from between the older
woman's teeth.

The wolf had expected the girl to protest, but she continued
eating the flesh and drinking the blood that he served her
until her clothes were wet and matted, until her mouth was
stained the color of her cape. Their goblets overflowed, then
tipped and dripped onto the cottage floor. The grandmother
was a bigger woman out of her skin than she had seemed in

it, so the wolf, tired from his gluttony, yawned once, twice, a third time. He could not stop yawning. With his head thrown back and his engorged throat exposed, he realized too late that the girl was crawling across the table, her face filthy with the wet horror of their meal. Clenching her fork and knife in her tiny fists, she searched the empty platters, and when she found nothing else to eat, she clambered quickly toward the yawning wolf, hungry for more.

The girl was surprised when she slid her hand between the wolf's muscular, furred legs to find that he was a *she*, something she had never considered, not even when she saw her dressed in her grandmother's clothes, so calm and perfect, reclining gorgeous against those many plush pillows.

He was a pup, a boy, a wolf, a man, a wolfman, a woodsman. He was all of these, but never more than one at a time. He changed with the moon and then, later, according to his own whim. When he came to her at night, it was always as a wolf, a shape she grew to love, even though it had cost her everything she had once known. Even after the deaths of her mother and grandmother, she preferred the wolf to the man, to that shape that had failed to protect her time and time again, without ever understanding that her choice was no choice at all.

The wolf was trapped as soon as he dressed himself in the grandmother's clothes. The bonnet grew tighter and tighter, its taut ribbons cutting into his throat while the nightgown's sleeves immobilized his forepaws, made useless his claws. When he tried to take a deep breath to give air to a howl, he found only whimpers left within his lungs, all the air crushed out of him by the constricting nightclothes.

By the time the women came for him, the wolf was past pitiful. Weaker women might have let mercy temper their vengeance, but not the grandmother, and certainly not her daughter's daughter, whose flat smile betrayed a heart as hard and heavy as an unskippable stone. With their saws and their hatchets and their sharp knowledge of knives, they fed the wolf piece by screaming piece to their fire, and when they were finished with him, they buried the slim remains — teeth and eyes and spleen and genitals — beneath a pile of rocks so unremarkable that they could never quite remember where in the wide woods it was.

After the mother and grandmother both passed away, the wolf took their places, so that the girl he secretly adored would not have to go without. The wolf raced back and forth between their two houses, switching between the mother's apron and the grandmother's gown, raising his voice as high as it would go. For her part, the girl pretended not to notice, but it was hard, and sooner or later she knew she would slip, or else he would, and then they would have to act like girls and wolves were supposed to act, with howling and screaming and the gnashing of teeth and knives, until they were each alone once again.

The woodsman and the wolf had been friends once, and what happened between them in the grandmother's cottage a mere misunderstanding. Seeing the wolf there in his mother's clothing, the woodsman mistook him for the woman he had come to kill. It wasn't until after his ax blade slowed — when he was able to see past his blinding matricide to the fur coating the floor — that he realized his mistake, and was ashamed.

The grandmother hungered, consumed with her sickness, and in her crazed state she tore the young girl's limbs from her body with fever-strong twists, devouring each one over the course of several screaming days. When the wolf came to visit, he saw what she had done, and in his mercy he devoured the grandmother too, so that she would not have to live with the sin, so that others would not know what this once-great woman had become.

The wolf grew skilled at counterfeiting the girl's voice. He gained entry into many of her haunts in this way, murdering her family and friends as he went, until his belly dragged on the ground as an animal, hung over his belt as a man. Sometimes, when she joined him in their bed, she laid her cheek upon the fur of his belly and listened to the grumbling from within, to the voices of all her kith and kin he had devoured on his way to loving her. They cried out for her to save them, but she had her wolf, and he was all she needed.

Come get into bed with me, said the wolf, said the grandmother, said the woodsman, said the girl. Each of them made their voice exactly what another wanted to hear, using the perfect enunciation and tone to lure another as completely as possible, and to each other they were lost.

Satiated, the wolf slumbered. His belly rose and fell with each breath, each drunken snore. Inside his swollen stomach he'd trapped little girls and mothers and grandmothers, woodsmen by the dozens. All around them were trees and deer and rabbits and birds and flowers, even the remains of a river, drunk greedily a week or a month before. The wolf himself couldn't remember, had been nearly mad with hunger and thirst, and in his madness had consumed all that he could. The wolf slept on, and when he awoke he was surrounded by the shattered ruins of a cottage, and beyond that a vast field of furrowed, rent dirt. He could no longer feel all those he'd swallowed kicking at his stomach, trying to force their way back out. Satisfied, the wolf grinned—a wolf's grin, all teeth—and then he tried to rise, only to find that his feast had turned hard and heavy as stone. No matter how he struggled, he could not stand, nor crawl against the distended weight of his belly, and soon there was nothing left within the reach of his desperate jaws.

If I told you the wolf deserved this lonely end, that his slow, struggling starvation was justified, then that would be one kind of tale. But he was not a moral wolf, and this was never about to become a moral story, no matter how it ended.

So little yet endured! Just the girl, with her red hood, her red cape, her red-slicked knife, with which she was still slashing her own story to pieces, still discovering new and radiant shapes of pain and pleasure, until all that remained was the last dirge of the wolf, howling with hungered frustration, joined by the cries of her own failing voice, each matching the other's song note for bloody note.

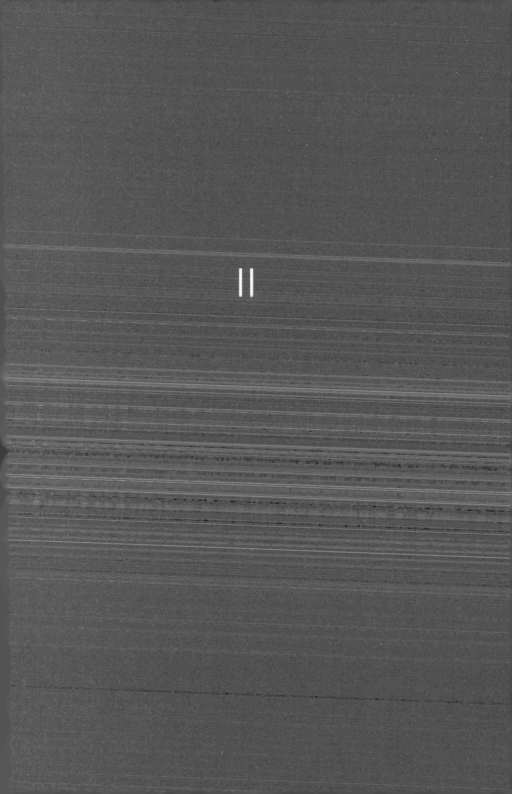

Her Ennead

HER BABY IS A JOKE, a tiny bundle of cells dividing, too small to be taken seriously. For another week or two, it will still be smaller than the benign tumor she had removed from her breast two years ago, a realization that leads to her touching the place where that lump once was. She jokes about this to her friends, who don't find it funny. She doesn't either, but she can't stop herself from sharing about her tumor-sized baby, growing and growing, taking over her body. This time, no one wants her to stop it or get rid of it. This time, people say congratulations and hug her instead of pretending she's contagious, instead of forgetting her number until they hear she's better. Like before, she's only angry because everyone always assumes they already know exactly how she feels. She is careful to keep her true feelings to herself, to see that, as with the tumor, there is much she could lose.

Her baby is a seed, barely planted but already pushing roots through its waxy coat, searching for the dank soil it needs to grow inside her. She pictures it flowering but knows it'll be years before her baby is old enough for flowers, for seeds of its own. Her doctor emphasizes nutrition, suggests she drink six to eight glasses of water every day. At home, she holds her face under the faucet, her throat pried open to swallow all the water she can. When she stands, her face and neck and shirt are soaked through. She puts her lips back to the flowing water and drinks again, as deep as she can, as deep as she knows she must.

Her baby is a stone, cool and dark, something formed not in an instant—as she always assumed her baby would be—but instead over an age, an epoch. Everything about her pregnancy progresses slower than she'd imagined it would. She pictures her stone skipping across the hidden darkness of a lake, each point of contact a ripple expanding and then disappearing. She practices skipping stones herself while she waits for the baby to come, transforming every ditch and puddle and pond and lake into a microcosm, into a point of departure, a possible place where one day she will have to let go.

Her baby is a thunderstorm, a bundle of negatively and positively charged ions about to interact violently. It is a hurricane or a monsoon or a tsunami, but she doesn't know which, doesn't know how to tell the difference. She feels it churning inside, growing stronger with each revolution. What happens after the baby comes will be different than what happened before. This is storm as cataclysm. Whole countries she once knew will be swept away, their inhabitants scattered and replaced by new citizens, other mothers and other children in whose company she knows she will spend the rest of her life.

—◠—

Her baby is a bird, mottled with gray and brown feathers that will last only until the end of its infancy, when it will molt into splendor. Its mouth is open wide, waiting expectantly. Sometimes when she lies still in her quiet apartment, she can hear cawing from her round belly. She has cravings, contemplates eating quarters, little bits of tinfoil, even a pair of silver earrings. She hopes her baby is building a beautiful nest inside of her. She wants to give it everything it needs so that it might never leave. Nest as lie, as false hope. Her baby is a bird of prey, something she has never been this close to before. All those talons. All that beak. It hooks her, devours her. They're both so hungry. She eats and eats. Before this, she never knew birds had tongues.

Her baby is a knife. A dagger. A broadsword, sharp and terrible. Her baby is dangerous, and if she isn't careful, then one day it will hurt her, hurt others. When it kicks, she feels its edges pressed against the walls of its sheath, drawing more blood in a sea of blood. She is careful when she walks not to bump into solid objects, not to put herself in harm's way. She wonders how it will hurt to push it from her body, to have the doctor tug her baby from her body as from a stone.

Her baby is a furred thing, alternately bristled and then soft. She hopes it isn't shedding, wonders how she'll ever get all that hair out of her if it is. She searches online for images of badgers and then wolverines, looking for something to recognize in their faces. She types the words *creatures that burrow*, then adds a question mark and tries again. The baby is so warm inside her, curled in on itself, waiting for winter to end, for a day to come when all the breath it's been holding can finally be expelled, like heat fogging the air of a still cold morning. Sometimes, when the baby rolls over and makes itself known, she can almost smell it.

Now the water breaking. Now the dilation of the cervix. Now the first real contraction, more potent than any of the false warnings she experienced before. Now the worry that this is too early, that she hasn't learned yet what her baby is supposed to be. Now the lack of thought and the loss of discernible time. Now the pain, which is sharp and dull and fast and slow, which is both waves and particles at the same time. Now the hurry, the burst into motion after the near year of waiting. Now the push, the pushing, the rushing stretch of her suddenly elastic body expanding to do this thing, to give birth to this baby. Now the joke, the seed, the stone, the storm, the bird, the sword. Now the tiny mammal, warm-blooded and hot and, yes, now the head covered in wet hair. Now the shoulders, now the torso and the arms. Now the hip bones and the thighs and the knees and the feet. Now the first breath. Now the eyes opening. Now the cry, calling out to her like déjà vu, like the recognition of someone from a dream.

Now the baby.

Now the baby.

Now the baby — an event repeating for the rest of her life.

Her baby is a boy. Her baby is a girl. Her baby is potential energy changing to kinetic, is a person gaining momentum. Her baby is a possibility or, rather, a string of possibilities and potentialities stretching forward from her toward something still unknowable. With the baby in her arms, she smiles. She coos. She tells her baby it can be whatever it wants to be. She tells her baby that no matter what it turns out to be, she will always recognize it when it comes back to her. There is no shape that could hide her baby from her, no form that would make her turn her back on it. She says this like a promise, swears it like she can make it true, like it's just that easy. Some days, no matter what she says, her baby cries and cries and cries.

The Stations

ONLY AFTER THE MOTHER IS gone does the boy imagine the man's hand reaching in, through the gap
between the doorframe and the lowered window glass.
The boy puts his own hand into that gap, feels how it
might feel to some other, perhaps this man at the other pump
watching him, then imagines how the man might experience this same difference between the escaping cool of the
car's interior and the summer heat outside. Below the glass
there is a crank for adjusting the window's height, the rela-
tive safety of the boy inside the car. The boy grips this action
but does not turn it. It is too hot to close the window, but the
window being open does not make the boy safer or the car
significantly cooler, and he knows he is not to roll it down
any more than the mother already has, not for anyone.

The mother is inside the station, glassed behind windows spackled with ads for cigarettes, coffee, two-for-one
milk. The mother is supposed to be coming right back,
but the boy marks her moving past the counter instead,
walking the aisles where there is every kind of candy, cold
glass sodas behind frosted glass doors, glass inside of glass
inside of glass.

The boy knows. He has been where the mother is, could

see what the mother sees, but for now he focuses not on her but on the distance between them, on the danger increasing with that distance.

The boy sweats his story, gathers its telling to him. He swelters, stifles, as the minutes of the mother's absence stretch away, their potential blooming, and when at last time becomes something he can see shimmering in the hot air, then he cups one hand to capture it, closes his fingers and clutches it tight, puts his other hand over it so his grip contains a space of seconds and also some leaking air, a single breath pregnant with potential, a small heat hot as the stuck air of the uncrowded car.

The boy lifts the gathered lie to his mouth, sucks it fast inside his lungs.

What the boy breathes: First, the window, barely open, almost closed, surely one or the other, the difference a matter of the saying and nothing else. Then the man, approaching the window, leaning near, nearer. Then the man's hand, contacting the surface, then the man passing his hand through, breaching the gap.

Then the man's fingers, grasping for the lock-nub, the other mechanics of entry.

The boldness of this imagined man. The stink of this man willing to risk, brave enough to take the boy in view of the mother, the station, the clerk and the other pumpers, believing the distance between the boy and the others enough to render him apart.

The salt-smell of the boy getting brave too, getting ready to scream before the man can open the door, then the boy screaming.

The boy saving himself, because, left alone, there is no else to save him, and this is what it is, this is the worst of it: not the leaving, but the without leave. The anger of being pushed into the pool even after learning how to swim. The shock making you forget how to be alone under the water.

Then the closing of the windows, the checking of the locks, the waiting for the return of the mother, and all along the boy holds his long breath to bursting, holds the lie inside the breathing. He is still wearing his seat belt, as if even when stopped he could crash or be crashed into, and now he opens the clasp, scrambles across the mother's seat. He rolls up the windows for evidence, then rebuckles, sits with his hands landed in his lap. The trapped heat explodes. Sweat wicks, soaks through. He smolders but does not relent, does not lower the window or let out the other hotness either, the one clutched in his lungs, getting big inside him.

A door opens, the mother enters. The boy jumps, but he holds on to what sound he has gathered. The mother buckles her own seat belt, then tries to hand the boy a candy bar — A prize, she says, and also, Why are the windows rolled up, how can you stand the heat — but the boy's hands are already full of his fists. The candy bar falls away, tumbles through the car's other leavings, and as it hits the floor the boy exhales, expels his lie.

To say it without stoppage: the boy knows this is how to make the mother hurt most, and so that is how he tells it.

The mother waits until he finishes, then starts the car, pulls away from the pump. She checks for oncoming traffic, steers the car toward home. Eyes careful through the windshield, the mother says he did good, the screaming for help, the locking the doors and closing the windows, the staying in the car.

She repeats his lie, says, It is important to stay in the car.

The boy does not like the way his words sound from her mouth. He checks every obvious mistake, any error making room for new failure. What he hears is no longer as good as it was before, when it was still withheld within.

The boy says, Do you believe it happened? That the man at the pump tried to take me after you left, left me behind?

He says, Do you believe me?

The mother says she does. She tells him to reach down and get his candy, to eat it before it melts.

She says, It's so hot in here.

I'm buckled in, he says.

Then unbuckle yourself, she says. Nothing worse is going to happen to you today.

The mother says this, and then a weird smile crosses her face.

The car is in motion. The boy does not want to remove his seat belt. He does not want to tempt the crashing of cars with his badness, with the absence of anything bad having really happened, but if he does not eat the candy, then the mother might not believe, and all this time the lie is out of the boy, but it is still lying all over.

The boy unbuckles his seat belt, disappears below the dash into the filth underneath. The danger extends itself, moves along the boy's inability to find the candy bar, and then there it is, at the end of those long few seconds spent among the cardboard burger boxes, the crumpled straw wrappers. He shakes as he straps himself back in, as he peels open the candy. He rushes, shoves the whole of it into his mouth, and still his fingers get dirty, still they stay sticky with the stuff all the way home, where he will rush to scrub his hands, and still it will be hard to get himself clean.

At dinner, the mother says nothing of what happened at the station. The boy waits for her to tell the father, to make some mention, but she never again shows which way it is, whether she believes or does not believe.

How long does she wait before she leaves him again? A week, a month? Some other amount, elongated or else shortened by memory, by the weird time of childhood? In this instance, he is left outside the doctor's office where she is inside learning how many new children grow within her, coming soon to swell her body and then the rest of their family, and in the distance between them the boy pushes in the car's cigarette lighter, catches it when it pops.

He holds its glow in his hands, watches it fade, fires it again.

How long can he bear to wait? How long before he brands this hot ring into his thumb, watching his mother's shape the entire time, as seen through the glass of the car, the glass of the office, the glass of the gathered world?

How long?

Less than a second, shaved down to its least hesitation.

When he has long been the oldest boy instead of just the boy, only then does he return home to remind his mother of the makings of his first lie, the first lie he can remember, his face alive with the shame of it, of the years in between. It is ten, fifteen, twenty years later, and now he is a boy with the body of a man grown up around him, but still he cannot confess cleanly, staring at his mother's kitchen table as he accuses without allowing her to stop him, because all this time passing and still he is the same shape when he says, Do you remember now? When you left me? When I pretended he tried to take me, so you would feel bad for leaving?

Do you remember the other time? When you came out of the doctor's office and then had to take me back in?

The smell of burn gel, he says. The doctor wrapping gauze around my thumb. You, crying.

The mother does not remember, not the one or the other. She refuses him his past even as he repeats the details, as he retrieves its remainder. He made it all up. He is lying to make her feel bad. She refuses to forgive him for something he did not do, that she did not make him do. He pouts his hands, scrubs them against his slacks, then retrieves his proof from within his fist. He presents his opened hand upon the table, palm up, thumb out, thin scars pointed toward the mother.

He says, How much I needed you back, back then.

The mother takes his hand in hers. Her hands are so cold. She lifts his hand to her face, she sees the old wound, or she does not. Mostly it's just a line in a mess of other lines, a scratch across the surface of the skin.

The Cartographer

O BEGIN, A KEY: THIS symbol is the place where the cartographer first met the girl. This symbol is the place where they kissed for the first time. This symbol is anyplace he told her he loved her, anywhere she said it back.

The cartographer wanders the city streets, crosses the invisible boundaries demarcating neighborhoods. He takes notes, studies the geometry of streets and sewers, of subway lines and telephone wires. His bag holds nothing of value beyond the tools of his trade: his pens and papers, his sextant, his rulers and stencils, his dozens of compasses, some worth a month's rent and others bought in bulk at dollar stores and pawnshops.

The compasses are disappointingly true, pointing north always when all he wants is for one to dissent, to demur, to show him the new direction he cannot find on his own. Even the compasses that break to learn some new way never point him to her. At least not yet. It is not their fault but his. He knows he's making the wrong kind of map, but he does not know the kind of map he needs.

Different maps have different requirements, and trying

to make the wrong kind of map in the wrong way is an obvious mistake. Less obvious is how making the right map in the wrong way will also fail completely, with no indication of how close he is to his goal. There is no partial success. He will either find his way to her or else he won't.

This symbol is anyplace where he believed he saw her after her disappearance. It is anyplace he circles back to, week after week after week.

From the very beginning of her sleepwalking, neither of them knew where she was trying to go or why she was going there. She became an expert at slipping out without him noticing, at opening the bedroom door and then the apartment door without making a noise.

How long was she gone before he awoke? He never knew. Some nights he found her quickly, sitting in the lobby of their building or on a bench a block or two away. Other nights he'd search for hours, only to return home and find her asleep in their bed, her nightgown streaked with mud.

Her worst episodes kept her away for days, days he didn't sleep or eat or work, instead wandering the city with someone else's map in his hand, some official version of the city drawn by a company or a commission, a useless fiction. Afterward, she could never explain where she'd gone or what she'd felt while sleepwalking. All she'd ever say was, Let's enjoy the time we have together, and then she'd cling to his body as if it were the mast of a sinking ship, like she'd lashed herself to him.

One time, near the end, the cartographer found her in a subway station at the end of their line, sitting beside the train tracks, crying into the red scarf she always wore layered around her neck. When he asked why she was crying, she said she'd just missed it, that she'd been so close this time. She said the word *skinny* over and over, but he didn't ask what she meant. He'd stopped asking long ago, when she'd begged him to, when she couldn't or wouldn't answer his questions.

Besides, she herself was skinny now, had lost so much weight in the previous months. How was he supposed to know her *skinny* meant something else entirely?

He'd looked down the empty tracks, into the open mouth of the subway tunnel. He worried she'd hurt herself, that if he didn't stop her she'd do something terrible. Now she was gone, and it was he who was hurt: by her absence, by not knowing where she went, by not knowing a sure way to follow.

This symbol is anyplace she woke up after sleepwalking, anyplace he found her, disoriented and scared and begging for help, secretly determined to try again.

It is never enough to assume that the reader of the map will approach it with the same mind-set the cartographer does. Even omitting something as simple as a north arrow can render a map useless. There must be a measurement of scale, and there must be a key so that annotations and symbols can be deciphered, made useful. Other markings are just as necessary.

Even though the map is for only himself, it must still be as perfect as possible.

As practice, the cartographer compulsively maps everywhere he visits, draws on any surface he can find. At the bar down the street from his house, he draws topological renditions of the layout of the tables, of the path from his stool to the bathroom, of the distribution of waitresses or couples or smoke. There are many kinds of maps, but none of these gets him any closer to where he needs to be. He keeps drawing anyway, keeps drinking too, until he feels his head begin to nod. He pays his tab, gets up to leave. If he walks home fast enough, he might be able to fall asleep without dreaming. Most mornings, he still smells her when he wakes, smells all her scents at once: vanilla perfume, hazelnut coffee, apple shampoo; her skin, her breath, her hair. She is only a breeze of memory. As soon as he opens his eyes, as soon as he moves his head, she will be gone.

This symbol is anywhere they had a minor fight, this symbol anywhere they had a major one. These are the places where he regrets, where he goes to say he's sorry when each new map ends in failure.

Her sleepwalking wasn't the only thing wrong with her, but it wasn't until after she disappeared that he opened his mailbox to find the first medical bills, sent from hospitals all over the city. She'd been hiding them from him, keeping him safe from how sick she was.

Opening each envelope, he saw the names of procedures she'd undergone, the dollar amounts she owed after the insurance paid its share: Blood tests. X-rays. EEGs, EKGs, acronyms on top of acronyms. Prescriptions for antiseizure medications, for sleeping pills in increasingly powerful dosages. *Electric shock treatments,* the phrase bringing him near tears the first time he read it, racking him with gasping cries when he began to see it over and over and over.

The cartographer received dozens of these letters in the months after she left, and it was only then that he realized the full scope of her problems.

Sleepwalking, sure, but this too: she was sick, possibly dying, had been almost as long as he'd known her. And she hadn't wanted him to know.

This symbol is any hospital she went to before he met her, and for the hospitals and specialists she went to later, after the sleepwalking began, after the seizures got worse, after she had something to hide.

The cartographer has traveled to these places. He has talked to her nurses, her doctors, her fellow patients. He has shaken their hands, introduced himself, explained his relationship to her. They remember her with fond laughter and sad smiles, but none of her caretakers has ever heard of him. This is how thoroughly she had protected him. This is how she kept her illness a mist-shrouded country, barely even imaginable from across a vast sea.

The cartographer cannot keep to ground truth, cannot render the streets and landmarks in precise relation to one another. No cartographer can. Rendering a three-dimensional world in a two-dimensional space means that purposeful errors are necessary to complete the drawing. Worse than the change in perspective are the lines that must be shifted, moved out of the way so that names can be affixed to symbols, so that this symbol can be distinguished from this one. So that these identical markings can become specific places instead of generalized symbols. Separating one location (basement apartment E5, where she lived when they first met) from another (the third-floor walk-up 312, her last apartment before they moved in together) requires space on the map, requires the physical world be made to accommodate the twin realms of information and emotion, the layers of symbols and abstractions necessary to represent the inhabitants of these parallel universes.

In even the best maps, all these short distances add up over time, until the city depicted is hundreds of meters wider than it should be. This is the second way he loses her, the way he feels her slipping away. He fights for accuracy by creating new symbols and more complex keys, each designed to end his reliance on language, on descriptions now unnecessary, obsolete. He saves his words, stockpiles them for the day he and his girl will be reunited.

This symbol is somewhere he thought he'd find her using his map. This symbol is false hope, easily crushed. One of their last dates before her disappearance was to see a show at the planetarium near the park. Hand in hand, they watched black holes bend light, obscuring everything nearby in their greed for photons. They watched supernovas, the death of one star, and they watched a re-creation of the big bang, the birth of many. He remembers how she

leaned in close and whispered that in a universe as myste-
rious as theirs, anything might be possible, and that it was
therefore completely reasonable to believe in miracles.

After another of her late episodes, the girl lay in their bed
and asked, Did you ever imagine there might be a place
just for us? That no one else could find?

The cartographer often lusted for such places, but when
he told her of his own imagined hideaways—a cabin in
the mountains or a ship floating in the middle of a vast,
unknowable ocean—the girl only shook her head.

That's not what I mean, she said. I mean somewhere no
one else could ever get to, no matter how hard they tried.

No one, she said, and no thing, either. Where we would
be untouchable and safe.

He hadn't known what she meant then, but he did now.

What scares him even worse than not being able to find
her is this: What if he finds her, only to discover that this
secret place is for her alone, that he can't follow where she
has gone?

It has been years, but in his heart, he is still true to her. He
has doubts, but he does not allow himself to express them.
To do so would be the end of him, of all he has become, of
all he has reduced himself to.

He is only the cartographer now, and so he must continue to believe.

The cartographer once thought this would be the last
map he would ever create, that his profession would end
with the culmination of this quest, but he knows that it
might not. What awaits might be another world, unmapped

and unknown. Sometimes he imagines the place he'll find her as a limbo, a purgatory, a place neither as bad as this world nor as good as the one they are truly destined for. It will take another map to escape that place, to complete the destiny he feels in his bones, in his sextant, in his many compasses. In their many needles, each aching to point the way.

X:

X is the store where he bought the ring he never got to give her.

X is the restaurant where he planned to propose, where he had already made the reservation.

X is the speech he rehearsed, that he practiced saying slowly, carefully, so that she would not mishear even a single syllable.

X is nowhere, X is now, X is never mind.

X is everything that ever mattered.

X is all he has left.

What follows the realization of his mistake is as intuitive as breathing, as involuntary as sleepwalking. He spreads his map before him, messy with a thousand corrections, and then, eraser in hand, he tries, tries again. One by one, he eliminates all his symbols, destroys them and replaces them with words. Mere words, great words, words that denote and words that describe and words that will direct him in the way he needs to go. Ground truth disappears, is replaced by something else, by truth as meaning, as yellow brick road, as a key to a lock to a door to an entrance.

He widens the error in his map one phrase at a time, each annotation requiring its own accommodations. He writes their truth upon the city, and the city bends to it, its streets and avenues warping around his words: This is the place where we met. This is the place where we kissed. This is the place where we fell in love, and so is this one and this one and this one. This is our first apartment. This is where we bought our first bed, the first possession we owned together. This is where we went for breakfast on Sunday mornings. This is our favorite restaurant, our favorite coffee shop, our favorite movie theater. These are all the places I found you when you were lost. This is the storefront where you bought the red scarf you cherished so much, that you were wearing the day you disappeared. Where you shopped while I stood outside smoking, where I looked through the window glass and saw how beautiful you were.

This is where I was going to tell you what I wanted to tell you, where I was going to ask you the question I wanted to ask. Where I decided I would ask to marry you, that I would be your man forever.

He annotates until the city appears as a bloated, twisted thing, depicted by a map too full of language and memory to be useful to anyone but himself. Until there are spaces that simply do not exist scattered everywhere, one of which will be the right one. After he finishes, he upends his bag on the floor of his apartment. He rifles through the spilled pile of his tools until he finds his favorite compass, the one she bought him for Christmas their first year. He holds it up, sees true north for the last time. He slips it into his pocket beside the only other object he needs, the small black box. He puts on his coat, then steps out the door with his map in hand. He looks like a tourist, but he's not. Somewhere the city opens, like a fissure or a flower. Inside, she is waiting.

For You We Are Holding

WE ARE WAITING ON THE streets in front of and beside the office. The number of us can be many but rarely is. The number can be none, but it is never that. Whatever the number, that is who we are. Another number of cabs and buses and elevated trains is dispatched into service, to carry those of us who no longer drive away from the end of our working to some other destination: Here is the shop selling suits that was once a shop selling dresses. Here is the restaurant that takes down our names when we call, then expects that we will arrive together, at one particular future. Here is the bank whose ledger is filled with names, some of which are ours, all of which can be organized according to various metrics of finance and circumstance, interest and time.

On the train, we open our phones to track our locations, watch the blue dots cut through the city's grid, across its streets and avenues. Once we rode the trains to get lost, to be anonymous, to be somewhere no one knew we were. Now there is always something locating us by minutes and degrees. The train goes through a tunnel, and for a moment the blue dot stops following. We are free for some

few seconds, and then it is with us again, an on-screen rep-
resentation of we who are traversing a city writ miniature,
pocketable. We press a button and the city disappears into
a menu of other options, other ways to disperse our time.
Our distractions trail us, make waves. We are traveling, but
we are mostly doing so by standing still, by holding on to
the provided railings, lest we be thrown free of this quick-
moving space we have chosen to occupy.

We can be separated by turnstile, by revolving door, by
threshold. Outside on the street, we are waiting to feel our
phones vibrate in our pockets. We are taking our phones
out and looking at the screens even when they do not.
These phantom feelings accumulate until we no longer
trust our senses, ourselves. To communicate we type with
our thumbs, walk with our heads down. When we look
up, our eyes meet from across the avenue. We recognize
each other, or else we think we do. We are the people who
are in a hurry, who are crowded together block after block
after block. We are close to other people but not the people
closest to us. We imagine them here too, imagine them filling this entire sidewalk, the block ahead, the block behind.
What a different city that city would be, filled with all those
missing or else lost. There we might glance upward and see
some her upon the balcony of her apartment, hung high
above us. We might see her, but we might also pretend not
to. It is easy enough to pretend when no one is watching.
She is far off, tiny with distance. She looks as alone as we
are, which is not to say that she doesn't have the remainder
of her family inside, waiting behind her sliding glass door.

We no longer know what that word means to us. *Family.*
Maybe neither does she, unless she turns around and looks.

Once, this bench was where we met on lunch breaks, at
this location an equal distance from each of our offices.
We shared different takeout each time, but often someone
at another bench had a meal that looked better, brought
from some new restaurant hidden in the blocks around the
park. It was hard to be satisfied with what we had when
there was so much more we could have had instead,
when there was all this city we hadn't yet found. We tried
to meet at our bench every day, but if it rained between
eleven and one, then we did not see each other. We tried
never to forget, but if it rained while we were at the park,
then sometimes we rushed back without remembering to
kiss goodbye. Then to spend the rest of the day dreading
car crashes, and what if we should die before we make it
home. *What happened happened but what is the chance of it happening again,* we said. We said, *It's not desperation if it's love,*
but maybe we were wrong.

When the rain starts, we are the number of people standing at this particular corner on this particular day. We
open our umbrellas, hide our faces from the rain but not
from one another. We clump, then disperse. We are going
in more than one direction. We will not remember each
other's faces, only fragments of clothing, posture, speech.
Only the size of an umbrella, the shape of a leg soaring
down and out of a skirt. Only the voice of a child saying *Hello,* saying *What is your name,* saying *Why won't you*

talk to me. Saying, *Mother, why won't he talk to me*. Only this tight sensation held behind our faces, that of our eyes fixed on a lit traffic signal, on the slim last second between not walking and walking. Even while we are walking away we are already walking with someone else.

At the store, we shop for fresh vegetables. We shop for cruelty-free meats. We put our purchases in reusable plastic bags made of recycled materials. The bags are printed with messages telling us we are saving the earth by what we choose to eat and drink, by what we feed our family and friends. Sometimes we wait in long lines; sometimes the train station is so thick with us that by the time we get home our meat is browning. Our lettuce is wilting, our strawberries are spoiled, and all must be wasted into a trash can or garbage chute. We imagine all that past and pointless sunshine, all that mother's milk, all those held breaths spilling out upon the slaughterhouse floor. We imagine that floor packed, crowded with unnamed beasts, defined best by their sudden awareness that they have been tricked.

The salesman at the running-shoe store explains that our shoes are no good for running. He tells us they are outmoded technology, then sells us something else, something better. We will be happier, he says, and healthier too. He says that in these new kinds of shoes we must run without socks. We wonder what about the shoes makes this so, but we don't ask. Not everything that seems to have causality actually does. Now look how long our stride is getting. Look how far we can run from where we were. When we turn around and head back, hear the difficulty in our breath, the discouragement at how far there still is to go. We stop, bend over, put our hands on our thighs. We are breathing hard while around us others are calmly walking. The sun is out, drying the afternoon rain from the sidewalks. The sun is out, but no one expects it to last.

We can be separated by termination, by resignation, by a move to another borough or another city. Sometimes we will think we see an estranged part of us in a department store window, in a bathroom mirror at a bar where we have been drinking. We see his face, his eyes, his hair, or his smile. He is holding a tie up to his reflection or he is lifting a scotch to his mouth. We call out his name, but he does not turn. Probably we did not see him. Probably he does not want to see us, or even look the same as he once did. All around are reminders of the people and places that were once us, images captured in glass and mirror, the shape of names etched into the bricks. In them we do not look unhappy. We are not an unhappy group of people. We have a job or else the prospect of job. We have an apartment we are pleased with. We are wearing suits that we have been told are fashionable so that we might start to meet women wearing dresses like those worn by the girlfriends of our friends, who are the kind of women our friends say we are supposed to be meeting. When our phones ring, it is a friend asking if we want to have drinks or a previous date asking if we want another one. We do want another, or else we do not. We are willing to continue trying, or else it is too early.

Perhaps if we are being honest we will say we only went on the first date because a friend insisted we try to start over. Maybe if we don't know when to stop talking we will say that we are still hoping to regain what we have lost, to repair what we have ruined. Our parents call every week to ask how we are holding up, how we are adjusting, if we are happy. We tell them what they want to hear. We smile, because we are told people can know we are smiling even on the phone. We say, *Yes, we are happy again.* We say, *We are trying hard to be as happy as we can be.*

In the evening we gather in front of an apartment building, then hail a cab. The cabbie is not one of us, not the us that is we who are sharing the cab together, not the us we will be when we are no longer in the cab. The cabbie is different, but he speaks our language. He looks at our suits and dresses and asks us where we are going, what we are doing this night. He asks, *What is the special occasion.* We say we don't know. We say it is our birthday, it is our anniversary, it is the evening after a funeral. There are reasons to celebrate or commiserate, enough people packed around with whom to do either. We have chosen these few others to be with. We have slipped our hands into their hands, have involved their fingers with our palms. Later we will break bread, clink glasses against other glasses. From a great-enough distance, it will be possible to mistake us equally for celebrants or mourners.

The waiter brings us food cooked by a man who yells, or else he gets a call from home, a message in his pocket bearing the first vibrations of bad news. We are the customers he is serving when he returns to our table with his red face and his white hands held above and around our plates. He asks, *Is everything all right. Is there anything I can do for you.* When he goes outside, we wait longer for fresh beverages or extra butter. We have conspired to eat our food in a place where the person who serves us is not a person who will eat beside us. When we leave the waiter at the end of the meal, we tip exactly what we would have tipped had he been perfect.

We stay together until the hour when the trains stop running the way they once ran, and afterward it is harder to get where we are going. Together we stand on the platform, take turns stepping over the line to look down the length of the tunnel, toward the lack of approaching light. Impatient, we stumble backward, shuffle our feet, run our fingers through our messed hair. We are either talking too much or else out of things to talk about. We are surrounded by the people we have been surrounded by all night, plus these others who are us too, if we become now the people waiting for this train. This time of night there are other options. Her number is stored in our phone but also remembered by our fingertips. We could call that number. We could apologize for the late hour, for sounding drunk because we are trying so hard to sound sober. We know we would not get what we are hoping for, but that doesn't mean we wouldn't try, if only there was reception this far beneath the earth.

On the way home, some part of the we takes a picture of the rest, promises to post it online after we are no longer together. Later some of us will write beneath it, craft sentences meant to make the photo seem offhand, incidental, the record of a gathering that could happen again anywhere, anytime, even though perhaps it never will, not even if we want it to. And how we want. And how we are always wanting. To hold on, to recapture what we have lost, what we are losing. Not what, but who. On the streets it is raining again, and again we are wet and tired and ready to be home. Beneath our feet the puddles pool and we plunge ahead until the cold water uncouples us into the night.

Awake alone, then panic again into questions. *Where is he. Where did she go. Where am I.* To be alone is the worst thing, so do not be alone: Open the laptop and watch it fill with glow. Put your fingers to the keys: *Can't sleep. Who else is awake. What are we all doing up.* Watch the screen for responses, then pour a drink while waiting for the coffee to brew. The coffee smells different here, this apartment still unfamiliar after all these months. Check the clock, then take a shower, get dressed. Better to stay awake than to allow the dream to resume its teasing. Morning is here again, but that doesn't mean the lonely nights aren't getting longer.

We can be separated by custody hearings, by the back and forth of the court-ordered visitation weekends that follow, or else by a failure of forgiveness, a persistence of penalty, an inability to beg right our pardon. Living elsewhere now is the boy who is harder to call our boy than he once was, harder to call our oldest son when there is no one left to be older than. Again and again he becomes a stranger in the times between our togetherness. We ask him, *How did you get so big,* and mean every syllable. We ask, *What do you want to do today,* because we fear we no longer know the right answer. We bring him a present, but it is something he already has. He is bored before he opens the package. *Now you have two,* we say. *Now you can keep one at your house and one at mine.* We say, *It's okay to miss your brother. I miss him too.* Over and over we speak these statements, each too much like a question, each clumsied out of our mouth. Always now there are two where once there was one. Always now the one left in this apartment lags behind, stuck in a Sunday evening, while the other rushes ahead, into and out of the coming week. Without us, away from us, the boy is becoming, the boy becomes. He becomes, but we don't know what. We don't know if we will ever know ever again.

In the end, we can be separated despite our best efforts at staying together. We can be separated by tragedy, then by arguments, by fair and unfair blame, by couples' therapy. Then by divorce and new addresses. Now we are too far away and want to get closer. If we still owned a car we would park it up your street. If we owned a bike, we would ride it past your apartment. Instead there is only the bus, the cab, the train. There is only the running, sockless in our new shoes. All day we make the blue dot follow us to the places of our previous habits. They are all diminished now, but we go anyway: Here is the park. Here is the restaurant. Here is the shop and the store and the bank. Tourists would need maps to find these places, but these are not the places tourists would think to find. We have lived here too long for their kind of maps. Our maps are stretched tight across our skin. We carry them everywhere with us so that when we are lost they might carry us home.

We ride and ride until the dot stutters, until we are disappeared between buildings or under the ground. It is only temporary, but it is all the chance we need or have ever needed. Unwatched by anyone, we call your number to ask if you are home. We send a message to tell you we are on our way. We press a button that causes a buzzing in your apartment to notify you that we are downstairs, that we want to come in. Maybe this time will be the time you press a different button that gives us access to what you have: your lobby, your elevator, your hall, your door. If so, then maybe we are knocking now. Maybe then the door is opening, then the door is open. Maybe a cab is waiting for us downstairs, and we are waiting for you, for the two of you. We are waiting for you to join us. We are waiting for you to again please say that you will. *Look how little we are holding without you,* we say. *Without you, look how hard we are trying to hold.*

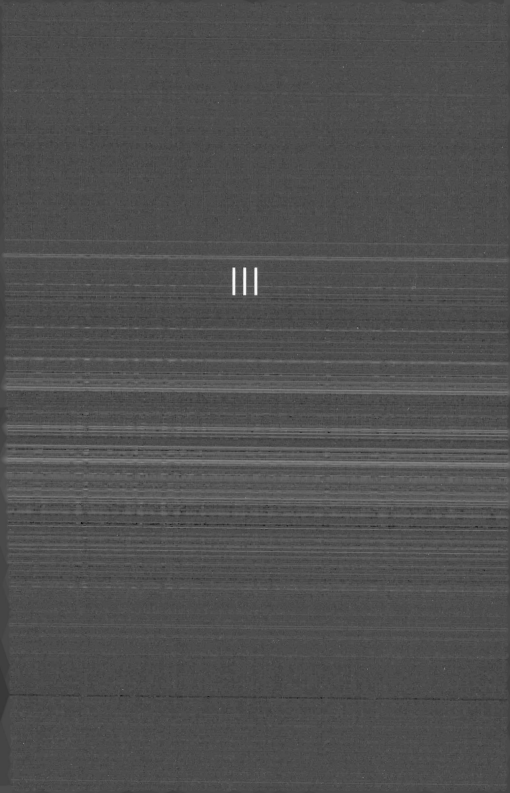

The Migration

AFTER EACH KILLING THE MIGRATION would quicken.
The men killed one, and another migrated. The
men killed two, and a dozen left. This was the method
of the migration, of its start and its continuation and its
quickening.

This is what the men who killed believed. This is the
belief they killed for, for which they continued to kill.

Over some number of nights the men killed a man and then
a man and then a man and then two men, then another
number of men they did not count. They killed them with
ball bats and pipe lengths, with bricks held in leather work
gloves, by pushing them over the railings of overpasses.
They ran some others down in the streets, dragged their
bodies beneath the carriages of crowded cars accelerated
quickly, braked hard and late.

The men who killed, they did not make anything look
like an accident, because they did not want those who
would migrate to believe anything was.

The men who killed talked about killing more, killing
faster, about buying dynamite, about making firebombs,
but mostly they could not afford to kill if they could not

use what they already owned, what they found ready inside house and garage and basement: one killing they made with a crowbar, a tool meant to tear drywall and to lever apart two objects, a tool that worked the same upon a person. Like rope, like wire, like a hammer.

Throughout the killings, there were some who used their boots, and some others used their fists, and afterward some of those men scrubbed themselves raw in the long dark of their sleepless hours. Some of these men who could not sleep had their doubts, but they did not give these worries voice nor allow the others to voice theirs, not even after the killing of the woman, after what happened because of her killing.

The men who killed the woman had not meant to kill the child inside her, had not known she was with child. They had not *seen* her, not as they laid their hands upon her, not as they held her down, not as they pinned her legs, not as they wrapped their hands around her face, quieting her mouth with heavy fingers. And not in the first minutes after either, when they stood close by in the pooling dark, unable to rightly reckon what else they had done.

After all, the child they could not see—the child inside the woman—it was only the size of a fist, and already there were so many fists that what was the presence of one more?

It was only later that they were told about the child—after the boots were removed, after the bat stopped its swinging against her body, after the child was found beneath the layers of its mother's bruises—after men in uniforms arrived at the doors of the men who killed to bind them with cuffs and herd them into the locked backs of waiting cars, their heads pushed low to protect them from injury.

From the first, they said they had not meant the second portion of what they did, were even some of them sorrowed — but they were not sorry enough, and for this crime they were locked into a building they could not escape.

The men who killed knew they had been locked up because they would not stop the killing, because even if they were freed they would not leave the city.

No, they said. They were not the ones who would migrate. They were the ones who would return, who would stay and kill more, because they wanted the migration to continue, wanted it to quicken and quicken.

Even with the men who killed locked in the building, even then it did quicken, and everywhere it went, there were televisions, and everywhere the televisions were, there were other men behind their screens, men in suits who said the killers had killed out of some long hate, out of old wrongs come back around and gone bad again.

But that was not what the men who killed said.

The men who killed were sometimes in the television too, and in the television they said they did not want much.

All they wanted, they said, was this where this went, that where that should go.

It is not complicated, they said. Just us and them. Not together but separate.

We are not the same, they said. They said, We do not belong together.

Some of the men who killed agreed with these experts, the men in suits and ties who did not believe the migration would ever be finished, because those who would migrate were not all of one mind.

Some were stubborn, the experts said, and would require more killings to be quickened, if they could be quickened at all.

The experts said that before they became those who would migrate, many of those who lived there had been trying to get out but didn't have the money to leave, nor the credit to borrow the money, and so no matter how many were killed some number would always live there.

In the ways of their finances and also in other ways, the men who killed and those who would migrate were not so different, but this the men did not believe.

Different is all we are, they said, all we will be.

The experts explained that the houses of those who would migrate had long ago been the houses of men like the men who killed. They had been the houses of women and children, of families, a father, a mother, children or else the absence of children, the trying for. The men who killed thought this was the way it had always been, the way they wanted it always to be. But that world seemed no longer to exist, no matter who they killed, no matter how many were made to migrate.

The sorrow this brought the men, it made them sorrier than killing the woman and the child ever had, but this they did not tell anyone. They did not need to. They had already said it, in every manner but speech.

According to another expert, you could tell the kith and

kin of the men who killed from those who would migrate by some matters of degree.

They were skinned differently, for one thing, and their skins did not take the same dressings.

Also there were matters of music, the next expert said. The men who killed did not like the music of those others who lived among them, of those who would migrate. They did not like even one single note of that sound, but their daughters did, and so also their sons. The music had grown louder and now if the men who killed heard this music moving down the street they would yell from their porches, their yards, their sidewalks, they would grind their teeth, harden their hands to fists. And when their hands were hard enough the men would use them to kill.

Just a theory, the expert said. Just a story, how we got from there to here.

The migration continued even without the men who killed, and without them the world bloomed and then burnished, went orange, and the women of the men did not know what to do. Their houses were hot with what their men had done, with what the women had known or not known, and in the heat they sweated in their kitchens, sweated in their bedrooms, sweated wherever the television held the faces of their men or else those who spoke for them, about them.

It was always their men they thought of, and their anger or disbelief or fear, and the heat already in the air and on the street entered and dwelled within the women until they struggled to work, to care better for their children, to gather peaceably in churches where they might see one another's sadness, the anger at being left behind.

The women of the men could not be fired for having a man who killed, but they could be made to quit, and so some of the women quit while others stayed and bore it, bore it as they bore the capture of their men, as they bore the sudden burden of a family they had to care for all alone. In the bars where some worked, a man would buy them a drink and then another drink and then he would say, Maybe you need help at home, and sometimes the women did and sometimes they did not and sometimes they were not sure and so they took the men home anyway to see what use they might be and then afterward they sat in the beds of the men who killed with these new men who had not and together they watched the television say *fair trial* and *impartial jury* and *change of venue*, and in those repetitions the women heard how even after it was over it would never be ended, not the migration and not the heat and not the women of the men who killed getting by less well and less often.

And what could the women say and what could the women do?

In the supermarkets some women worked and some women shopped and it was not the same women at the same time. Some women went to work in the factories where their men had once worked and some where those who migrated once worked, but maybe some of the women got worse jobs than the others, because of the differences in who they were, in who they replaced.

On the evening news an expert said, There were

differences in their lunch boxes, in the food they chose to bring for lunch. What parts of the cow they ate, how they prepared their potatoes.

Another expert straightened his already straight tie and said, They did not drink the same drinks, and he was right on this as he was on the surface of all things.

Sometimes when the women of the men who killed left work early to pick up their sons and daughters from their schooling, sometimes they saw them playing with the sons and daughters of the killed.

And what this meant to the women.

And how hard it was to watch.

And how hot it made them to tell their sons and daughters no; to tell them, Never again; to tell them, What would your father say. And then it was summer and there was no more school and the differences between burned all the brighter, for being farther apart, for being harder to see.

Those who would migrate were women and children, and also men who had lived, who had not been killed. Maybe these men did not want to migrate, but maybe their women did, maybe their children deserved it, and anyway there was no more work, even less work than when the migration had begun, because the factories and the shops and the supermarkets were migrating too, closing down, locking up. Some of the men did not have the means to take their families away, lacked exactly what the television experts said they lacked, and so the men who would migrate did so without their women and their children, to other cities where they were paid less, where they lived in smaller apartments, where it was hotter or it was colder and where some of them were still killed.

One expert said, This migration will not be isolated. It will spread city to city, until it is finished or until it is stopped.

But another asked, Where will those who migrate go? Who will receive them, house them, take them in?

The men who killed were also allowed to speak, and together they said, Someone else, and, No one, and, We do not care as long as they migrate, as long as their migration quickens until it is finished.

Some others had less reason to stay or to return, and so they locked their front doors for the last time. Their migrations were the easiest, because their reasons to remain were the weakest—although they were not nothing, and still there was cost—and those without men or children or women left their houses and their apartments, and then those homes sat empty, their windows black accusations, and then no one would take their place, no one would move into their emptied but still-hot rooms.

In the courtroom, the men who killed were not allowed to wear their own clothes, and so each man sat dressed in the same colors, in similar shoes. They tried to appear changed, different from the days when they slept each in their own houses, beside their women or else alone, but different was not always an improvement—and when the photographs of the woman before and the woman after were shown on the screen only one of the men who killed cried—and then they were each called by name to offer their testimony, which was of two parts, always or almost always.

We killed the woman, they said. We had warned her before. She shouldn't have been out so late.

During the day, she could have gone to the store or the laundromat, and they would not have seen her. They would have then been decent men, workingmen. Not yet the men who killed.

At night, we killed the woman, they said, but wasn't it her fault, for being where she was not wanted.

She should have left, said the men who killed. They all should have migrated. They should have been quicker to do one or the other, they said, and all this was only always the first part.

Now the city was emptying, its citizens leaving by the freeways, and in the television the experts said there were no more jobs anywhere, not in the neighborhood or in the city or the county, not even in other states, and those who were migrating would not all find anything better than what they had once had.

One expert said this was the year the factories closed and then reopened, and maybe you got your old job back and maybe you didn't, but if you did it was not the same job anyway, not at least in matters of pay, of benefits.

And then his image was replaced by footage of the trial, of the judge and the men and the women of the jury, and also the men who killed, taking the stand and taking the stand, a progression of men who had killed, of those who were left, who had not been killed themselves by those other killers also imprisoned, the ones they were most afraid of—and again there were problems of rough description, problems of calling this rightly what it was, because so few men were made different enough.

Identifying marks, an expert said. This is how you tell them apart. There are tattoos and scars, each located on a particular part of the body, and each differentiated in purpose by class, by education, by neighborhood and affiliation.

Fear, said another. The tattoos are about fear.

But the men who were killed had tattoos too. Like the men who killed.

Yes, agreed the experts. Yes, and all such men are afraid of each other equally.

What the men who killed now knew: it was possible to be sure you were right and still be punished for what you had done wrong. This is what they told themselves, when they were alone in their cells, through the nights stretched so long in the building where they were guarded, where their worst parts twisted in around the remains of the better.

In the courtroom the prosecution said there was danger in the men who killed, and if they would not claim it for themselves, then it was the duty of the state to place it upon them. To set them apart and then to punish them for their apartness. There was evidence against them which could only be mitigated by matters of degree, by dividing accusations of who had held the weapon the longest, who made the most blows against the body of the woman, and this was the second part of their defense: not the difference between not guilty and guilty, but between this guilty and that guilty, the determination of which was worse, the killer who did most of the killing or the killer who waited behind a steering wheel for it to be done or the one who kept watch, ensuring it would not be interrupted.

One of the men said, I would never kill a woman. I could not look either, or stand too close to listen.

But the migration, he said. And so me, waiting on the sidewalk, watching the street, protecting my friends.

My wife left, he said. She took my children and I don't know where they went.

It wasn't her I was trying to make migrate, he said, and haven't I been punished enough, and this was the man who had cried, and now he cried again, and in his tears he knew it was not enough, that it would never be enough, and he did not know how to stop his begging, his wanting for what mercy he did not deserve or understand.

Another of the men who killed took the stand, and then another and then another, one who placed his hand upon a Bible and then denied placing his same hand upon the bat.

Only her mouth, said the man. I held her head in my lap, held her screaming inside her while the others did what they did, what I will not tell you whether they did or not, or who did what part.

I did not murder the woman, said the man. I only quieted her awhile, until she was quiet herself.

Another admitted it was his bat—those were his fingerprints, among and under the fingerprints of the others—but he did not admit to anything else.

This man, he did not admit to swinging the bat over

and over, did not admit to the breaking of the ribs and the breaking of the fingers and the breaking of the femur and the hip.

The bruising of the organs, the prosecutor said, and the man said, That wasn't me either.

And the baby, he said. I had nothing to do with what happened to that baby.

The baby, he said, was someone I didn't even know, and why would I want to hurt what I didn't know?

The migration continued, quickened by the trial, the reminder of the killings enough, and there were reminders everywhere in our neighborhood: here was the laundromat where the woman was leaving with her clothes in her basket, with her baby in her belly, a sliver curled beneath, and here was the distance away where we were too, we who must not pretend anymore that we were not there, and here was where we heard the sirens and here was where we were when we knew they wouldn't get there in time, and also where we never called out, never begged anyone to help, to stop what was coming.

Here was where we were when we did not stop what was happening to these others, who were not us or ours.

Here was where we did not help because we did not want to be made to migrate too, here was where we decided whether or not to join the men who killed, our brothers and uncles and fathers and neighbors, who we had never stood apart from before.

Here was where we decided we required one who could be blamed until he might stand before us scapegoated, so his shape might be broken and his limbs torn from his unforgiven and sacrificial body, an act best accomplished by deed, or else by law and letters, the judgment of myth.

What we decided: that not all the men who killed had been caught, locked up, brought to trial. Still there was the one who remains.

The one who remains, still he was housed with his woman and his children, still he was employed at his place of work, still he was drinking after, he smoked or did not smoke. He had a woman or did not, he loved his kids, probably, but maybe he did not even have kids—and we have to admit we do not know, we have not thought so far ahead. We argue that it does not matter. Whatever separated him from those around him, even those skinned as he was skinned, clothed as he was clothed, it was perhaps very little. Whatever it was, he could have been anyone. He drove a car or he took the bus or he walked, because his house like all the other houses stood in the shadow of the factory where he worked, the factory he'd told the others might cut his job, might terminate their employment at any time.

The one who remains, he might or might not have played ball, but either way he knew how to swing a bat.

On the television, he watched the prosecutor move his accusations across a chart, explaining the configurations of the men who killed, the proportions of guilt each might hold—but the figures did not add up, skewed inaccurate.

The prosecutor said, Someone is lying about what he did.

The one who remains, he sucked a splinter from his thumb, then the blood from the splinter's wound. When he removed his mouth, the blood welled, stained the skin around his thumb, darkened it darker.

The one who remains, his skin was the same color as the men who killed, his skin was different than that of those who would migrate, and it was the surface of a man only different by chance, and what differences there were within were believed to be of another category, created by a man's own designs, his own making—or else this was only what we told ourselves, that the one who remains had been this way, a man who kills, even from the first of all the many times he moved among us.

In the television, we saw the men and the women of the jury, bored and restless.

The men and the women of the jury were united in purpose, anything but in mind. And what that meant for arriving at conclusions, consensus. And how there were some who believed in the guilt of the men who killed and some who believed only in the difficulty of their prosecution, in the lack of clear blame—and should the man who held the woman down be sentenced the same as the man who drove the car as the man who swung the bat, if that man was even on trial, a now-doubted assertion?

What is proof, the men and the women of the jury asked.

What is enough proof, they asked one another, and their words seemed so familiar, and each man and woman worried at this, feared some assigned and acted-out role, but each day they said nothing to any other, and what good could these thoughts have done if voiced, and so despite their doubts they voted, and then the vote was split and then the men and the women of the jury admitted to the judge they had not yet made a decision and they were sequestered in rooms that did not contain their families when all they wanted was to go home to rooms that did. *Sequester* as a synonym for *imprison*. In the night the men and the women of the jury lay awake and this was the night they decided they would change their vote and then after all those long and stalling deliberations they at last voted as one, and then in the morning the men who killed stood to hear the foreman read the jury's decision, the foreman sweating with heat under his collar, a hotness that did not abate when he finished speaking, when the end of his speech set off what was always coming after.

Now all the men who killed were crying or else stricken silent, temporarily ghost white, and around them the room erupted into hot sound and hot fury as the judge's gavel banged on, and on the steps of the courthouse one of the experts faced the camera and said, Now the migration will never end. Now it will quicken and quicken and worsen.

Another said, The savagery of man. The fault of the police. The incompetence of the prosecution.

A third expert looked nervously at the camera, then nervously away. This is the summer of rage, he said. This is the summer of the furies. Now they will take to the streets, righteous and terrible, and who knows where they will stop.

The streets already hot when the verdict came down, now getting hotter, burning up with what rolled across their cracked and potholed surfaces: Heat coming out of television sets and radios. Heat coming out of car engines, out of automobiles long ago assembled by the men who had killed, by the same hands with which they had killed. Heat coming out of the doorways of their homes and the doorways of those who remained but not the doorways of those who had already migrated, whose houses sat empty, shut up.

Then the heat in Oakland, in Detroit and Flint and Saginaw, in Chicago and Mobile and Oxford and Cincinnati. The heat rising in St. Louis and Bismarck and Lincoln, in Albuquerque, in Pittsburgh and Bethlehem and Baltimore.

Then the heat hottest in the neighborhood where the men who killed once lived, where their women and children lived still, where those who would migrate remained in great numbers, despite the danger and the anger, at the end of the summer, at the end of the trial, at the ends of this city, at the terminus of one city the city might have been, and the heat came up off the concrete and down out of the sky until it filled the space in between, and anyone caught on the street near burst with it, their skinned bones wet with sweat begging to get out, and when the houses were too hot to hold the men and the women and the children, then each house was opened and each spilled its inhabitants out onto the street, where they became a crowd — and then the crowd filled the streets — and then the crowd in the streets began to move.

The crowd in the streets moved not as one body but as many bodies moving together, and while some were angry at the sky, others were angry at the ground. Some were angry at store windows and shattered them with bricks and stones and pipes and boards, some were angry at the objects inside the stores and so they smashed them too, or else carried some objects off into the streets, where they were also smashed or secreted away, while others were angry at cars and trucks and vans and so together they worked to overturn one and then another and another, and to set them ablaze, and some of the vehicles they burned were ones they had built themselves in the last days of their working, and in the flames there burned some part of themselves.

Some were angry at their God, but whether they prayed or cursed there was no one to hear but themselves, all others blunted mad and mute, smote dumb by watching.

Some were angry at those who most resembled the men who killed, and they dragged them from the cab of their trucks or from behind the counters of their shops. And so again the killed and the killers became confused, and in their confusion they died or were made dead, and the city burned, and the men who killed were still not released, because it was not safe for them on the streets, and each man cried out in his solitude, for what was happening was stronger than he had ever imagined the migration would be, and he knew he had done his part to make it so.

The men in uniform were armed with weapons that did not kill but would injure, carried grenades that did not burn but would choke. They did not want to fire these weapons, or at least they did not all want to fire all of them, but then the crowd in the streets arrived, at first standing a distance from these men, a divide too small. On the other side a uniformed man with a bullhorn and a helmet told the crowd to go home, saying, No one needs to get hurt, but he said it with such a quaver no one had to believe him, not if they didn't want to, and there were those who did not, who would never again believe anything any man in uniform had to say. And so instead they threw their voices and they threw their rocks and they threw their bricks, and when the men in uniform began to fire their weapons into the crowd, then most of the crowd ran, but some few rushed the wall of uniforms and shields, falling beneath boots and batons wielded by men who were not supposed to kill unless they had to, unless they were threatened, but who nonetheless sometimes struck with the same force as the men who killed, broke bones in those who should have migrated, the same bones others had broken before.

And what now, asked some expert, sweating before the camera. And what next? What would there be? What could there ever be again?

The one who remains stepped out of a bar or a house or an automobile, smoking or not smoking. He knew where his woman and his kids were or he did not. He wore a shirt with his name on it, but still we do not know his name, or else we will not speak it—or else it was an invention, and also it was invented that he had tattoos and scars, but not such that identified him for what he was, for who he is.

His hands were big, but perhaps his body was not. Again there was a baseball bat in his hands, probably, and steel sewn into the toes of his shoes, more than likely, and always there had been migration in his heart and always he had worked to quicken it, this separation of men from men, first alone and then with others.

The one who remains did not have his bags packed. The one who remains did not plan on running away. The one who remains did not know if he would be arrested, if his blows upon the woman and the baby would ever be properly counted and accounted for, translated into punishment, imprisonment.

The one who remains, he *remained*. He did not run, he did not move, he did not migrate.

The one who remains, this was his house.

This was his street.

This was his neighborhood, this was his store and his bar and his laundromat.

This was his factory, where he had spent all the working days of his life, where by some hard grace he worked still.

This was his city, and he would not leave it to those he wished would leave, nor would he forsake it to their music and their foods and the dressings of their different skins.

This was his city, as long as he remained, as long as he remained and the others were made to migrate, and now he walked out among those he hated so, a new bat hanging loose and easy from his hands, and at first he was not visible, although he should have been, because everything he was made of cried out from the etchings of the lines of his face and from within the black parts of his eyes, and around him and ahead of him the crowd in the streets surged against a wall of shields, those men in uniform, and there were gas and rubber bullets and beanbags fired into and through the air, and everywhere the one who remains strode there was crying and running, and also fire, flames lit amid broken skins and broken glass.

The city burned, and the one who remains did not smile at the sight. His face was a slab of slate, his eyes killer's eyes, black and blank. His movements were those of a ghost, and he thought of himself in this way, not flesh but this other thing, ghosted. The one who remains, this was his city, and yet he stayed invisible to it until he acted, until he swung the bat, until he connected its heft with the head of one of those he wished would migrate, and then there was blood on the wood, and there were splinters in his hands, the action vibrating through his arms and into his shoulders, a feeling so quickly expanding it nearly split him, and perhaps it would have done so, had he not made of himself an empty room, had he not earlier pried loose so many other holdings, the ones that might have made him different than he was.

In the television there was video from the sky, video from the streets, and on the streets as in the television a man in uniform brought his baton across a teenage face, and the crowd in the streets circled a car on fire, surrounded the shirtless man atop it, a gory glory triumphant, and all around there was paint sprayed on the bricks and blood sprayed on the paint and there were killers in the crowd and also mothers and fathers and sons and daughters, revolted and revolutionary, and those who would migrate were the crowd in the streets but they were not all the crowd, and all there combined into one creed, and this creed contained among its verses the absence of love and God and the possible death of every man and woman and child and the destruction of the city, and the heat was still so hot the air shimmered and sung, and the men in uniform gassed the crowd in the streets and the crowd in the streets charged through the gas, and the houses burned and the fuel stations were firebombed and the fire trucks were not enough and the men in uniform were not enough either and the crowd in the streets contracted and hardened, until it was all right to steal and it was all right to hurt and it was all right to sink to your knees with your hands in the air and your face streaming down your shirt and it was permitted to hold a trampled child and to comfort even what was not yours and it was permitted to rend your clothes when the gas streaked your eyes and you did not know which way to run; and it was permitted to run, so the crowd in the streets ran, so the men in uniform ran after, uncareful, each man maybe losing his head beneath his helmet so that he fired behind the backs of those who were running through the lists of smoke, who were falling to the concrete, bodies breaking upon the hard miles of the city even as the day dwindled toward the dark, and beneath the last rose of the dusk the one who remains continued on, farther against the sundered city.

The one who remains, he swung his bat and all gave way beneath his blows, and at last some others heard, at last some of us still scrapping turned to stop him instead, to stand opposed to what he was—and this is the story we tell ourselves about ourselves, a testimony sworn to, retold as often as we need it to be so, whenever we regret what else we remember we were: Down the street came a crowd made of one purpose, armed with bricks and stones and loud voices and bodies all around, and when the one who remains did not heed their call to stop they filled the air with more shouting. When they reached his shaded shape they saw all he had caused, and in their anger they knocked him to the ground and they lifted him from off the paved earth and they pried at the bat fisted within his hands, and the furious crowd tried to identify his face but he was no one anyone would recognize because while his face was still whole he looked like everyone else, and because while there was difference in his heart it was not always visible on his skin, which did not color with blood the way others' did, and even caught his face did not bloom, would not no matter how he might rage, and as the crowd in the streets and all around him became a single rushing awful mass, then the one who remains declined again to flee, but turned into them instead, grinning a joyless smile, and as they beat him he gave up his fingers to be broken from the bat and he gave up his teeth to be booted from his head and he gave up his cheeks to be dashed against the sidewalk and he gave up everything without giving up, and when they at last made him cry out the crowd in the street saw what they had become, and the one who remains saw too and was gladdened, even as his body came unsocketed by their hands, and by his long command he knew some in that crowd would yet die before the end of the day and some of them believed they would live forever or close enough, and those who lived would be the ones who remembered, and as the crowd in the streets left what was left, as they ran away from what animals they had made of him and of themselves, then they knew that at the end of those hot days there would be no answers and no punishment either, no reckoning except what remained of the migration, paused but not stopped, except the crowd in the streets cooled, made again those who migrate, made again the women and the children of the men who killed — and before the one who remains could die some men in uniform came down the streets in their helmets, locked side by side behind their shields to empty the crowd of its last resistance, and the flying rubber and stinging gas forced the people in the streets back home, back into their houses, each a powerless space where no lights burned, where no one waited for their return, where for some the word *home* would never apply again, and outside the city smoldered, and everywhere there was less than before, and it was not just people who could be made to migrate but all good things, and the sun and the stars and the moon were absent from the sky for a span, hidden by a foul tower of smoke, but then for some time the sun returned, and by its pink light other men found the one who remains, what of him there was, but they too did not know his name, nor how to recognize what was left, and some say that because they did not name him right then he never ended either, and some say he went ever on, anonymous, and the men in uniform lifted him onto a stretcher, lifted him broken into an ambulance, lifted him into surgery and repair and rest, and later he would leave the hospital unseen, wholer and still wrongly unaccused, and later the men who killed were for a time made freed men, and all the city's citizens were unsatisfied anew, despite what they too had done, and at the release of the men who killed a new expert spoke, said the migration was not finished, that forever it would quicken and quicken. The migration did not require men to continue to kill but only to not stop killing, and walking among us there were some who never would, and at the last they might be all that there was, men who killed turning upon one another until perhaps there would be only one, and all around that one some city like this city, ruined and burned and spent, broken off its bones, heaving haggard its best breaths, and those gathered did not want it to be this way, wanted to cry out some rebuttal. But if there was another story to tell, then it was lost to us that day. But if there was anyone with a better story to tell, then together we are all still waiting for them to speak.

His Last Great Gift

SPEAR HAS ALREADY BEEN LIVING in the cabin overlooking High Rock for two weeks when the Electricizers speak of the New Motor for the first time. Awakened by their voices, Spear feels his way down the hallway from the dark and still-unfamiliar bedroom to his small office. He lights a lamp and sits down at the desk. Scanning the press of ghastly faces around him, he sees they are all here tonight: Jefferson and Rush and Franklin, plus his own namesake, John Murray. They wait impatiently for him to prepare his papers, to dip a pen in ink and shake it free of the excess. They begin speaking, stopping occasionally to listen to other spirits that Spear cannot quite see, that he does not yet have the skills to hear. These hidden spirits are far more ancient, and Spear intuits that they guide the Electricizers in the same way that the Electricizers guide him.

What the Electricizers show Spear how to draw, they call it the New Motor, a machine unlike any he has ever seen before. He concentrates on every word, every detail, of their revealment: how this cog fits against that one, how this wire fits into this channel. In cramped, precise letters, he details which pieces should be copper, which zinc or wood or iron. The machine detailed in this first diagram is a mere miniature, no bigger than a pocket watch but twice as intricate.

It's too small, Spear says. He puts down the pen, picks up the crude blueprint with his ink-stained fingers. He holds it up to the specters. He says, How can this possibly be the Messiah you promised?

Jefferson shakes his head, turns to the others. He says, It was a mistake to give this to him. Already he doubts.

Franklin and Rush mutter assent, but Murray comes to Spear's defense. Give him time, the spirit says. At first, we had doubts too.

Murray touches Spear on the face, leaving a streak of frost where his fingers graze the reverend's stubbled skin. He says, Have faith. It is big enough.

He says, Even Christ was the size of a pea once.

The First Revealment

First, that there is a UNIVERSAL ELECTRICITY.

Second, that this electricity has never been naturally incorporated into minerals or other forms of matter.

Third, that the HUMAN ORGANISM is the most superior, natural, efficient type of mechanism known on the earth.

Fourth, that all merely scientific developments of electricity as a MOTIVE POWER are superficial and therefore useless or impracticable.

Fifth, that the construction of a mechanism built on the laws of man's material physiology, and fed by ATMOSPHERIC ELECTRICITY, obtained by absorption and condensation, and not by friction or galvanic action, will constitute a new revelation of scientific and spiritual truths, because the plan is dissimilar to every previous human use of electricity.

This mechanism is to be called the NEW MOTOR, and it is wholly original, a mechanism the likes of which has never before existed on the earth, or in the waters under the earth, or in the air above it.

In the morning, Spear descends the hill into the village below, the several pages of diagrams rolled tight in the crook of his arm. On the way to the meeting hall, he waves hello to friends, to members of his congregation, to strangers he hopes will come and hear him speak. He is confident, full of the revealed glory, yet when he reaches the meeting hall, he does not go in.

Spear's friends and advisers—the fellow reverends and spiritualist newspapermen meeting inside the hall—have followed him to Massachusetts because of the revelation he claimed awaited them here. Already he knows they will not be disappointed, but he worries it is too soon to tell them about the blueprints, to allow them to doubt what the Electricizers have given him. He leaves the meeting hall without entering, wanders the town's narrow streets instead, waiting to be told what to do next.

It takes all morning, but eventually Rush appears to tell him which men to pick, which men to trust with the knowledge of what will be built in the tiny shed atop the hill.

He chooses two Russian immigrants, Tsesler and Voichenko, who speak no English but understand it well enough. Devoted followers of spiritualism, he has seen their big bearded heads nodding in the back row at fellowship meetings, and he knows they will be able to follow the instructions he has to give them.

After the Russians, he selects a teenager named Randall, known to be hardworking and good with his hands, and James the metalworker, a man who has followed Spear since the split with the church.

He chooses two immigrants, an orphan, and a widower: men in need of a living wage, capable of doing the work and, most important, with no one close enough to obligate them to share the secrets he plans to show them.

Spear selects no women on the first day, but knows he will soon. One of the women in his congregation will become his New Mary, and it's she that will bring life to their new God.

The Fourth Revealment

Each WIRE is precious, as sacred as a spiritual verse. Each PLATE OF ZINC AND COPPER is clothed with symbolized meaning, so that the NEW MOTOR might correspond throughout with the principles and parts involved in the living human organism, in the joining of the MALE and FEMALE. Both the wooden work and the metallic must be extremely accurate and crafted correctly at every level from the very beginning, as any error will destroy the chance for its fruition. Only then shall it become a MATHEMATICALLY ACCURATE BODY, a MESSIAH made of singular, scientific precision instead of biological iterations and guesswork.

Spear gathers his chosen men together around the table in the shed, lays out the scant revealments he's received so far. He says, This is holy work, and we must endeavor at every step to do exactly what is asked of us, to ensure that we do not waste this one opportunity we are given, because it will not come again in our lifetimes.

He says, When God created the world, did he try over and over again until he got it right? Are there castaway worlds littering the cosmos, retarded with fire and ice and failed life thrashing away in the clay?

No, there are not.

When God came to save this world, did he impregnate all of Galilee, hoping that one of those seeds would grow up to be a Messiah?

No. What God needs, God makes, and it only takes the once.

Come closer. Look at what I have drawn. This is what the Electricizers have shown me.

They have revealed to us what he needs, and we must not fail in its construction.

As the work begins, Spear walks the perimeter of the room, listening to the Russians translate the blueprints into their own language before beginning construction, while at the other end of the shed, James shows Randall how to transform sheets of copper into tiny tubes and wires, teaching him as a master teaches an apprentice. Later Spear steps forward to weigh the tubes the two have produced so far, impressively narrow but still wider in diameter than the revealments require.

Smaller, he says.

Smaller is impossible, says James.

Have faith, says Spear, and faith will make it so.

James shakes his head, but with Randall's help he creates what Spear has asked for. It takes mere days to build this first machine, and when they are finished, Spear throws everyone out of the shed and padlocks the door.

He does not start the machine, cannot even see what it might do.

He thinks, Perhaps this is only the beginning, and he is right. The Electricizers return after midnight, and by morning he's ready to resume work. He calls back Tsesler and Voichenko and Randall and James and shows them the next blueprint. The new machine will be the size of a grapefruit, and the first will be its heart.

Franklin joins Spear on the hill while in the shed behind them the work continues. Spear has the next two stages detailed on paper, locked in the box beneath his desk, and he is no longer concerned about their specifics. Instead, he asks Franklin about this other person, the opposite of himself. He asks Franklin, Who is the New Mary? How am I supposed to know who she will be?

Franklin waves his hand over the whole of High Rock, says, She has already been delivered unto us. You need only to claim her, to take her into your protection.

He says, When the time is right, you will know who to choose.

But the time is now, Spear says. If her pregnancy is to coincide with the creation of the motor, it must start soon.

Franklin nods. Then you must choose, and choose wisely.

On the Sabbath, Franklin stands beside Spear at the pulpit, whispering into Spear's ears, sending his words out Spear's mouth. There are tears in Spear's eyes, brought on by the great hope the Electricizers have given him. To his congregation, he describes the reborn America the New Motor will bring, the most beautiful world Spear has ever imagined, complete with the abolition of slavery, the suffrage of women and Negroes, the institution of free love and free sex and free everything, the destruction of war and greed. Spear tells his congregation that with their support the New Motor will make all these advancements possible.

Franklin whispers something else, something meant for Spear alone. The medium nods, looks out at the congregation. One of these women must be the New Mary, and so Spear waits for Franklin to say a name, hesitating when the specter fails to reveal the correct choice. He considers the women in the restless audience, searches his heart for their qualifications. He thinks of the first Mary, of what he understands of her beauty, her innocence, her virginity. The girl he selects to replace her must be young, and she must be unmarried.

Spear does not know the women of his congregation well.

He can recognize them by sight but remembers their

names only when he sees them beside their husbands or fathers or brothers.

There is one he has known for a long time, one he has watched grow from a child into a young woman under the tutelage of the spiritualist movement. He has always felt discomfited by the attention he paid her, but at last he understands his lingering gazes, his wanting thoughts. From the pulpit, he says her name: Abigail Dermot.

He says, Abigail Dermot, please step forward.

He watches her stand, confused. As she approaches, he averts his eyes, both from her and from the front pew, where his wife and children sit.

The thoughts in his head, he does not want to share them with his wife.

He turns to Franklin, but the specter is gone. What he does next, he does on his own.

The Seventeeth Revealment

Among you there will be a NEW MARY, one who has inherited an unusually sensitive nature, refined by suffering. To her will be revealed the true meaning of the CROSS, as the intersection of heaven and earth, as positive and negative, as both male and female. She will become a MOTHER, but in a new sense: the MARY OF A NEW DISPENSATION. She will express a maternal feeling toward not just the NEW MOTOR but also to all individuals, who, through her instrumentality, will one day be instructed in the truth of the new philosophy.

After the services are over, Spear takes Abigail into his office in the meetinghouse and motions for her to sit down before taking his own seat behind the desk. He believes she is sixteen or seventeen, but when he asks, she says, Fifteen, Reverend. She has not looked at him once since he called her up to the front of the congregation, since he told the others that she was the chosen one who would give birth to the revelation they all awaited.

Spear says, Abigail, you are marked, by God and by his agents and by me. You are special, set apart from the others.

He says, Abigail. Look at me.

She raises her eyes, and he can see how scared she is of what she's been called to do. He stands and walks around the desk to kneel before her. She smells of lavender, jasmine, the first dust off a fresh blossom. His hands clasped in front of himself, he says, Can you accept what's being offered to you?

He rises, touches her shoulder, then lifts her chin so that their faces are aligned, so that her blonde hair falls away from her eyes.

He says, It is God that calls you, not me, and it is he you must answer.

The Thirty-Second Revealment

The MEDIUM is rough, coarse, lacking culture and hospitality, but with the elements deemed essential for the engineering of the NEW MOTOR, for this important branch of labor. At times he must be in the objective position [not in a TRANCE] while at other times he must be erratic, must ignore his family and friends so that he might hear our many voices. Acting upon impulse, this person will be made to say and do things of an extraordinary character. He will not be held accountable for his actions during the MONTHS OF CREATION. Treading on ground so delicate, he cannot be expected to comprehend the purposes aimed at. Do not hold him as a sinner during this time, for all will be forgiven, every secret action necessarily enjoined.

The services of many persons must be secured to the carrying forth of a work so novel, so important. The NEW MOTOR will be the BEACON FIRE, the BLOODRED CROSS, the GENERAL ORDER OF THE NEW DAY. Whatever must be sacrificed must be sacrificed, whatever must be cast aside must be cast aside. Trust the MEDIUM, for through him we speak great speech.

That night, Rush shows Spear the next stages of the New Motor, detailing the flywheel that will have to be cast at great cost. Spear is given ideas, designs, structures, scientific laws and principles, all of which he writes as quickly as he can, his hand moving faster than his mind can follow. When he reads over what he has written, he recognizes that the blueprint is something that could not have originated from within him. He can barely comprehend it as it is now, fully formed upon the paper, much less conceive how he would have arrived at this grand design without the help of the Electricizers.

Rush says, The motor will cause great floods of spiritual

light to descend from the heavens. It will reveal the earth to be a limitless trove of motion, life, and freedom.

Spear dutifully inks the diagram and annotates each of its intricacies, then asks, Did I choose the right girl?

Rush points to the diagram and says, That should be copper, not zinc.

Spear makes the correction, then presses his issue. She's only fifteen, from a good family. Surely she's a virgin.

He says, I have seen her pray, and I believe she is as pure of heart as any in the congregation.

Rush says nothing, just waits for Spear to take up his instrument. Spear apologizes, swallows his doubts. He silences his heart and opens his ears. He writes what he needs to write, draws what he needs to draw.

A week later, Spear sends Randall down into the village to fetch Abigail. When the boy returns with the girl, her mother and father also walk beside her. Spear tries to ignore the parents as he takes the girl by the arm, but her father steps around him, blocking the path to the shed.

The father says, Reverend, if God needs my daughter, then so be it. But I want to see where you're taking her.

Spear keeps his hand on the girl. He says, Mr. Dermot, I assure you that your daughter is safe with me. We go with God.

What is in there that a child needs to see but a man cannot?

You will see it, Mr. Dermot. Everyone will, when the time comes. When my task—your daughter's task—is complete, then you will see it. But not before.

Spear holds the father's gaze for a long time. He wants to look at Abigail, to assure her that there is nothing to be afraid of, but he knows it is the father he must convince. Behind them, her mother is crying quietly, her sobs barely louder than the slight wind blowing across the hill. Spear waits with a prayer on his lips, with a call for help reserved farther down his throat. Randall is nearby, and the Russians and the metalworker will come if he calls.

Eventually the father steps aside. Spear breaks his gaze but says nothing as he moves forward with the girl in tow. Out of the corner of his eye, he sees the curtain of his cabin parted, sees his wife's face obscured by the cheap glass of the window. He does not look more closely, does not acknowledge the expression he knows is there.

Inside the work shed, construction continues as Spear shows Abigail what has been done, what the New Motor is becoming. He explains her role as the New Mary, that she has been chosen to give life to the machine.

He says, I am the architect, but I am no more the father than Joseph was. This is your child, and God's child.

He says, Do you understand what I am telling you?

The Electricizers are gathered in the shed, watching him. He looks to them for approval, but their focus is on the machine itself. Inside the shed, the words he says to them never have any effect, never move them to response or reaction.

Work stalls while they wait for supplies to come by train to Randolph, and then overland to High Rock by wagon. For two weeks, Spear has nothing to do but return to the ordinary business of running his congregation, which includes acting as a medium for congregation members who wish to contact their deceased or to seek advice from the spirit world. A woman crosses his palm with coin, and he offers her comforting words from her passed husband, then he helps a businessman get advice from an old partner. Normally, Spear has no trouble crossing the veil and coming back with the words the spirits offer him, but something has changed with the arrival of the Electricizers, a condition aggravated since the beginning of construction on the Motor. He hears the other spirits as if his ears are filled with wax, and the real world seems as distant, as difficult to navigate.

By the time the spinster Maud Trenton comes to see him, he can barely see her, can barely hear her when she says, I'm hearing voices, Reverend. Receiving visitations.

She says, Angels have come to me in the night.

Spear shakes his head, sure he has misunderstood the woman. He feels like a child trapped in a curtain, unable to jerk himself free. He hasn't crossed the veil, merely caught himself up in its gossamer.

He says, What did you say?

Maud Trenton, in her fifties, with a face pocked by acne scars and a mouth holding the mere memories of teeth, she says, I told the angels I was afraid, and the angels told me to come to see you.

Jefferson appears behind her, with his sleeves rolled up, wig set aside. His glow is so bright it is hard for Spear to look directly at the specter, who says, Tell her that God loves her.

Spear's eyes roll and blink and try to right themselves. He can feel his pupils dilating, letting more light come streaking in as wide bands of colors splay across his field of vision. He's firmly on the other side, closer to what comes next than what is.

Jefferson says, Tell her we're thankful. Tell her we venerate her and protect her and watch over her. Tell her the whole host is at her service.

Spear is so confused that nothing comes out when he opens his mouth. And then the specter is gone, and Spear is freed from his vision, returned to the more substantial world, where Maud sits across from him, her eyes cast downward into her lap, her hands busy worrying a handkerchief to tatters. Suddenly Spear feels too tired to talk to this woman anymore or to concern himself with her problems.

Spear tries again to say Jefferson's words, but they won't come out, and although he knows why he blames her instead. He says, Woman, I have nothing to say to you. If you feel what you're doing is wrong—if you've come to me for absolution—then go home and pray for yourself, for I have not been granted it to give you.

At dinner that night, Spear's forehead throbs while his wife and daughters chatter around him, clamoring for his attention after his day spent down in the village. He continues to nod and smile, hoping his reaction is appropriate to the conversation. He can't hear his family's words, cannot comprehend their facial expressions no matter how hard he tries.

He does not try that hard.

What is in the way is the New Motor. The revealments are coming faster now, and Spear understands that there are many more to come. It will take eight more months to finish the machine, an interminable time to wait, but there is so much to do that Spear is grateful for every remaining second.

The New Motor is ready to be mounted on a special table commissioned specifically for the project, and so Spear brings two carpenters into his expanding crew, each once again hand-selected from the men of High Rock. The table is sturdy oak, its thick top carved with deep concentric circles designed to surround the growing machine. When the carpenters ask him what the grooves mean, Spear shakes his head. Their purpose has not been revealed, only their need.

Abigail becomes a fixture in the shed, spending every day with the men and the Motor. Spear sets aside part of every morning for her instruction, relating scriptures he finds applicable. The girl is an attentive student, listening carefully and asking insightful questions. Spear finds himself wishing his own children were so worthy, and more than once he finds the slow linger of a smile burned across his cheeks long after he and Abigail have finished speaking.

In the afternoons, he joins the others in the day-to-day work of constructing the machine, but even then he continues to watch her, to notice her. This is how he observes the way she sees Randall, the talented young worker who will have his pick of trades when the time comes. Metalworking, carpentry, even the doing of figures and interpreting of diagrams, come easy to Randall, the boy's aptitudes speaking well of his deeper, better qualities. Spear has often been impressed with the boy, but now, watching the quick glances and quicker smiles that pass between Randall and Abigail, he knows he will have to study him even closer.

He tells himself that it is not the girl he cares about, only the Motor. After she gives birth to his machine, Randall can have her. Let him be her Joseph then, but not before. Spear is sure that, like Mary, Abigail must be a virgin to bring the Motor to life, and he cannot risk Randall ruining that. Spear will take the girl home. It is only himself that he can vouch is above reproach.

Spear is no engineer, but he knows enough to understand that the New Motor is different. Where most machines are built in pieces, one component at a time, the Motor is being built from the inside out. It is being grown, with the sweat and effort of these great spiritualist men, all excellent workers, excellent minds. Tsesler and Voichenko especially seem given to the task; their ability to translate the complexities of the diagrams and explanations into their own language is almost uncanny. The others work nearly as hard, including Randall. Despite Spear's misgivings about the boy, he knows the young man is as dedicated as any other to the completion of their work. Six days a week, for ten or twelve or fourteen hours, they slave together in the forge-heated shed to fulfill the task handed down by the Electricizers. By the time snow covers the hill, the machine has enough moving parts that a once-useless flywheel becomes predictive, turning cogs that foretell the other cogs and gears and pulleys not yet known to Spear. The first gliding panel is set in the innermost groove of the table's concentric circles, moved all the way around the Motor once to ensure that it works the way it is intended to. The panel's copper face is inscribed with words that Spear does not know, words he believes are the long-hidden names of God, revealed here in glory and in grace.

On the day of the fall equinox, the men finish after dark, every one of them covered in sweat and dirt and grease and grime. Spear gathers the men to his side, then says, It took a quarter of a million years for God to design our last Messiah, who could only come in our form, created in our image, a fallen man. Our New Messiah will take only nine months to build, and when it is done it will show us who our own children will be, what they will become in the new kingdom.

This New Motor, he says, it will be the beginning of a new race, unfallen and perfect, characterized by a steam-work perfection our world is only now capable of creating. God has shown the Electricizers and they have shown me and I have shown you, and now you are making it so.

The New Motor is his task, but Spear knows that there are others working too, all of them assigned their own tasks somewhere out in America. He knows this because even on the nights when the others fail to materialize, Franklin comes and takes Spear from his bed and out into the night. The two men walk the empty streets, Spear shivering in his long wool coat and hat and boots, Franklin unaffected by the cold. The specter tells him of other groups sent to help, of other spirits in need of a medium: the Healthfulizers, the Educationalizers, the Agriculturalizers, the Elementizers, the Governmentizers, perhaps other groups unfamiliar even to Franklin.

Franklin says, I can't know everything. Like you, he says, I am merely a vessel. He puts a cold hand on Spear's shoulder, causing the medium's teeth to chatter painfully. If the specter doesn't release him, Spear worries he'll break his molars.

A new age is coming, Franklin says. The Garden restored.

He says, Fear not.

He says, Through God, even one such as you might be made ready.

As the Motor grows in complexity, Spear begins to lose his temper more and more often, always at home, always behind closed doors. He tells his wife that Abigail is not to work, that she is not to lift a finger, but more than once he comes home to find the girl helping his wife with her chores.

To his wife, he says, Why is it that you can't listen to even the simplest of my instructions?

She's pregnant, he says, with the growing king of our new world. Why can't you do what I say, and treat her accordingly?

Sounding as tired as he's ever heard, his wife says, That girl's not pregnant, John. The only reason she's here is that you want her instead of me.

To Abigail, Spear says, Child, return to your room.

He waits until Abigail has left the room before he strikes his wife across the face with the back of his hand. He says, Christ forgive me, but you watch your tongue. You either recognize the glory of God or you do not. Only you can choose which it will be.

By December, there are sixty-five revealments, and by the end of January there are thirty more. The New Motor grows larger, taking up the entire table with its array of sliding panels and connecting tubes and gears. Loose bundles of wires dangle from the construct's innards, waiting for the places where they will connect to give life to extremities that only Spear has seen, to other appendages even he can't imagine.

The machine does not resemble a man, as Spear once thought it would. He does his best to quell the workers' worries, but as the team grows they ask their questions louder and louder, until their concerns leak out of the shed and into the congregation below. The collections that once went to feeding the poor or funding abolitionist trips into the South have for months gone to the Motor, and so the congregation's patience grows thin, especially among those who haven't seen it, who cannot conceive of what it is, what it will be.

Spear counsels patience, counsels faith. From the pulpit, he says, We have been given a great gift, and we must not question it.

But he does. He questions; he doubts. He opens his mouth to speak again, but cannot. He hasn't eaten or changed his clothes in days, takes to sleeping in the shed beneath the copper reflection of the Motor. He does not go home to the cabin except to fetch Abigail in the mornings and to take her back home at night.

On the next Sabbath, he stumbles at the pulpit, but the Electricizers at his side catch him with their frosty hands and return him to his station.

Spear shivers, wipes the drool off his lip with the back of a shaky hand. He waves his hand, motions for the ushers to pass the collection plate. They hesitate, look to the deacons for confirmation, a gesture not lost on Spear. His authority has been questioned, his future made dependent on the outcome of his great project.

Spear closes his eyes against his congregation's wavering faith, then says, God blesses you in this kingdom and in the one to come. Give freely, for what you have you will soon not need.

Spear stifles a gasp when Maud Trenton comes into his office during the first week of February. She is as pregnant as any woman Spear has ever seen, her belly stressing the seams of her black dress. He can see patches of skin between strained buttons, and momentarily he desires to reach out and touch her stomach, to feel the heat of the baby inside.

Maud sits, her hands and arms wrapped around the bulk of her belly. She says, I need your help, Reverend.

With quivering lips, she says, I don't know where this baby came from, and I don't know what to do with it.

Spear shudders, trying to imagine who would have impregnated this woman. He realizes it has been weeks since he last saw Maud at services or group meetings. She's been hiding herself away, keeping her shame a secret. The villagers may not be ready to accept such a thing, but Spear prides himself on his politics, on the radical nature of his insight. This does not have to be the ruin of this woman, but there must be truth, confession, an accounting.

Spear says, Do you know who the father is?

Maud neither nods nor shakes her head. She makes no motion to the affirmative or the negative. She says, There is no father.

Through the curtain of gray hair falling across her downcast face, she says, I am a virgin.

She looks up and says, I know you know this.

Spear shakes his head. He does not want to believe, and so he does not. He says, If you cannot admit your sin, then how can you do penance?

He says, The church can help you, sister. I ask again, Who is the father?

Spear asks again, but she refuses to tell the truth, even when he walks around the desk and shakes her by the shoulder. He sends her away. She will return when she is ready, and when she is ready he will make sure she is cared for. There is time to save the child, if only she will listen.

At night, Spear wanders the floors of the small cabin, checking and rechecking the doors. He locks Abigail's room himself each evening but often still awakens in the night, sure her door is open wide. Some nights, he stands outside her door with his face pressed to the wood, listening to the sounds of her breathing. Others he dreams he has been inside the room, that he has said or done something improper, only later he can never remember what. More than once, he wakes in the morning curled in front of her door, like a guard dog or else a penitent, waiting to be forgiven.

The Electricizers flood Spear's bedroom with more specters than ever before. He can see some of the others, the older spirits he long ago intuited, can hear the creaky whisper of their instructions. These are past leaders of men, undead but still burdened by their great designs, and Spear can sense the revealments these older ghosts once loosed from their spectral tongues: their Towers of Babel, their great Arks. His fingers cramp into claws as he struggles to write fast enough to keep up with the hours of instruction he receives, his pen scratching across countless pages. Near dawn, he looks down and for one moment he sees himself not as a man but as one of the Electricizers, his faded muscles aching with iced lightning, shooting jolts of pain through his joints. Spear understands that Franklin and Jefferson and Murray and the rest are merely the latest in a long line of those chosen to lead in both this life and the next, and Spear wonders if he too is being groomed to continue their great works. He looks at Franklin, whose face is only inches away from his own. He sees himself in the specter's spectacles, sees how wan and wasted he looks.

Spear says, Am I dying?

The ghost shakes his head, sadder than Spear has ever seen him. Franklin says, There is no longer such a thing as death. Now write.

February and March pass quietly, the work slowing, then halting altogether as supplies take longer and longer to reach High Rock through the snow-choked woods. Spear spends the idlest days pacing alone in the snow atop the hill, watching the road from Randolph obsessively. There is so much left to do and always less time to do it in.

In June, the nine months will be over. The Motor must be ready.

Spear spends the short winter days in the shed, rechecking the construction of the Motor, but the long evenings are another matter. Being trapped in the cabin with his wife and children is unbearable, and being trapped there with Abigail is a torture of another kind. From his chair in the sitting room, he finds his eyes drawn to her flat belly, to the lack of sign or signal. His gaze wanders to her covered breasts, to the pale skin that escapes the neckline of her dress, the hems at the wrists of her long sleeves. He watches her while she plays with his own children on the floor, searches for the kindness and grace he expects to find in his New Mary.

Mostly what he sees is boredom, the same emotion that has overwhelmed him all winter, trapped by snow and waiting for the coming thaw that feels too far off to count on. While they wait, he expects some sign, something to show her development into what she must become. He knows she will not give birth to the Motor, not exactly, but she must give it life somehow.

Spear wishes he could ask the Electricizers for reassurance, but he knows they will not answer. Despite their long-winded exposition on every facet of the Motor's construction, they have been silent on the subject of Abigail since he first plucked her from the flock.

Spear decides nothing. He stops touching his wife, stops holding his children. He tells himself he is too tired, too cold. Food tastes like ash, so he stops eating. The Electricizers keep him up all night with their diagrams and their inscriptions. Jefferson tells Spear that by the end of the month he will know everything he needs to know to finish the New Motor. The revelation will be complete.

By the end of the month, Spear replies, I will be a ghost. He spits toward the ancient glimmer, sneers.

The specters ignore his doubt. When he resists, they press harder, until eventually he goes back to work. He writes the words they speak. He draws the images they describe. He does whatever they ask, but in his worst moments he does it only because he believes that by giving in he might one day reach the moment when they will at last leave him alone.

The One Hundred Seventy-Sixth Revealment

The PSYCHIC BATTERY must be cylindrical in shape, constructed of lead and filled with two channels of liquid, one containing a copper sulfate and the other zinc. Copper wires will be run from the GRAND REVOLVER into each channel, with great care taken to ensure that none of the wires touch each other as they ascend into the NEW MOTOR. There is a danger of electrocution, of acid burns, of the loss of life and the destruction of the machine. From the moment of

CONCEPTION to the moment of BIRTH, always the NEW MOTOR has been in danger, and in these stages there is no safety except for the careful, the diligent, the righteous. When the PSYCHIC BATTERY has been successfully installed, the NEW MOTOR will be complete in one part of its nature, as complete as the MEDIUM alone can make it. Men have done their work, and now it is woman's turn.

In the morning, the leaders of the congregation are waiting for Spear when he steps out of the cabin. On his porch are other preachers, mediums, the newspapermen who months before published excited articles in support of the project. The men stand in a half circle in front of his house, smoking their pipes and chatting. Their voices drop into silence as Spear descends the steps from his porch onto the lawn.

One of the preachers speaks, saying, John, this has to stop. Whatever you're doing in that shed, it's bankrupting the community.

A newspaperman nods and says, We thought this was a gift from God, that his spirit spoke through you, but—

He breaks off, looks to the others for support. He says, John, what if what you're making is an abomination instead of a revelation?

And what about the girl, John? What are you doing with the girl?

The others mutter their assent, close ranks against him. Spear doesn't move. They aren't physically threatening him, despite their new proximity. He holds out his small hands, displays the creases of grease and dirt that for the first time cross his palms.

Spear says, I am a person destitute of creative genius, bereft of scientific knowledge in the fields of magnetism and engineering and electricity. I cannot even accomplish the simplest of handy mechanics. Everything I tell you is true, as I do not have the predisposition to make any suggestions of my own for how this device might function or how to build what we have built.

He says, This gift I bring you, it could not have come from me, but it does come through me. It comes through me or not at all.

The men say nothing. They tap their pipe ash into the snow, shuffle their feet, and stare down the hill. There is no sound coming from the shed, even though Spear knows the workers have all arrived. They're listening too, waiting to hear what happens next.

Spear says, Three more months. All I need is three more months. The Motor will be alive by the end of June.

He promises, and then he waits for the men to each take his hand and agree, which they eventually do, although it costs him the rest of his credibility, what little is left of the goodwill earned through a lifetime of service. It does not matter that their grips are reluctant, that their eyes flash new warnings. Whatever doubts he might have when he is alone, they disappear when he is questioned by others, as they always have. The Electricizers will not disappoint, nor the God who directs them.

While he is shaking hands with the last of the men, he hears the cabin door open again. Believing Abigail has come to join him in the shed, Spear turns around to see his wife instead, standing on the porch, leading his older child by the hand. Their other child is balanced in the crook of her arm, and all are dressed for travel. He looks from his wife to the men in his yard—his friends—and then back again. Spear watches without a word as the men help his wife with the two chests she has packed. Even when his family stands before him, he has no words.

He looks at this woman. He looks at her children. He turns, puts his back to them, waits until they are far enough that they could be anyone's family before he looks once more.

He watches until they disappear into the town, and then he goes into the shed and begins the day's work, already much delayed. He sets his valise down on the worktable at the back of the shed, unpacks his papers detailing the newest revealments. While the men gather to look at the blueprints, he wanders off to stare at the Motor, gleaming in the windowless shed, the lamplight reflecting off the copper and zinc, off the multitudes of burnished magnetic spheres. He puts his hand to the inscriptions in the table, runs his fingers down the central shaft, what the Electricizers call the grand revolver. It towers over the table, vaguely forming the shape of a cross. There are holes punctured through the tubing, where more spheres will be hung before the outer casing is cast and installed.

It is this casing that he has brought the plans for today. Spear does not need an explanation from the Electricizers to understand this part. Even he can see that the symbols and patterns upon the panels are the emblematic form of the universe itself. They are the mind of God, the human microcosm, described at last in simple, geometric beauty. He does not explain it to these men who work for him, does not think they need to know everything that he does.

The only person he will explain it to is Abigail, and then only if she asks.

With his family gone back to Boston, the cabin is suddenly too big for Spear and Abigail, with its cavernous cold rooms, but also too small, with no one to mediate or mitigate their movements. Everywhere Spear goes, he runs into the girl's small, supposedly virginal form. Despite her bright inquisitiveness whenever she visits the shed, she is quieter in the cabin, continuing her deference to his status as both a male and a church leader. Abigail keeps her eyes averted and her hands clasped in front of her, preventing her from noticing that in their forced solitude Spear stares openly at her, trying to will her to look at him, to answer his hungry looks with one of her own, only to punish himself later for his inability to control these thoughts.

By May, he is actively avoiding her within his own home, so much so that he almost doesn't notice when she begins to show around the belly. The bulge is a hand's breadth of flesh, the start of something greater yet to come.

He is elated when he sees it, but the feeling does not last.

Spear knows he has chosen wrong, has known for months that the Electricizers' refusal to discuss the girl is his own fault. In the shed, he stops to take in the New Motor, growing ever more massive, more intricate. There is much left to do before June, and now much to pray and atone for as well. He is sorry for his own mistakes, but knows Abigail's pregnancy is another matter altogether, a sin to be punished separately from his own. Spear drags Randall out of the shed by his collar and flings him into the muddy earth. The boy is bigger than he, healthier and stronger, but Spear has the advantage of surprise. He cannot stop to accuse, to question, must instead keep the boy on the ground, stomping his foot into the teenager's face and stomach and ribs. The boy cries out his innocence, but Spear keeps at it until he hears the unprompted confession spray from between the boy's teeth.

When Randall returns to the shed, Spear will welcome the boy with forgiveness, and then he will send him to collect Abigail and return her to her father's home. Let Abigail's father deal with what she and Randall have done, for Spear has his own child to protect.

Even after Abigail leaves, Spear waits to go to Maud Trenton. He walks down the hill to his offices in the meeting hall, a place he hasn't been in weeks, and sends one of the deacons to summon her. When she enters his office and closes the door behind her, Spear barely recognizes the woman before him.

Her face is clear, her acne scars disappeared, and the thin gray hair that once hung down her face is now a thick, shining brown, healthy and full. Even her teeth have healed themselves, or else new ones have appeared in her mouth, grown in strong and white. She is shy, but when he catches her gaze, he sees the glory in her eyes, the power of the life that rests in her belly.

Spear says, Forgive me, Mother, for I did not know who you were.

He gets down on his knees before her and presses his head against the folds of her dress. He feels his body shudder but does not recognize the feeling, the new shape of sadness and shame that accompanies his sobs. While he cries, she reaches down and strokes his hair, her touch as soothing as his own mother's once was. In a lowly voice, he gives thanks that his lack of faith was not enough to doom their project, or to change the truth, finally revealed to him: this woman is the Mother and he is the Father, and together they will bring new life to the world. He reaches down and lifts the hem of her dress, working upward, bunching the starched material in his fists. He exposes her thick legs, her thighs strong as tree stumps but smooth and clean, their smell like soap, like buttermilk and cloves. He keeps pushing her dress up until he holds the material under her enlarged breasts, until he exposes the mountain of her swollen belly, her navel popped out like a thumb. He puts his face against the hot, hard flesh, feels her warmth radiate against his skin. She moans when he opens his mouth and kisses the belly, and he feels himself growing hard, the beginning of an erection that is not sex but glory. Maud's legs quiver, buck, threaten to collapse, and he lets the fabric of her dress fall over him as he reaches around to support her. He stays for a long time with his face against her belly and his hands clenched around her thighs. He waits until she uncovers him, until she takes his weeping face in her hands. She lifts gently, and he follows the movement until he is once again apart from her, standing on his feet.

Maud kisses Spear's forehead, then crosses herself before turning away, keeping her back to him until Spear leaves her there in his office. He walks outside into the warmth of a sun he has not felt in months. He has supplicated himself, has seen the mystery with his own eyes, and he has been blessed by this woman, the better one he failed to choose. It is enough to put faith in God and in what God has asked of him. It is enough to cast aside all doubts, forevermore.

Jefferson wakes Spear with a touch to his shoulder, the specter's hand a dagger of ice sliding effortlessly through muscle and bone. Jefferson says, Come. I want to show you what will happen next.

The reverend gets up and follows the spirit outside, where they stand together on the hill and look down at High Rock, at the roads that lead toward Randolph and the railroad and the rest of America.

Jefferson says, As the Christ was born in Bethlehem and raised in Nazareth, so the New Motor has been built here by the people of High Rock. When it is finished, it must go forth to unite the people, and you with it.

Spear says, But how? It gets bigger every day. Surely it's too large to rest on a wagon.

Jefferson shakes his head. He says, Once the machine has been animated, you will disassemble it one more time, and then you will take it to Randolph where you will rebuild it inside a railroad car.

Spear says, The railroad doesn't go far enough. We'll never make it across the country that way.

Jefferson ignores his objection, saying, One day it will, and in the meantime the Motor will grow stronger and stronger. You will take our New Messiah from town to town, and he will reach out and speak through you to the masses. He will use your mouth and your tongue to relay his words, to bring about the new kingdom that awaits this country. This is why your family was taken from you. This was why we could not allow you to keep the girl, even after the Motor was finished.

He says, As much as you have given, there is more that may be asked of you. You must forsake everything you have to follow the Motor, as the disciples did before you.

Spear looks at Jefferson, stares at his ghostly, glowing form. He wants to say that there is nothing left to give, that already he is a shell of a man, reduced to a mere vessel, an empty reservoir, but it is too late to protest, too late to go back. Whatever else remains, he does not care enough for himself to refuse.

The Two Hundredth Revealment

BIRTH will commence upon the arrival of the NEW MARY, who will appear pregnant with the energy necessary to bring the machine to life. Through the WOMBOMIC PROCESSES, the NEW MARY will be filled with the THOUGHT-CHILD, the necessary intellectual, moral, social, religious, spiritual, and celestial energies that will fill the PSYCHIC BATTERY and give BIRTH to the new age. The BIRTH will be attended by the MEDIUM, who will become more-than-a-male — a FATHER — even as the NEW MARY becomes more-than-a-female, a MOTHER. The womb has had its season of desire. It has had its electrical impartation. The organism of a choice person was acted upon by our LORD and MAKER. The NEW MARY is a person of extraordinary electric power, united in a harmonious, well-balanced physical, mental, and spiritual organism, and when she is brought within the sphere of the NEW MOTOR she will give it life.

The first week of June, Maud Trenton struggles up the hill in the predawn dark, her arms wrapped under the largesse of her belly. She climbs alone, as she has done everything else in her long life, but she also feels watched, as she has since even before the stirring in her body began. She feels the presence of spirits, of angels, of men who care for her, protect her, keep her safe. When she stumbles to the stony path, it is these angels who give her the strength to rise again, lifting her with hands as warm and soft as they are invisible. The rest of the climb, they hold her by the elbows as she walks, keeping her ankles from twisting, from casting her again to the ground beneath her feet.

At the top of the hill, both the cabin and the shed are dark and quiet. She looks up into the sky, into the pink dawn obliterating the star-flecked heavens by degrees. She moans, squatting over her knees to wait out the horrible pressure of the next contraction. She wants to go to the cabin to wake Reverend Spear, but even a mother as inexperienced as she knows time is short. The angels whisper to her, guide her away from the cabin and toward the shed instead. She must be inside when she gives birth, must be near this New Messiah the reverend has revealed to her.

At the shed's wide, sliding door, she sees the lock clasped around the latch and despairs, but then—after another crushing contraction—the door slides open at her touch, helped along its tracks by her angels. The room within is dark and cool, the dimness softened by the slow sunlight following her inside. At the direction of the angels, she moves to lie down on the floor, to lean her head back on the dusty floorboards, but only after she stares at the machine, at its metallic, crafted magnificence. She does not understand its purpose, but its beauty is undeniable.

There is no midwife to guide her, no husband to comfort her, but Maud requires no earthly assistance. The angels are beside her, and with them is her God. It is enough. Her whole life, he has come when she has called, and it has always been enough.

Spear watches from the cabin windows, waiting for the Electricizers to leave Maud's side and fetch him, but they stay with her and envelop her with their light. Eventually, Spear leaves the cabin himself and goes to the shed, where he sits down beside Maud and takes her in his arms, holds her sweating, convulsing body to his. He watches her clenched jaws and closed eyes, watches her legs kick out from her body. He tries to remember the birth of his own children, finds he cannot, then puts his past from his mind. He whispers to Maud, telling her about the great purpose of what she is doing, about the great world she is bringing into being.

At last, he says, Push, and then she does. She spreads her legs, and her womb empties. What comes is only a gush of blood, the smell of sweet flowers, a sodden heat spreading through the air. Spear and Maud and the Electricizers all wait, endure together a long moment when Spear feels nothing except for the breath trapped in his lungs, the woman in his arms, the way his heart beats both fast and slow, as if it might stop at any moment, as if it might go on forever.

The New Motor pulsates subtly, a motion so minute Spear sees it only if he looks at the machine sideways, detecting a slight swaying in the hanging magnets of the grand revolver. How will this infant energy mature into the great savior he has been promised, that he has promised himself?

Her pregnancy ended, Maud Trenton is light, her body barely skin, barely bones, her cries producing so little water they are barely tears. He lifts her in his arms, carries her gently from the shed into the cabin, where he lays her down on the bed he once shared with his wife. He waits with her until she falls asleep. It takes a long time, and it takes even longer for Spear to realize she was crying not in pain but in frustration. A lifetime of waiting and a near year of effort, and still she is without a child to call her own. Now Spear understands the terror that is the Virgin, the horror that is the name Mary, the new awfulness that he and the Electricizers have made of this woman.

Whatever she has given birth to, it will never be hers alone.

He whispers apologies, pleas for penance, into her dreaming ears, and then he gets up to leave her. He will go down into the village and fetch the doctor, but only after he attends to the Motor. He must lock the shed's doors and be sure that no man crosses that threshold until he Spear is ready, until he can explain what exactly it is that has happened to his machine.

The next morning, he invites the other leaders of the congregation to view the Motor, to see the slight pulsation that moves inside it. They listen attentively, but Spear sees the horror on their faces as he tries to point out the movement of the magnets, as he grows frustrated at their inability to see what he sees. After they leave, Spear stands at the top of the hill, listening to their voices arguing on the way down the crooked path. Their deliberations are complete by evening, and when the messenger arrives at the cabin with a letter, Spear knows what it says before he reads it: he has been stripped of his position in the church, and of the church's material support.

Spear locks himself in the shed with the Motor, where he watches it pulsate until morning, when there is a knock at the door. He opens the door to find Maud waiting for him. She is beautiful, transformed by her pregnancy, and she takes him by the hand, saying, This machine is ours to believe in, ours to take to the people.

She says, I have listened to your sermons, have heard the words you've spoken.

She says, You cannot give up. I won't allow it.

Spear nods, straightens himself, and looks back at the machine he's built. There is life in it, he knows. He looks at Maud's hand in his. It is but a spark, but one day it will be a fire, if only he nurtures it.

—

There is no more money to pay for what Spear needs—
wagons and assistants, supplies for the great journey
ahead—and so Spear splits his time between the shed and
his desk, between preparing for the disassembly of the
Motor and writing letters begging for financial support.
He writes to New York and Boston and Philadelphia and
Washington, asking their spiritualist congregations to trust
him, to help fund this new age that is coming.

He writes, *The Glory of God is at hand, and soon I will bring
it to each and every one of you, if only you will help me in these
darkest of hours.*

The words he writes, they are his alone, and he finds
himself at a loss to explain the New Motor without the
help of the Electricizers. He calls out, begs for assistance.
In his empty office, he cries, All that you helped me create
is crumbling. Why won't you tell me what to write?

His words are met with silence, as they have been since
the birth of the Motor. The Electricizers are no longer
distinct to him, just blurred specters at the periphery of
his vision, fading more every day. Their abandonment is
near complete when Maud begins to help him instead,
comforting his anxiety and giving him strength with her
words. She has not gone down the hill since the day she
gave birth, and Spear knows that this is the reason his
family had to leave, that his congregation had to abandon
him. Even the Electricizers leaving him, he recognizes it
not as an abandonment but as making room for what is
to come next.

Like Mary and Joseph's flight with the newborn Jesus
into Egypt, he and Maud will flee with the New Motor

across America, taking it by railroad to town after town, waiting at each terminus of the line for more rail to be laid.

Like Mary, Maud will not love him, only the Motor she has birthed.

Like Joseph, he will have to learn to live with this new arrangement, this adjusted set of expectations.

Spear tears up all the letters he has written so far, then starts new missives infused not with the bitterness he feels but with the hope and inspiration he wishes he felt instead. Soon, the Motor will begin to speak to him, and he must be ready to listen.

It takes a month for the letters to come back, but Spear receives the responses he requires. He runs into the cabin, where Maud awaits him. He says, They're coming to help us, with money and with men. They'll be waiting for us in Randolph, ready to assist me in reassembling the Motor.

He hesitates, then says, I'll start tonight. I'll disassemble the Motor and get it ready for travel, and then I'll send word to Randolph for a wagon to transport it. The worst is nearly over, and soon our new day will begin.

Maud rises from the dining table and takes Spear in her arms, cradling his head against her shoulder. She does not tell him what the angels have told her about what must happen instead, about what has always happened to those who have served God with hearts like his, too full of human weakness, of pride and folly and blinding hubris. She does remind him of Moses at the border of the Promised Land, of Jonah in the belly of the whale. She could, but she chooses otherwise, chooses to repay his onetime lack of faith with her own.

Despite his intentions to start immediately, Spear finds that he cannot. Once he has locked himself in the shed with the New Motor, he is too in awe of its ornate existence, the shining results of all the months of effort and prophecy that went into its construction. He is awed but dismayed, no longer remembering the details of the revealments or the purpose of the grand revolver, the many plates inscribed with holy messages or the intended sequence of motion through the many interlocking gears. He watches the pulsation of the hanging magnets and tries to understand what they might mean, what message might be hidden in the infant energies of their attractions and repulsions. He believes it must be made clear soon, even without the Electricizers' help.

Spear sits down on the floor and crosses his legs, preparing for the first time in many months to go into a trance, to purposefully pierce the shroud between this world and the next. The trance comes easily to him, in all of its usual ways: a prickling of the skin, a slowing of the breath, a blurring of the vision. He stays that way for many hours, listening to the other world, and so he does not hear the knock at the door or the raised voices that follow. By the time something does snap him out of his trance—the first ax blow that bursts open the shed door, perhaps—it is far too late to save himself.

The men of the village surround him, swearing they have come to help, to set him free. Men who were once

Spear's friends promise he won't be hurt if only he'll lie still, but he can't, won't, not in the face of what they've come to do. Held between the arms of the two Russians, he watches disbelieving as one of High Rock's deacons steps to the New Motor, emboldened by the permission of the others. The deacon reaches up toward the grand revolver to take hold of one of the magnetic spheres suspended from its crossbeams, and then he rips it away from the Motor.

Spear waits for intercession, for Electricizer or angel to step in and stop the destruction. He struggles against his attackers, tries to warn them against what they plan to do, against the wrath of God they call down upon themselves, but they do not listen. Eventually he twists free and attempts to take a step toward the Motor, where others have joined the deacon in dismantling the hanging magnets. The Russians stop him, knock him to the ground, fall upon him with fists and boots, and when they tire of striking him they step aside so that others might have their turn.

Spear no longer cares for himself, only for his new God, for this mechanical child gifted not just to him and to Maud but also to all of mankind, if only they would accept it. By the time Maud arrives in the doorway to the shed, he is already broken, in body and face and in spirit. The Motor is crushed too, ax blows and wrenching hands tearing its intricate parts from their moorings, rendering meaningless the many names of God written in copper and zinc across its components. He cries to her for help but knows there's nothing she can do. All around him are the men he once called to himself, who followed him to High Rock and up its steep hill to this shed, where he had meant for them to change their world. He watches the Russians and James the metalworker and the carpenters, all of them striking him or else the machine they themselves built. When they finish, when his teeth and bones are already shattered, he sees Randall, the now-scarred youth he once admired above all others.

Spear accepts the vengeance the boy feels he's owed, but before the beating ends he lifts his head to look up at Maud, to take in her restored youth and beauty. For the last time, he sees the Electricizers, sees Jefferson and Franklin and Rush and Murray and all the others. He cries out to them for protection, for salvation, and when they do not come to his aid he looks past them to Maud, who glows in their light, but also with a light of her own, something he wishes he had seen earlier, when there was still some great glory that might have come.

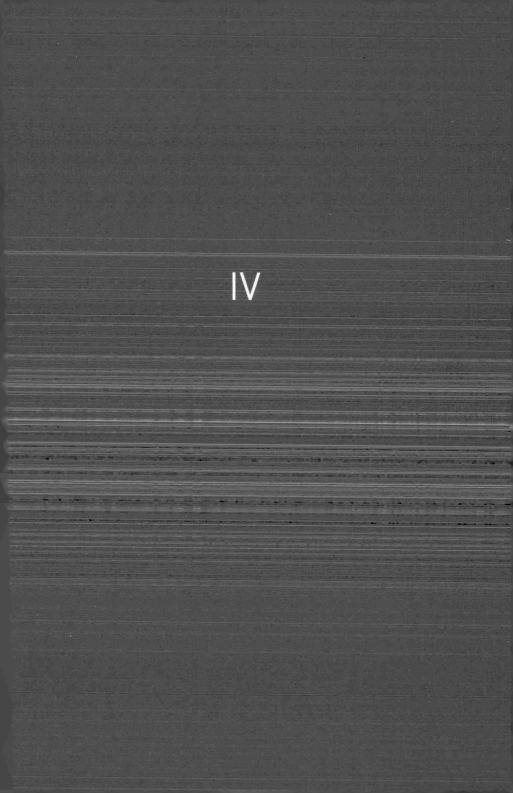

IV

A Certain Number of Bedrooms

THE BOY CARRIES THE BLUEPRINT catalogs everywhere he goes. At school, he keeps them in his backpack, only occasionally looking inside to spy their colorful covers, comforted simply by their presence, their proximity. It is different at home. After school, he locks himself in the empty house and sits at the kitchen table, where he fans the catalogs out in front of him as he eats his snack. He compares the artist's renditions on the left page with the floor plans on the right, then moves to the living room floor, where he watches television and turns the thin catalog pages. He mutes his cartoons so he can hear himself enunciating the names of the homes he hopes his father will build.

Ranches: Crestwood, Echo Hills, Nova.

Split-levels: Timber Ridge, Elk Ridge.

The Capes: Cod, Vincent, and Chelsey.

Two-story houses, like the one they live in, in ascending order by size: Walden, Westgate, Somerset, Carbondale.

The boy has not been reading long. He wants to be sure that when the time comes he can spell the new house's name, that he can say it. He pronounces slowly. He wants the new home to be built from the ground up, so it will not have anyone else's history attached to it, so he can know that no one will have died in the garage. He wonders if they would be better off without a garage at all.

Only after his father's obsession with the catalogs passed did the boy take them to his own room. He thought he'd get in trouble for claiming them but never did, not even later when he started sneaking them to school in his backpack. The boy is years away from the time he steals his first porno magazine from beneath his father's mattress, but when he does he will remember the catalogs, remember the feel of their crinkly, hand-worn pages. Once again, he will find himself too young to understand what he has or why he wants it, the magazines reminding him only obliquely of this earlier time, when so much hope is invested in so little paper.

At dinner, the boy tells his father about the houses he likes best, about how he is having trouble deciding between the Crestwood and the Cape Cod. The father glances at the pages. A month ago he smiled at the boy's enthusiasm, even joined in with his own comments, but now he is less demonstrative with his opinions.

The boy has been in so few other houses that picturing the interior of any other home means simply reconfiguring the rooms of their own house into his conception of the new one. The floor plans he likes best are ones he can most easily shoehorn his own into, using the homes of his grandmother and of the neighbor boy his mother once forced him to play with to fill in the bigger houses. To make up for his father's reticence, the boy talks more than he is comfortable with, not because he wants to but because he cannot bear the silence at the table, the reminder of what they're missing, how without her they are alone even when they are with each other.

Suicide: car running, windows closed, parked in the garage. No one would ever drive it again, and two months after her death it would be sold at a loss. The boy was not supposed to find her. She did not know that school had become a half day, that everyone had been sent home early because of the impending snowfall. The note taped to the outside of the driver's window was addressed to his father, not to him. The boy could barely read then, but decided to try anyway. He pulled the note off the window, leaving a stain of Scotch tape behind.

Mother: Hidden underneath. Fallen against the window, the steam from her breath slowly disappearing from the cloudy glass. The last time he saw her.

9-1-1: The boy had learned the number in school, but he had not been taught that it was not fail-safe, that it did not save everyone. For months he thought about raising his hand and telling his teacher about her error, but they had moved on from health and safety and would not speak of it again.

Extolling the virtues of the houses to the father, the boy lists the numbers of bedrooms and bathrooms. He wonders what half a bathroom is but does not ask. He explains that all the houses from American Homes have R-19 insulation, which the catalog assures is the very best kind. He shows his father the cross-section of a wall and repeats from memory the phrase *oriented strand board*. The boy pronounces many words wrong. He does not realize that learning words by sounding them out has left him with false pronunciations, sounds that as an adult he will be constantly corrected for. No matter how hard he tries to hide it, he will not speak the same language others speak.

Father: Quiet. Sluggish. Often watches the news from his easy chair with his eyes closed. A tumbler of melting, browning ice dangles from his fingertips. He has apparently forgotten how to play catch or even how to get to the park.

Father (previous): Fun. Loud. Told jokes the mother disapproved of but that the boy loved. Often rustled the boy's hair, which the boy pretended to hate but secretly didn't. Missing in action.

Father (future): Defined by the loss of his partner in a way he was never defined by her presence.

The boy reads the catalogs in the evening while his father naps in his recliner. His father rarely makes it to the bedroom anymore, and so sometimes the boy sleeps on the couch to be near him. More often he goes to his own room, where he reads the catalogs until he is too tired to keep his eyes open. Each night, before he sleeps, he chooses the home he thinks they need, his decisions changing quickly, like moods or Michigan weather. Sometimes he falls asleep with the light on, and those nights are the ones he stays in his bed.

On other nights, the boy wakes up shaking, then walks

into the living room where his father sleeps. Standing beside the recliner, the boy tries to will his father to wake up before starting to shake him. Neither tactic works. The father snores on, even when the boy begins at last to talk, begins to insist that his father talk back, that he take them away from this home which is no longer any such thing.

Eventually his teacher notices the black rings below his eyes and keeps him inside at recess. She asks him if there's anything he wants to talk about, if maybe something is happening at home. He knows she knows, but if she will not say so, then neither will he. The boy does not show her the catalogs, hides their meaning from anyone who might accidentally see and ask. Curiosity is not the same as caring.

The new house will end up being an apartment, a word the boy doesn't even know yet, and then later the new house will be his grandma's basement. The boy will lose the catalogs on one moving day or another, but by then he will have memorized them completely. They will be part of who he is. As he grows, he will make friends and then lose friends, realizing years later that he is unable to remember their names or faces but can still recount the number of bedrooms in their houses, how many bathrooms and a half they had. When he thinks of his old house, the one he had been born in and his mother had died in, he will picture it as a spread in one of his catalogs, imaginary fingers tracing the picture of the remembered home, the hard blue lines of the floor plans.

Home: Three bedrooms. One bath. Storm windows and a thirty-five-year guarantee on the shingles.

Family: Two parents. One child. One dead with two survivors.

This is a home. This is a family. This is what happens in a home when a family breaks down a fault line, when a foundation suddenly shifts because once it got wet when it should have stayed dry, because that wet spot was sealed beneath the floorboards, because it hid there for years and years before cracks began showing around doorways and windows, before one day whole chunks of plaster fell from the ceilings and walls as something fundamental within gave way to ruin.

The Collectors

1A. HOMER STANDS, FALLS, STANDS AGAIN

How long has Homer been sitting here in the dark? A decade, a year, a day, an hour, a minute, or at least this minute, the one where his eyes pop open and his ears perk up, listening for the voice howling in the dark. Somewhere in the house, Langley is yelling for Homer to help him, has perhaps been doing so for some time. Homer leans over the edge of his tattered leather chair — the chair that once belonged to his father and has been his home since he lost his sight — then sets down his snifter, the brandy long ago emptied. He stands, legs shaky. For a moment he thinks he will fall back into the chair's ripped excess, but he finds his balance, takes a step or two forward, then loses it, crashing forward onto the damp floor covered in orange peels and pipe ash, the remains of the only forms of nourishment he's allowed.

Homer calls out for Langley, who calls out for him, and together their voices echo through the twisted passageways and piled junk of their home.

Homer's eyes long gone, everything has become touch, life a mere series of tactile experiences. He pushes himself

upward, his hands sinking into the orange peels, their con-
sistency like gums pulled away from teeth. He's disgusted,
but has been for so many years that this newest indignity
barely registers.

In a loud voice, he tells Langley that he is coming, but he
doesn't know if that's true. There's so much between them,
much of it dangerous, all of it theirs.

3A. INVENTORY

Some of the items removed from the Collyer House
include hundreds of feet of rope, three baby carriages,
rakes and hoes and other gardening implements, several
rusted bicycles, kitchen utensils and at least four complete
sets of china, a heap of glass chandeliers unfastened from
the ceilings to make room for the piles and the tunnels, the
folding top of a horse-drawn carriage, a sawhorse, a room
full of dressmaking dummies, several portraits of family
members and early century presidents Calvin Coolidge
and Warren Harding, a plaster bust of Herman Melville,
a kerosene stove placed precariously close to the stacks
of newspapers in Homer's sitting room, a variety of children's furniture and clothing, the chassis of a Model T Ford
that Langley had apparently been trying to turn into a gen-
erator, hundreds of yards of unused silk and other fabrics,
several broken clocks and piles of clock parts, one British
and six American flags, piles of tapestries and rugs, whole
rooms filled with broken furniture and bundled lumber.
There was also the matter of their inheritance from their

father, which included all his medical equipment, plus his thousands of medical and anatomical reference texts, greatly expanding the already large, impenetrably stuffed Collyer family library.

Also living in the house were eight cats, an emaciated dog, countless numbers of vermin. By the time Langley was found, the dog had eaten most of his face, and the rats were beginning to carry off the rest.

2A. THOSE WHO CAME FOR YOU FIRST

It began with the newspapermen, their tales of the gold stashed in your halls, of stockpiled gems and expensive paintings and antique jewelry. None of it was true, but none of it surprised you either. The reporters had never worried about the truth before, not when it came to you and yours.

So the articles run, and then they come: not your real neighbors, but these new ones who replaced them. The first brick through the window is merely irritating, the second more so, and after the third and the fourth you board up all the windows. You have to go out at night and scavenge more wood despite Homer's protests, his pleas for you to use the piles of lumber already in the house. He doesn't understand that what you have gathered so far has its own purpose, is stock against future tragedies.

The bricks are only precursors, warnings: there is a break-in, and then another. The first time you fire a gun in the house, Homer screams for two days, refusing to calm down no matter what you say. You count yourself lucky that he's gone blind, or else he might have come down himself, seen the blood soaked into the piles of newspapers bordering the basement door.

It is your family's history they are after, the city's that will keep them out. You move even more newspaper to the basement, stacking the bundles to the ceiling, layering them six feet deep, hoping no burglar will be able to push his way through the thickening newsprint, so heavy and damp and covered in mold and rot.

4A. HOW I CAME IN

I came in through a history of accumulation, through a trail of documents that led to you, Langley, and to him, Homer. I came in through the inventory of your home, through the listing of objects written down as if they meant something, as if they were clues to who you are.

Obsessed, I filled one book and then another and then another.

What I learned was that even a book can be a door if you hold it right, and I held it right.

When I arrived at your home, I did not climb the steps or knock on your door. Instead, I waited and watched and when you came out I followed behind you.

I watched your flight through the dark night air, watched as you pretended skittishness in the streets. I followed you from backyard to alley to dumpster, lingered behind as you scavenged for food and pump-drawn water and shiny objects to line your halls. I watched you take each new prize and clutch it to your breast, and when you were ready to return, I followed you inside.

I want to tell you now that I am a night bird too, just another breed of crow.

Like the bird we each resemble, I am both a scavenger of what has happened and an omen of what is to come.

Despite your fears, I am not your death.

Despite this assurance, you will not be saved.

I promise I will be here with you when you fall, when he fails. After you are both gone, I am afraid that I will still be here.

3B. INVENTORY

Individually, the phone books are another pile of junk, but read as a collection they are something else. The names change, a process that doesn't happen all at once but slowly, like the mixing after a blood infusion. Read like this, they are yet another type of wall, one that is both harder to see and yet obvious enough once you know the color of the bricks.

1B. HOMER HATES THE WEATHER IN NEW YORK CITY

Rainwater seeps in through the ceiling, trickles from floor to floor, from pile to pile. The wood of every chair and table feels warped and cracked while nearby newspaper bundles grow slippery with ink leaking downward into the carpet. Things float in the water or, worse, swim, like the rats and cockroaches and whatever else lives in the high press of the stacks. Other floors are similarly obscured by the often ankle-deep torrents, hiding broken glass, sharpened sticks, knives and scalpels, the dozens of lightbulbs Langley broke in a fit when the electricity was shut off for nonpayment.

Once, Homer remembers, it snowed in his sitting room, the flakes settling on his face and tongue and clothes. He'd had only Langley's word and the freeze of the air to tell him it was snow that fell that day. Reaching out his tongue, he feared he'd taste ash instead, but said nothing as his brother laughed and refilled their snifters.

3C. INVENTORY

Inside much of the house, the only navigation possible was through tunnels Langley had carved into the piles of garbage that filled each room. Supported with scraps of lumber and stacked newspapers or cardboard, these tunnels appeared to collapse frequently, forcing Langley to start over or to create alternate paths to the parts of the house he wished to access.

Some of the tunnels were wide enough that a person could crawl comfortably through them, and in places even walk in a crouch. Others, especially on the second floor, were much smaller. Langley might have been able to fit through them, but not the heavier Homer. The tunnels were the closest thing the house had to doors, and beyond them were secrets the older brother had most likely not shared in decades.

Langley once claimed to be saving the newspapers so that when his brother regained his sight he would be able to catch up on the news. It wasn't a funny joke, but Langley wasn't a funny man. The earliest newspapers dated from 1933, the year Homer went blind, and they continued to be delivered until weeks after the house began to be emptied and inventoried. Even allowing for twelve years of uninterrupted delivery, there were still far more newspapers in the house than expected, stacked and bundled in every room, in every hall, covering the landings of staircases and filling closets and chests.

If Homer had somehow learned to see again, this was never going to be the best way to rejoin the world.

1C. HOMER TAKES HIS MEDICINE

After Homer lost his sight, his brother put him on a diet of oranges, convinced the fruit would restore his vision. Homer wasn't sure, but he couldn't go out and get food himself — only Langley ever left the mansion, and even then only at night — and so Homer had no choice but to take what was offered. Every day, he ate a dozen oranges, until his breath stank of rind and pulp, until the undersides of his fingernails were crusted with the sticky leftovers of his meals. Langley claimed that if Homer could eat one hundred oranges a week his sight would return, but

Homer couldn't do it, no matter how hard he tried. It was too much of one thing, a deadening of his taste buds as complete as the deadening of his irises, his corneas, his optic nerves that still sent useless signals down the rotted pathways of his all-too-useless brain.

2B. THE ONLY THING YOU HAVE CAUGHT THUS FAR

You started improvising the traps soon after the break-ins began and never stopped revising and improving this new class of inventions. You rigged trip wires and deadfalls, hid walls of sharpened broomsticks behind the moist surface of newspaper tunnels, poured loose piles of broken glass beneath intentionally weakened floorboards.

You made other traps and then forgot them, until you were unsure of your own safety. More and more, you had to tell Homer that maybe it would be best for him to stay in his chair.

The one that caught you was a trip wire in the second-story hallway leading from the staircase to the master bedroom. You were hurrying, careless for one moment, long enough to trigger the wire that released the trap, burying you beneath a man-made boulder, a netted mass of typewriters and sewing machines and bowling balls hung from the ceiling.

Only your right leg is pinned and broken, but it's enough to doom you. You cannot see behind you well enough to know how bad the wound is, but even through the mold and must you smell the blood leached from your body, soaking the already ruined hallway carpet.

1D. HOMER IS MERCIFUL

It doesn't take long for Homer to lose his bearings and get lost, turning randomly at each intersection in the tunnels. Without sight, there's no way to check the few clues that might yet remain, the pattern on the ceiling or the moldings in the corners. He reaches out with his hands, stretches his fingers toward whatever awaits them, every inch a lifetime's worth of danger, this hallway filled with tree branches, a homemade bramble slick with rot and sticky with sap. Homer recoils at the sound of movement nearby—insect or rodent or reptile, Homer can't know which—and with his next step he crushes something beneath his foot, the snap of a vertebra or carapace muffled by the sheer bulk of the room. He stops for a moment to stamp the thing out, to be sure it is dead. Somewhere his brother moans in the stacks, and there's no reason for whatever creature lies beneath his heel to suffer the same.

2C. JUSTIFYING YOUR GATHERING

When your father left you and your brother and your mother, he took his medical books and his anatomical drawings and his specimen jars. He took his suits and his shoes and his hats. He took his golf clubs and his pipes and his records, and when he was gone, your mother scrubbed the house from top to bottom in her grief, removing every last particle of dust that might once have been him. He left her, and in return she eradicated him so thoroughly that for twenty years he stayed out of the house.

And then he returned, bundled in the back of a truck and disguised as gynecological equipment and ornate furniture, bound into chests and sacks and bundles of paper.

Just because your stolen inheritance one day came back doesn't mean you didn't hurt during the years it was gone. Now you have your father trapped, boarded behind the doors of the second floor: every stray hair still clinging to a shirt collar, every scrap of handwriting scrawled in the margins of his texts, all of it is him, is who he was. It is all that's left, but if you keep it safe, then it is all you'll ever need.

3D. INVENTORY

In the master bedroom, hundreds of letters were tied into bundles organized by month and year. The letters begin arriving in 1909, then increased in frequency during the following decade until a letter arrived almost every single day. After this peak, the correspondence slowly tapers off before stopping in 1923. The bulk of the unopened mail is from Herman Collyer, each letter a single entry in a series of entreaties dating from his abandonment of his family to the year of his own death. Whether Langley ever showed his brother these sealed envelopes is open to debate, but his own stance on his father's writings is more definitive: each letter remained an apology unasked for, unwanted, and unopened, from the day it was received until the day Langley died.

2D. THE FIRST HOARD

Was inherited, not gathered. Your father died, and suddenly all his possessions were yours, spilling out of your rooms and into your halls. As if you knew what to do with the evidence of a lifetime. As if you could throw away your father, or sell him off to strangers.

It wasn't long after that when you started adding to the piles yourself, was it?

If only you gathered enough, then maybe you could build a father of your own. Gather a mother up in your arms, like all these piles of porcelain knickknacks. Design a family from the best things left behind. Replace birth with theft, life with hoarding, death with destruction. This house is a body, and you and Homer move within it. Rooms like cells, floors like organs, and you two—like what, exactly? Pulses of electricity, nervous messages, the tiny sparks that one day might bring this place to life?

Listen! Somewhere, Homer is crying again, isn't he?

4B. WHERE I AM IN RELATION
TO WHERE YOU ARE

The thin biography tells me nothing, doesn't help me penetrate past the birth and death dates, the one extant photograph, the mere facts of your father leaving you and of your mother dying and of the great divide opened between you and your brother by his blindness. I am divided from you too, by decades I could not cross in time. The only way I feel close to you is when I read the list of objects you left behind, because I know that in your needy acquisitions there is something of me.

Are you listening? Breathe, Langley. *Breathe.*

1E. HOMER REMEMBERS HIS FACE

Homer crawls on his hands and knees, searching for signs of his brother, whose voice is a cricket's, always out of reach, the sound coming from every direction at once. Homer is hungry and tired and wants to go back to his chair, but he perseveres. His brother would do it for him. His brother has been doing it for him. On each of the thousands of days since Homer went blind, Langley has fed him and clothed him and kept him company—has kept him safe from the intruders Homer isn't supposed to talk about—and now, on the day when Langley needs his help, he is failing. Homer's face is wet, but he doesn't know if the wetness is tears or sweat or something else, something dripping from the ceiling and the stacks. He doesn't think he's crying but feels he might start soon, might start and never stop. Whatever it is, he doesn't reach up to wipe it away. His hands are filthy, filthier than anything that might be there on his face.

His face: once, before his blindness but after he

stopped being able to look himself in the mirror, Homer dreamed he was a man made of mud, a pillar of dust, some delicate creation waiting to be dispersed or destroyed.

It was a dream, he knows, not motivation or reason for staying in his chair as long as he has. Not the cause of his nothingman life. He wishes he could go back, forget he ever left the chair, ever left the sitting room, ever reentered the world of pain that had always been there waiting for him. His bathrobe is torn, his hands and feet bloodied and bruised, and his face —

Over the years, he has forgotten his face, its shape, the angle of his nose, and the thickness of his lips and the scars or lack of scars that might distinguish it from another. He has forgotten how it feels to see a brow furrow in pain, to see a mouth contort in frustration and anger.

He has forgotten, but he is trying to remember.

Whatever his face is, floating in the dark around his eyes, it is wet again.

3E. INVENTORY

Fourteen pianos, both grand and upright. A clavichord, two organs, six banjos, a dozen violins (only two of which are strung), bugles, accordions, a gramophone and an exhaustive record collection, two trumpets, a trombone, and what appears to have once been an upright bass before it was smashed beyond easy recognition. Both brothers were accomplished musicians, and it is possible to imagine them sitting and playing music together in happier days and then, later, after the lights went out and they began to fight, playing their instruments apart, their only points of connection the accidental melodies they made in the dark.

1F. HOMER PLAYS THE PIANO

After Homer trips over the bench in front of the parlor's piano, he sits down and rests his fingers on the keys. Wherever Langley is, he's quiet, resting too, or else something worse has happened already, something Homer doesn't want to think about. His lungs ache and his ankles throb, the arthritis in his leg joints a lightless fire. He centers himself in front of the piano and starts to play, then stops when the sound comes out wrong. He sighs, starts over with more realistic expectations. The piano is almost completely buried by the mounds of trash that fill the room, the heaps of paper and metal and wood, the objects breaking down again into their constituent parts. Homer's fingers are gnarled ghosts, flickering over the keys in an approximation, the memory of music. The sound comes out of the piano muffled and muted. It does not fill the room but goes into it instead, Homer's fingers driving each note through the piled garbage and into the rotting walls like a nail, like a crowbar, like something meant to hold a thing together, like something meant to tear it down.

4C. MOTIVATION

I'm sifting through their possessions, crawling through the ruins of their lives, searching for those lost, for the remains of a family: I am in the master bedroom, reading letters they never read. I am in the parlor, wiping the grime off a generation of portraits. I am in the hallway, setting thousands of mousetraps all in a row.

I am on my hands and knees, scrubbing the floor without success, as if there could ever be enough soap to remove this particular stain.

There is so much to see here, but only in fragments, in peripheries. Every step across the floorboards brings this house of cards closer to collapse, and so I must move backward and forward in time, balancing the now and the then.

I am a collector too, but it is not their possessions I have clutched close and hoarded.

I am holding Homer's face in my hands, staring into his milky eyes, whispering to him as he searches in starved sadness. I am kneeling beside Langley like a detective, my bent knee slick with his blood, looking through the rote clues to discover what happened to him.

I am conducting an investigation. I am holding a wake. I am doing some or all or none of these things.

2E. THE CRACK IN YOUR FOUNDATION

You howl, hurling the curse of your brother's name down the corridor. For hours you have heard his bumbling, and still he is no closer to you, his blind search for you as failed as your own cursed attempt to reach the master bedroom. You picture him crawling forward on his hands and knees, unable to see through to the end of each tunnel, unable to know how much farther there is still to go.

For years, he has kept to his chair in the sitting room, leaving you to deal with the collapse of the house, the danger it poses to all of your possessions. The house is both protector and destroyer, both safety and threat, and it is you who tips the scales, not him. It was you who braved the streets night after night to bring back food and water, to gather all the supplies essential to your lives. Homer knows nothing of what you've had to do, how you've moved from one halo of lamplight to the next, avoiding the dark men who rule the streets. You see their eyes sometimes in the shadows, peering at you from front steps and street corners, hurrying you on your way through this ruined city that was once your home.

The pain is too much. This time when you scream, your brother answers, but from too far away. The slow sticky warmth emanating from your crushed thigh has reached your crotch, your belly. It's easy to reach down and feel the slippery copper heat of your blood. There's so much, more than you expected.

You close your eyes. Not much longer now.

Even surrounded by all your possessions, dying is so much lonelier than you expected.

Whisper your brother's name. Whisper the names of your father and your mother. Whisper my name, and pray that I might save you, but understand that even though I have already changed the truth merely by being here, I will still refuse to change it that much.

1G. HOMER LOSES FAITH

The house bucks and shudders, settles or shifts. Homer stumbles but doesn't fall down, knows that if he does he might never get up. He stops and listens to the creaking of the floorboards, the scuttle of the rats. Says, Langley?

Homer wants to yell his brother's name again but doesn't. It's been a long time since his brother answered, and without sight there is no light and no marker of time. Homer doesn't know if it's morning or night, if a few hours have passed or if it's already been days. He's so tired and so alone, lost inside his own house, remade in whatever crooked shape Langley has envisioned.

He thinks about all Langley tells him to do because he cannot tell himself.

Homer, go to sleep, it's midnight.

Homer, wake up, I've got your breakfast.

Homer, it's time to play your violin.

It's time for me to read to you.

It's time for a drink, time for a smoke, time to eat another orange.

Homer's so tired, and all he wants is to be back in his chair, but for once Langley needs his help, and Homer doesn't want to let his brother down.

The thing is, he doesn't know if Langley is still there to be helped.

2F. YOUR WEIGHTY GHOSTS

No father without medicine, without dictionaries, without reference texts full of once-perfect answers slowly rotting themselves wrong.

No mother without silk, without satin, without wool and cotton. No mother without a closet full of shoes, a hundred high heels spilled out into a trapped nest of spikes.

No brother without a piano, without a bathrobe, without a chair, a pipe, a mouthful of oranges and black bread.

No self without these ghosts. No ghosts except in things.

They surround you, press closer, waiting for the rapidly approaching moment when you too will be only an object, a static entity slowly falling into decay. That moment so close you can smell it, like the breath of rats, like the rot of oranges, like blood and dirt mushed into new mud.

4D. MARCH 21 (EARLY)

I know you were hurrying through the second floor hall because you knew what you needed to do to complete this place, to bring an end to the endless gathering and piling and sorting. You were hurrying because it had taken you so long already, and you didn't want to waste another second.

Even now, at the very end, you tell yourself that if only you could have completed your project, then it would have been enough to stop all this. It could have been different. You could have taken Homer and left this house. You could have started over somewhere else, which is all you'd ever wanted.

You were hurrying, and you were careless, and now it's too late.

Your lungs heave, trying unsuccessfully to clear their bloody fractures. When you are still again, I reach down to touch your face, to turn it toward my own.

With my fingers twisted around your jaw, I say, Homer isn't coming.

I say, Tell me what you would have told him.

I can see the sparks dancing in your eyes, obscuring the last sights you'll ever see, so I say, Close your eyes. You don't need them anymore. Not for how little is left.

For these last few moments, I will see for you as you saw for him.

In the last seconds of your life, I will tell you whatever you want to hear, as long as you first tell me what I need.

I say, Tell me how to finish the house.

I say, Tell me what I have to do to get out of here. And then you will, and afterward I will lie to you, and despite my whispered assurances you will know I am not real enough to save you or him, and then it will be over.

1H. HOMER FINDS THE FARTHEST ROOM

Homer experiences the lack of guideposts, of landmarks, of bread crumbs. He tries to remember if he climbed the stairs or if he crawled upward or if he is still on the first floor of the house, twisted and turned inside it. He tries to remember the right and the left, the up and the down, the falls and the clambering to his feet, but when he does the memories come all at once or else as one static image of moving in the dark, like a claustrophobia of neurons. He wants to lie down upon on the floor, wants to stop this incessant, wasted movement.

He closes his eyes and leans against the piles. His breath comes long and ragged, whole rooms of air displaced by the straining bellows of his lungs. He smells the long-dormant stench of his sweat and piss and shit, come shamefully back to life now that he's on the move again.

Somewhere beyond himself, he smells a hint of his orange peels, the last of their crushed sweetness.

Homer opens his eyes, useless as they are, and points himself toward the wafting rot of his last thousand meals. He holds his robe closed with one hand, reaches out with the other toward the dark. He puts one foot in front of the other, then smiles when he feels the rinds and tapped ash begin to squish between his toes.

He slips, and falls, and crashes into the tortured leather of his favorite chair. He pulls himself up. He sits himself down. He puts his heavy head into his hands.

3F. INVENTORY

In the lockbox: thirty-four bank books, all from different banks. Irving Trust Company. Fillmore-Leroy. Liberty National. Park Avenue. Seaboard. Albany City Savings. Temple Beth Israel. Alfred Mutual. ABN. Alliance.

Amalgamated. American Bond and Mortgage. Jefferson Savings. Associated Water Companies Credit Union. Assumption Parish. Canaseraga State. Dry Dock. Eighth Avenue. Fallkill. Queens County. Glaser Mercantile. H&K. Village. Industrial Bank of Ithaca. Kings County. Manhattan Trust. State Dime Savings. Bank of Brooklyn. Oneida. Rockaway. Union National Bank of Friendship. Beacon Federal. Whitehall Trust. The Zurich Depository.

A total of three thousand and seven dollars and eighteen cents. The very end of a fortune, kept in Langley's name, inherited by Homer, and then, after he died too, taken by the state.

11. MARCH 21 (LATE)

Homer squirms on the high throne of his last decade, every pose the wrong one. His back aches and his legs jerk no matter how he adjusts himself. Everything is physical, every craving desire a need for his brother, for his abandoned Langley. Homer would give everything away for a glass of water, would go into equal debt for a snifter of brandy or a pipe or even one of Langley's goddamn oranges. Anything that might bring relief. Anything that might bring with it absolution or forgetfulness. He licks his lips and tastes mud. He puts his fingers to his mouth and sucks and there it is again. His face, his beard, his clothes, all are mud. Homer puts his hand back in his mouth, sucks and swallows until it is clean. He repeats the process with his other hand, and then he cleans himself like a rodent, using his hands to bring the dirt off of his face and neck and arms to his mouth, where he devours it. Homer's throat chokes shut. He closes his eyes to block out the last blurs of gauzy light his blindness still allows. He is inside the house and the house is inside him, a nesting of labyrinths. Lacking the tools to solve himself, he gives up. The process starts in this one second but takes a week to finish. He does not cry out again. He does not beg. He does not want, not for food or water or companionship. He could, but he does not. This life has been an abject lesson in the limits of wanting. He has learned all he cares to learn.

5A. WILLIAM BAKER

William Baker breaks a second-story window from atop a shaking ladder. William Baker peers into the darkness and then signals to the other officers that he's going in. William Baker uses his nightstick to clear all the glass out of his way. William Baker climbs through the window into the room beyond. William Baker gags but does not vomit. William Baker turns his flashlight from left to right, then back again, like a lighthouse in a sea of trash. William Baker thinks, Not a sea but a mountain rising from a sea, a new, unintended landscape. William Baker begins to take inventory in his mind, counting piles of broken furnishings, books molded to floorboards. William Baker puts his hands to a wall of old newspapers and pushes until he sinks in to his wrists. William Baker finds the entrance to the tunnel that leads out of the room, then gets down on his hands and knees and crawls through. William Baker passes folding chairs and sewing machines and a wine-press. William Baker passes the skeleton of a cat or else a rat as big as a cat. William Baker turns left at a baby carriage, crawls over a bundle of old umbrellas. William Baker crawls until he can't hear the other officers yelling to him from the window. William Baker is inside the house, inside its musty, rotted breath, inside its tissues of decaying paper and wood.

William Baker disappears from the living world and doesn't come back for two hours, when he appears at the window with his face blanched so white it shines in the midnight gloom. William Baker knows where Homer Collyer's body is. William Baker has held the dead man, has lifted him from his death chair as if the skin and bones and tattered blue-and-white bathrobe constitute a human person, someone worth saving. William Baker thinks it took a long time for the man to die. William Baker counts the seconds that pass, the minutes, the days and the years. William Baker has no idea.

5B. ARTIE MATTHEWS

Artie Matthews doesn't understand how a house can smell so bad throughout every inch of its frame. Artie Matthews thinks the garbage should have blocked the stench at some point. Artie Matthews smells it on the sidewalk, smells it in the foyer, smells it in the rooms he and the other workers have cleared, and he smells it in the rooms they haven't. Artie Matthews wears coveralls and boots and thick leather gloves and a handkerchief over his face and wonders if it's enough to protect him from what happened here. Artie Matthews has arms that ache and knees that tremble from yesterday's exertions as he climbs the stairs to the second floor. Artie Matthews throws cardboard and newspaper out a window. Artie Matthews throws out armfuls of books that reek of mold and wet ink. Artie Matthews pushes a dresser to the window and empties its contents onto the lawn below. Artie Matthews wonders who these clothes belong to, wonders if there is a wife or a mother or someone else still trapped in the house, or if this woman left long ago. Her brassieres and slips and skirts fall to the ground. Artie Matthews watches another worker trying to gather them up before the pressing crowds can see them. Artie Matthews wonders why the worker is bothering, why anyone would worry that the people who lived in this house have any dignity left to protect. Artie Matthews thinks that what they are really removing from the house is shame made tangible as wood and steel and fabric.

Artie Matthews will find Langley Collyer, but not for two more weeks. Artie Matthews will find him buried beneath a deadfall of trash ten feet from where his brother died and wonder why he didn't yell, why he didn't ask Homer for help. Artie Matthews will not realize that Langley did yell, did howl, did scream and cajole and beg and whimper. Artie Matthews will not be able to hear how sound moved in this house before all the walls and tunnels of trash came down. Artie Matthews will never understand how a man might cry out for help only to have his last words get lost in the deep labyrinth he's made of his life.

3G. INVENTORY

Besides the letters, there was one final object found in the master bedroom, hidden beneath a canvas tarp. It is a model, a dollhouse, a scaled approximation of the brownstone home. Inside, the model's smooth wood floors are stained and then carpeted, the walls all papered or painted with care. There is an intricately carved staircase that winds to the second floor, its splendor shaming its murderous real-life counterpart. Tiny paintings hang on the walls, painstaking re-creations of the smeared and slashed portraits found downstairs. Miniature chandeliers dangle from the ceilings in nearly every room.

There are tiny beds, tiny tables and chairs, tiny pianos. There are tiny books with tiny pages, a violin so small that it would take a pair of tweezers to hold its bow. In the downstairs sitting room, there is a tiny version of what Homer's chair must have looked like before the leather tore open, before its stuffing leaked onto the floor.

This is a house without traps, without tunnels, without stacks and collections never completed.

In the absence of photographs, this is who these people used to be.

The wood floor around the model gleams, its surface scrubbed and polished, contrasting with the filth and rot of the rest of the room, left unprotected by the tarp.

Outside this circle, there are dozens of prototypes for what would have been the model's finishing touches: Four figures, repeated over and over in different mediums. A man and a woman and two small boys, rendered from wood and clay and string and straw and hair and other less-identifiable materials. All discarded, cast aside, and no more a family than anything else we found lying upon the floors of the Collyer House.

4E. DECAY

I wanted to leave after both of you were dead, or at least after your bodies were bagged and covered and taken out into the sunlight that awaited you, that had always been waiting. Instead, I remain here, walking these emptying halls. Without you to talk to, I become desperate for connection, for these workers tearing down your tunnels to see what you had become, what you might have been instead. I tap a new father on the shoulder so that he turns and sees the child's mobile hanging in a newly opened space, its meaning slanted by your own childlessness. I open a medical reference text to the page on treatments for rheumatoid arthritis or diabetic blindness, then leave it on top of the stack for someone else to read, to note what is absent, to see that nowhere on the page is the cure of the hundred oranges you prescribed your brother. I whisper theories into curious ears, explain that what you had planned to do with all these piles of lumber was to build a house inside the house, to build a structure

capable of holding a family together, something the previous one had failed to do.

I try to explain how close you were, how close I am, how
with a little more help I could solve this puzzle. They don't
understand. They are not trying to understand you.

They are trying to throw you away, and they are suc-
ceeding.

Before they finish, I go up to each nameless sanitation
worker and offer him a facet of your lives, a single dusty
jewel plucked from the thousands you had gathered.

To each person, I try to give whatever he has been looking for, to offer him a history of you that will clash with
the official version, with the version of the facts already
being assembled by the historians and newspapermen. I
want them to see you as I wanted to see you when I first
came to this place, before I started telling your story to my
own ends.

I leave minutes ahead of the wrecking ball. All your possessions have been carted away to be burned or else tied
into garbage bags and discarded. What took you decades
to acquire took other men mere weeks to throw away, and
now all that you were is gone. Despite the many oppor-
tunities to take whatever I wanted, I have left all of your
possessions behind, with only a few exceptions: I have
taken one of Homer's orange peels, with hopes that it
might help me see, and I have taken the makings of one
of your traps, on the off chance that it might protect me
better than it did you. I have left everything else for the
historians and garbagemen to do with what they will.

The workers want to throw you away, but the historians who follow will want something else altogether. They will gather you into inventories, into articles and biographies, hoarding the facts, annotating time lines, reciting their theories on television shows and in packed lecture halls. They will collect more of you and Homer than anyone should need or want, and then they will collect some more, never satisfied with what they have, always greedy for more facts and more theories.

Once, I wanted to be just like them.

Once, I built a trap out of a few obsessed pages, and when I fell in, it crushed me too. Sometimes I am still there, calling out for help to anyone who will listen.

An Index of How Our Family Was Killed

BSENCE OF LOVED ONES, NEVER diminishing no matter how much time has passed.

Accidents happen, but what happened to us was not an accident.

Alarms that failed to go off, that have never stopped ringing in my ears.

Alibis, as in *Everyone's got one.*

An answering machine message, never deleted: my sister's voice, telling me she's okay, that she's still there.

Arrest, to bring into custody.

Arrest, to bring to a stop.

Autopsy, an investigation conducted as a means of discovering the cause of death.

Autopsy, or else an index, a collection of echoes, each entry suggesting a whole only partially sensed.

Ballistics, as method of investigation.

Blood, scrubbed from the floor of bedrooms and barrooms and hospital beds, sometimes by myself, more often by others, by strangers, by men and women in white clothes, unaffected by the crime at hand.

Brother, memory of: Once, my brother and I built a fort

in the woods behind our house by digging a pit and covering it with plywood. Once, we put the neighbor kid down
in that pit and covered the hole. Once, we listened to him
scream for hours from the back porch, where we ate the
snack our mother prepared and misunderstood what it
was we were doing wrong.

Brother, murdered. Murdered by a woman, a wife, his
wife, the wife he had left but not divorced. Who he had
left for another woman, a woman who could not protect
him even with a house clasped tight with locks. Murdered
in his sleep, with a blade to the eye. Murdered beside his
new woman, who woke up screaming and didn't stop for
days.

Bruises so black I couldn't recognize her face, couldn't
be sure when I told the coroner that yes, this is my mother.

Bullets, general, fear thereof.

Bullets, specific: one lodged in my father's sternum,
another passing through skin and tissue and lung, punc-
turing his last hot gasp of air.

Bullets, specific: Pieces of lead, twin mushrooms clatter-
ing in a clear film canister. Sometimes I shake them like
dice, like bones, but when I pour them onto my desk they
tell me nothing, their prophecy limited to that which has
already come.

Call me once a day, just to let me know you're still safe.

Call me X, if you have to call me anything at all.

Camera, fear of, need for. To document the bodies, to
show the size and location of wounds, to produce photographs to explain the entry and exit points of weapons.

Car accidents, as in *It is easier to say it was a car accident than to tell our friends what really happened.*

Caskets, closed.

Control, impossibility of.

Crimes, solved: murders of father, mother, brother.

Crimes, uncommitted (and therefore as yet unsolved): murder of sister, murder of self.

Curse, as possible explanation.

Do not.

Do not answer the phone.

Do not ask for assistance.

Do not associate with one-armed men, men with tattoos, men with bad teeth or bad breath or bad dispositions.

Do not be the messenger, for they are often shot.

Do not believe everything you hear.

Do not break down on the side of the road.

Do not call out for help—yell *Fire* instead. It will not save you, but at least there will be witnesses.

Do not cheat at cards or darts or pool.

Do not cheat on your spouse.

Do not cross the street without looking.

Do not date, no matter how lonely you get.

Do not disagree with people with loud voices or short fuses.

Do not discuss religion or politics.

Do not dress in flashy or revealing clothes. Do not ask for it.

Do not drink in bars.

Do not fight for custody of your children. Better they see you one weekend a month than in a casket.

Do not fly in airplanes.

Do not forget that you are destined for death, that your family carries doom like a fat bird around its neck, that it is something you will never be rid of.

Do not forget to set the alarm when you leave the house, when you go to sleep at night.

Do not fuck around.

Do not get divorced.

Do not get in fights.

Do not get married.

Do not go looking for trouble.

Do not go outside at night or during the day.

Do not go skinny-dipping in dark ponds with anyone.

Do not have acquaintances.

Do not have friends.

Do not hire a private detective. They may find what you are looking for, but they will also find out about you.

Do not hitchhike or pick up hitchhikers.

Do not hope too much.

Do not leave trails of bread crumbs showing which way you have gone.

Do not leave your phone number written in matchbooks or on cocktail napkins.

Do not linger outside of buildings. Do not smoke or wait for buses or cabs.

Do not look back when you should be running away.

Do not love a man with a temper.

Do not love men at all, or women either.

Do not make enemies, if you can help it.

Do not meet strange men or women you find on the Internet in coffee shops or bars or motels.

Do not play with fire.

Do not pray for salvation, for protection, for deliverance.

Do not push your luck.

Do not put your trust in security guards, in the police arriving on time.

Do not raise your voice in anger.

Do not sleep, for as long as you can avoid it.

Do not smoke marijuana, as you are paranoid enough already.

Do not take any drugs at all.

Do not take shortcuts.

Do not take the same way home twice.

Do not telegraph your punches.

Do not telephone home and say you'll be out all night.

Do not think that not doing any of these things will be enough to save you.

Evidence, locked away in locked cabinets inside locked rooms.

Evidence, not harmless, even behind all those locks and doors.

Evidence as symbol of a crime committed, of a deed done.

Ex-wives, as likely suspects.

Eye, as in *Keep an eye out*. As in *Keep your eyes peeled*.

Eye, as point of entry, as wound.

Eyewitnesses, reliable enough for the courts, but not for me. They never tell me what I need to know.

F, tattooed on my left bicep, the first initial of a father lost.

Family, as in mother and father and brother and sister and me.

Family, as something broken and lost.

Family, as something destroyed by external forces deadly as tornadoes, destructive as wildfires.

Fate, as explanation, as probable cause.

Father, memory of: I see him shutting the door to my bedroom, refusing to leave the light on, even after he gave me something to be afraid of. I see him shutting the car door, locking me in for delirious summer hours while he drank, sitting near a window so he could keep an eye on me. I see him walking out the front door of our house, suitcase in hand, vanishing forever.

Father, murdered. Gunned down by a complete stranger, outside a bar, in Bay City, Michigan. They had not been fighting, nor had they even spoken, at least according to the murderer. This murderer, he said he didn't know why he did it, why he felt compelled to pull the pistol out of his jacket and shoot my father dead. We didn't know either. We hadn't talked to our father in five years, didn't even know he was still in Michigan, waiting to be killed.

Fingerprints, hard to get ahold of, but not impossible. These five-fingered imprints of the men and women who have torn my family to shreds, I have placed my own fingers over theirs, but they do not match. I am not accountable, at least not in this most surface of ways.

Fingerprints: once you know your own, you can dust your house, can prove that no one has been there but you.

Fire, as possibility, since it did not claim any of the others.

Forensics, as method of investigation.

Gunpowder, smell of: my father's face, when I bent down to kiss him in his coffin.

Hair samples, stored in plastic bags inside folded manila envelopes. Labeled with name, date, relationship. Fragile, dangerous to handle.

Her, the only one of them that remains.

Her, who has separated herself from me, for her safety, for my own.

History, familial, patriarchal, and matriarchal: This is not just us, not just my mother and father and brother and sister and myself. This is uncles killed in poker games, aunts smothered in hospitals. This is babies exposed in vacant lots and brothers holding sisters underwater until the ripples stop. This is history as an inevitable, relentless tide.

History, of an event, of a series of events.

History, personal and also partial, as in this index.

Hospital: the place we were born, the place we go to die, the place we will be declared dead.

Identity, as in *Can you identify this body?* As in *Is this the body of your father/mother/brother?*

Identity, as in *If I could identify my sister's future killer, could I stop her murder from taking place?*

If I can't have him, no one can. Words overheard but ignored. A lesson about the importance of warning signs.

Index, as excavation, as unearthing, as exhumation.

Index, as hope, as last chance, as method of investigation.

Index, as task to be completed before I die.

Index, as understanding, however incomplete.

Inevitability, as a likely end to this story.

J, tattooed on the inside of my right wrist, first initial of a brother lost.

Jars, for holding each organ individually after they are weighed and categorized and examined for meaning.

Jars, full of brains and livers and hearts. They will not give these to me, no matter how persistently I ask.

Knife, as weapon, if you hold it right.

Like being torn from the arms of the father.

Like being wrenched from the bosom of the mother.

Like closed caskets, like graves all in a row, like the last two plots, waiting to be dug out and filled in.

Love, as necessity.

Love, not nearly enough.

Luck, as in *bad luck*, for all of us.

Madness, temporary, blinding.

Manslaughter implies that what happened was a mistake. In my family, we do not believe in manslaughter.

Memory, doing the best it can.

Memory, failing to do enough all by itself.

Memory, inconsistent, remembering the wrong events, seeking significance and signs where probably there are none.

Memory: When my brother and my sister and then I went off to school, my mother gave us each a Saint Christopher medallion. When she placed mine around my neck, she told me it would protect me, that it would keep me safe from accidents, from accidental death. As if that was all we had to worry about.

Mirror, the only place I see my father's hairline, my mother's nose, my brother's ears, my sister's thin, frightened lips.

Mother, memory of: Lonely before our father left, then worse after. There were men with good jobs and men with no jobs, men with tempers and men with appetites, men who were kind to us and men who used us as punching bags, as whipping posts, as receptacles for all the trash they carried inside themselves. Of all those who failed to protect our family, she was only the first.

Mother, murdered. Died strapped into the passenger seat of a car, unconscious from a head wound, from a wound to the head. I have heard it said both ways. Her boyfriend—a man she started dating after our father left but before he was dead—thought he had killed her with his fists, but was wrong. It was the drowning after he dumped the car that did it.

Motives are almost the opposites of alibis, but not quite.

Mug shots: One, two, three, all in a row on the wall of my office. A reminder of who they were.

My brother's dog, which I take care of but do not trust.

He failed to bark in the night once before, and he could do it again.

Mystery, unsolved, even after all this investigation.

Nothing: as inevitable as an ending.

Nothing: impossible to index, to quantify, to explain.

Overprotectiveness is something you always learn too late.

P, tattooed on the left side of my neck, first initial of a mother lost.

Persistence of destiny, of fate, of karma, of a wheel turning and turning, crushing whatever falls beneath its heel.

Phones, both answered and unanswered. Bearers of bad news.

Phones, ringing and ringing and ringing.

Photographs, blown up and then cropped until the wounds disappear beyond the borders of the frame.

Photographs, mailed to me from Michigan, of my father's body, as unrecognizable as the distance between us.

Photographs, plastered like wallpaper until all I can see from my desk are familiar clavicles and jawlines and hands placed palms up to expose too-short lifelines.

Photographs of crime scenes, always the same series of angles, repeated for each murder.

Photographs of my brother, dead before he could scream.

Photographs of my brother's eye, of the knife wound left where it used to be.

Photographs of my brother's lips, pressed together in sleep, then death.

Photographs of my mother's face, bruised and broken.

Photographs of my mother's teeth, on the floor of the car.

Photographs of our family of five, and then of four, and then of three. There are no photographs of our family of two. We do not gather. We do not congregate.

Questions, how can there not be questions?

Risk, always there is the risk that at any moment one wrong word or action might bring upon we who are left what has already been brought to bear on those who are gone.

Rope: there are so many cruelties that can be done with rope that it is hard to know what to be afraid of.

Search party, looking for my mother, before we knew she'd gone through the surface of the lake.

Sister, memory of: Happy in the fourth grade when she won the school spelling bee. Happy at her confirmation, when God promised to protect her forever. Happy at my brother's wedding, dancing the polka. Happy, happy, happy, until she wasn't happy anymore or ever again.

Sister, survivor. She has tried to live a life free of dangers. She follows every rule, every instruction, takes every precaution. She does not talk to strangers, either men or women. She does not talk to children or babies. She does not pet dogs or hold cats or touch any other small domestic animals. In her purse, she keeps both mace and pepper spray, but she never walks anywhere. She has a Taser in her glove box, but never drives. If she walks or if she drives, then she will die. If she rides in cars with others, then they too will die because she is with them. She says there are no knives or forks or shovels or tire irons in her house. She does not answer her phone or check her e-mail or open her door, ever, even if it is me knocking. She has done everything she can, but it will not be enough. I have not seen her in months, but that does not mean I believe she is safe. Sooner or later my phone will ring and then I will know that she too is gone.

Sometimes, I go to department store perfume counters and spray my mother's scent onto a test card. In the back of my wallet are dozens of these now-scentless things, marked only by the splotch stained across the white card stock.

Sometimes, I think of my father without realizing he's gone, my heart numb as an amputee's fingers, as a lost hand trying to pick up a telephone over and over and over.

Sometimes, while I'm petting my brother's dog, I have to stop myself from hurting it, from punishing it for its failure to bark, to warn, to save its owner's life.

The sound of a black bag being zippered shut.

The sound of a brother comforting a brother, ignorant of the doom between them.

The sound of a bullet making wet music in his organs.

The sound of a car breaking the surface of a lake.

The sound of a confession, taped and played back.

The sound of a gunshot reverberating, echoing between concrete facades.

The sound of a knife, clacking against bone.

The sound of a message played over and over until the tape wears thin.

The sound of a phone going unanswered.

The sound of a police siren, of multiple sirens responding to multiple events.

The sound of a sentence heard three times, which means loss, which means murder, which means another taken from me.

The sound of a sister crying and crying.

The sound of a sister saying goodbye, saying that this will be the last time you will see her, for both your sakes.

The sound of a woman screaming for hours.

The sound of an alarm ringing.

The sound of sirens, a Doppler effect of passing emergency.

The sound of testimony, of witnessing.

The sound of words left unsaid.

Strangulation, as possibility. To be that close to the killer, to see his eyes, to feel his breath, to press my windpipe against his grip. After all I have endured, after all I have imagined, this is one of the most satisfying ways I can see to go. This is a way that at least one question might get an answer.

Survivor, but probably not for long.

Tattoo of my sister's first initial, eventually to be inked but not yet necessary.

Tattoos, as reminders, as warnings, as expectations of loss.

Understanding, as in *lack thereof.*

Vengeance, but never enough. Always state sanctioned, always unsatisfying.

Victim is a broad term, a generalization, an umbrella under which we are all gathered at one time or another.

Violations of the law symbolize violations of the person, of the family, of the community. This is why they must be punished.

We regret to inform you.
　　We regret to inform you.
　　We regret to inform you.
　　What it takes to cut yourself off.
　　What it takes to defend your family.
　　What it takes to hide forever.
　　What it takes to kill a man.
　　What it takes to see this through to the end.
　　What it takes to solve the crime.
　　What it takes to take back what is yours.
　　Why, as in *Why us?*
　　Witness, general.
　　Witnesses, specific: The other men and women who were with my father that night, plus the other people who were walking down the street when the shots were fired. The bartender and two waitresses, plus the policemen who arrived on the scene. I have interviewed them all myself, months later, after the conviction of the killer. The crime already solved, but not yet understood.
　　Wound, as in *bullet hole*, as in *burn*, as in *puncture*, as in *slashing*, as in *fatal*.

X, as in *to solve for* X, as in *to complete the equation*.

X, tattooed on my chest, above my heart.

X, that calls out to he who will commit this deed, to she who might end all that I am.

X, that marks the spot.

X, that will come to be.

X, which could stand for absolutely anything.

Y, the shape of an autopsy scar zippering the chest of a loved one.

Y, the sound of the only question worth asking.

Y, the sound of the question I cannot answer.

You, reading this.

You, you, and you. You may not know yet, or maybe you always have, have felt the fist of the deed clenched in your heart for years. Please, do not wait any longer. I am tired of the day after day after day.

Zero, as brother.

Zero, as father.

Zero, as identity.

Zero, as memory.

Zero, as mother.

Zero, as name.

Zero, as self.

Zero, as silence.

Zero, as sister.

Zero: what will remain.

V

The Receiving Tower

OST NIGHTS, WE CLIMB TO the tower's roof to stand together beneath the satellite dishes, from whose shadows we watch hundreds of meteorites fall through the aurora and across the arctic sky. Trapped high in the atmosphere, they streak the horizon, then flare out, with only the rarest among them surviving long enough to burst into either mountains or tundra, that madness of snow and ice beneath us, around us.

Once, Cormack stood beside me and prayed aloud that one might crash into the receiving tower instead and free us all.

Once, I knew which one of us Cormack actually was.

The tower is twenty stories tall, made of blast-resistant concrete and crowned by two enormous satellite dishes twisting and turning upon their bases, their movements driven by powerful electric motors installed in the rafters between the listening room and the roof. The larger dish is used for receiving signals and messages from both our commanders and our enemies, the latter of which we are expected to decode, interpret, and then reencrypt before sending them to our superiors using the smaller transmitting dish.

It has been months since the larger dish picked up anything but static, maybe longer. Some of the men talk openly about leaving the tower, about trying to make our way to the coast, where we might be rescued by the supply transport that supposedly awaits us there. These men say the war is over, that — after all these years — we can finally go home.

The captain lets the men speak. When they are finished he asks each of the dissenters where they are from, knowing these men will not be able to remember their hometowns, that they haven't been able to for years.

The captain, he always knows just how to quiet us.

As I remember it — which is not well — young Kerr was the first to grow dim. We'd find him high in the tower's listening room, cursing at the computers, locking up console after console by failing to enter his password correctly. At night, he wandered the barracks, holding a framed portrait of his son and daughter, asking us if we knew their names, if we remembered how old they were. This is when one of us would remove the photograph from its frame so that he could read the fading scrawl on the back, the inked lines he eventually wore off by tracing them over and over with his fingers, after which there was no proof to quiet his queries.

Later, after he had gotten much worse, we discovered him sleeping on the roof, half frozen beneath the receiving dish, his arms wrapped partway around its thick stem, his mind faded, his body lean and starved and blackened with frostbite.

None of us realized he was missing until we found his

body trapped in the ice, still inside the compound's gate. What pain he must have felt after he threw himself from atop the tower, then tried to crawl forward on crushed bones, heading in the direction of a coast he must have known he would never live to see.

My name is Maon, according to the stitching across the breast of the uniform I am wearing and of all the others hanging in the locker beside my bunk. This is what it says beside my computer console in the listening room, what the others call out when they greet me. It is what the captain snarls often in my direction, growling and waving his machine pistol to remind me that he is the one giving the orders, not me.

My name is Maon, pronounced *moon*: some mornings, I stand before my mirror and speak its syllable again and again, reminding myself as I stare at my reflection, surprised anew by the gray of my hair, by how the winter of my beard mimics the snow and ice outside. I have begun to fatten, to find my stomach and face thicker than I believe them to be away from the mirror. Caught between the endless dark outside the tower and the constant fluorescence of our own gray halls, it is too easy to mistake one time for another, to miss meals or repeat them. My mouth tastes perpetually of cigarettes and salted beef. My belly grows hard and pressing against the strained buttons of my uniform. Sometimes I can't remember having ever eaten. My stomach is so full of food I am often sick for hours.

It was only after Kerr died that I discovered our personnel records had been deleted: birth dates, hometowns, the persons to be notified in the case of our deaths, all these crucial facts gone. From that moment on, we had only our tattered uniforms to prove our ranks, only the name tape attached to our chests to remind us who we each were.

Without the personnel records, it became impossible to determine the date we were to be released from service and taken to the coast for transport home. According to the captain, this meant no one could go home until we reestablished contact with the main force, something he seemed increasingly uninterested in trying to do.

Once, Macrath and the others came to me and asked me to speak to the captain, to inquire after our missing records. The next morning in the mess hall, I did my best to convince him to honor their requests.

It would only take a few minutes, I said. You could do it right now. Probably there's no one out there listening, but even if there is, they won't respond without your authorization codes.

The captain finished chewing before looking up from his breakfast of runny scrambled eggs and muddy coffee. His eyes flicked from my face to where Macrath stood behind me, then back again. He said, Are you trying to give me an order, Maon?

No, sir. A suggestion, maybe.

The captain's voice was stern, providing no room for argument. When I turned to leave, I saw Macrath still standing there, his eyes murderously red rimmed and locked onto the captain's own implacable black orbs, on those irises as shiny and flat as the surface of burned wood. Macrath only wanted to go home. He thought he had a family, a wife and children, a little house, a car he liked to tinker with on weekends. That was what he always told us, what he believed he remembered.

When the captain acted, it was not me he targeted but Macrath, ordering some of the men to haul him into the frozen courtyard, then following behind to deliver the fatal bullet himself. The captain explained that the orders to execute Macrath had come from higher up the chain of command, in a coded communication meant for his eyes only. Even though it was I who had manned the silence of the listening room all morning, I said nothing, counseled the others to do the same. As I had once warned Macrath: We must not cross the captain too often. Certainly not when he is in a killing mood.

The captain is unshakable in the face of our questions, but perhaps he too knows nothing more than what we know ourselves: that there are no more signals, no signs of either friend or foe. When we ask if our transport is still moored at the coast, waiting for our return, he refuses to answer. He says that information is classified, that we don't need to know. But if the ship is still waiting, then we could make a try for the coast, leaving this wasteland behind. Perhaps then we could find a way to stop our fleeing memories, to slow the dimness that replaces them. In the meantime, we blame our forgetfulness on anything we can, scapegoating the tower first, then the components of our lives here. It could be radiation from the satellite dishes, or the constant darkness, or the fact that the only foods we eat are yeastless wafers of bread, jugs full of liquid egg substitute, tins of dried beef, plus powdered milk and powdered fruit and powdered everything else, the same few meals day after day, our taste buds grown as dull and listless as the brains they're connected to, until the repetition steals away our past lives, until our minds are as identical as our gray beards, our curved paunches, our time-distressed uniforms.

Standing in the dark among the mechanical workings of the two satellite dishes, I work swiftly to repair a series of frayed wires splayed out from the larger dish, my fingers shaking beneath the tight beam of my headlamp, frozen even through the thickness of my gloves. It has been dark as long as I can remember, long enough that the sun grows increasingly theoretical, abstract. My own memories of it faded long ago, so that all remembrances of places lit not by torches and floodlights are suspect, at best more evidence of a past increasingly faked and unlikely, stolen from the remnants of the others who share this tower.

When I finish my task, I stand and look out from the tower's edge, studying the ice and snow and wind and above it all the aurora, its bright curtains of color cutting a ribbon through the darkness, obscuring much of the meteor shower that continues to fall. I linger until the cold penetrates the last of my bones, then I turn the metal wheel atop the frost-stuck hatch, descend the rickety ladder leading back into the tower.

An hour later, lying in bed, I am unable to remember the colors of the aurora or even what exactly I went outside to fix. The events of my life increasingly exist only in the moment, too often consumed by their own bright fire, lost as the many meteorites tumbling and burning out across the already unimaginable midnight sky.

After we're sure the captain is asleep in his quarters, we gather in the basement of the tower, amid the stacked pallets of canned and powdered foodstuffs, the whole rooms of spare wiring kits and computer parts and drums of fuel oil, where there is enough of everything to last another hundred years. There are six of us who meet, the only ones who still remember enough to work, who can still log in to our computers. Weeks ago, we changed our passwords to *password*, everyone's first guess, so that as we continue to dim we will still be able to log in and listen for the orders we hope we might yet receive.

In the basement, we take turns telling whatever stories we can. Tonight, Camran tells us about playing baseball in high school, about how the smell of the grass stuck to everything, to his clothes and hair and fingers, and then about the sound of the bat striking the ball, how he once hit three home runs in a single game. With his gravelly voice, Lachlann brags about all the sex he had before coming here, going on and on about tits and ass until we beg him to stop torturing us with what we cannot have.

Earc speaks of his parents at length, a strange but touching attachment for a man his age, and then Ros tells us about his favorite dance club back home, about the heaving crush of the dancers. We look around at the meagerness of our group. We try to imagine hundreds of people in one place but find that we cannot.

I talk—as I always do—about the ship and the base camp and the coast. I have forgotten everything so that I might remember this, for myself and for the rest of us. Better that I never again recall my family, my friends, my former home, if it means remembering the ship, our last hope, because if I forget, the captain will have won, and none of us will escape this tower.

We go on speaking until we've exhausted ourselves, until we've shared everything we still have left to share. Every week, this takes less and less time. Once there were eleven of us, but soon there will be only five, then four, and then three and two and one, until the treason of these meetings ceases to exist altogether.

The next morning, Camran is dead by the captain's hand, shot at his station in the listening room. The force of the bullet shatters his face, spraying his monitor and lodging wet flecks of skull and teeth between the once-cream-colored letters of his keyboard. The captain surveys our shocked expressions, then accuses Camran of trying to use the transmitting dish to send an unauthorized message. As we watch, unable to see around the bulk of his body, the captain silently reads the sentences typed across the flickering green screen, his lips moving wordlessly as his eyes scan from left to right. When he is finished, he fires a bullet into the computer, showering the leftovers of Camran with sparks. We beg him to tell us what the message said, so he gestures to his lieutenant, Dughall, the only other who'd seen the screen.

The captain puts away his pistol, then takes a deep

breath, sucking in a lung's worth of cordite and bloodsmoke. He says, Let Dughall tell you, as he told me.

But of course Dughall has already forgotten. It has been months since he's been to one of our meetings, so there is no one to tell us what message might have gotten out. All we want is something to hope for. This is what the captain refuses us.

We could push the captain further, but there is only so much we can risk. The threat of automatic fire from his machine pistol prevents us from asking too many questions, from arguing against even his harshest orders. We all have our sidearms, but he's the only one who still has bullets, having convinced us to surrender our own to his care some time ago, when our troubles first began.

After silencing our protests, the captain orders Dughall and some of the other dim to carry what's left of Camran down the stairs and out into the courtyard. The rest of the men go back to their work, but not me. I climb to the roof, where I watch the dim stack Camran atop the pile of our other dead, our frozen and forgotten friends.

The captain is in a foul mood today, in response to our persistent nagging about Camran, and to our continued speculation about the chances of making it to the coast if we were to try as a group. He rants at us for planning to abandon our posts without leave, then decides to make an example out of two of the longtime dim, Onchu and Ramsay, both so far gone they can barely speak. He dresses them in their furs, then hands them packs already provisioned to the point of bursting, as if the captain knew this day was coming. He pushes them both out the door, kicking at them and threatening with his pistol when they protest. He points toward the south, the opposite of where I see the auroras over the mountains, then forces them across the courtyard, through the gate, and out onto the ice. Within minutes they're out of sight from the ground, but from the roof we watch through our night scopes as they wander against the wind and blowing snow, unable already to remember which direction they've come from or where they're going.

Only a few hundred yards from the gate, Onchu sits on the ground, facing away from the tower, too far to see or hear us above the howl of the wind. We scream anyway, begging him to get up, to keep moving, to make for the coast, to save us all. He doesn't move. He draws his limbs in, hanging his hooded head between his knees. By morning, he will be frozen to death, and then, sometime after, we will forget his name.

Later, Ramsay somehow finds his way through the dark and the blowing snow back into the courtyard, where the captain shoots him dead, as he has so many others who have refused to go gentle into the wastes, who have returned without his leave.

One night, there is a meeting at which I wait alone until dawn before returning to the barracks. With no one to tell stories to, I walk the rows of bunks instead, watching my men slumber, their gray heads full of dim dreams. A week later, I find Lachlann dead by his own hand, hanging from the rafters in the supply closet. The captain cuts the body down himself, has it dragged outside and stacked with the others. He asks if anyone would like to say a few words in Lachlann's memory, shakes his head when we cannot.

I wait until it is night again—true night, not just dark, as it always is—and then fill my backpack with foodstuffs and bottles of water, with chemical torches and the thickest blankets I can find. I am leaving, but first I consider murdering the captain in his sleep. Perhaps smothering him with one of his own battered pillows. Perhaps choking him with my hands. I sneak easily past the sleeping, dim guards outside his quarters, then through the creaking door of his bedchamber.

Once inside, I stand beside the captain's bed and watch his creased, stubbled face until I experience an unexpected moment of doubt: If it is only he and I who still remember anything, then who will be left to lead these men after he is dead and I am gone? If one day the signal does come, who will be here to lead them out of the receiving tower and across the ice?

What I have to admit is that, in the face of my pending abandonment, perhaps even this captain is better than no captain at all.

I wake him up and we talk for the last time. Seated across from me in his room, the captain makes me promise that I will leave the tower when we have finished, no matter what he tells me.

Three questions, he says. No more.

I ask him if there are other receiving towers, and he

says there are, but when I wonder aloud who mans these towers, he offers nothing beyond shrugging misdirections and half-truths.

Next, I ask him if others will come to take our place after we are all dead. He looks over my provisioned pack, my donned furs, then says, No. You are the last Maon. I am the last captain. Everyone here is so old now, and all of them have finally grown dim. What we did, no one else will have to do.

The last question is even harder for him to answer, but I press him, begging for honesty, for confirmation, and finally he nods his head, his coal-black eyes saddened for the first time I can remember, but maybe, I realize, not for the first time ever.

He tells me how, long ago, when we were both young and strong, we stood atop the receiving tower in the dark, watching the waves of satellite debris tear endlessly through the atmosphere, their terrible truth not yet disguised as innocent meteorites.

Already this was years after the war ended, after we'd each accepted we'd never go home, that there was no home to go to.

Already this was after we'd started to forget, to go dim. Not all at once, not everyone, but enough of us, starting with Kerr.

The dim demanded to know why they were being kept in the receiving tower, why they couldn't travel to the shore to be relieved of their duties. They grew restless and angry, and before long there were enough of them that something had to be done.

The captain says, Everything we did next was your decision.

He says, Before there was Maon, there was the major, and for a second I can see us atop the tower, grimly shaking hands. I hear myself say to him the name that was once his, the one I have claimed myself for so long, ever since I stepped down from this command.

By my orders, he tells me, the captain took over my abandoned duties administrating the useless routines of the receiving tower, while I joined the men in the ranks so that I could better watch over the dim and keep them safe. A major no more, I held midnight meetings with those whose wits remained, explaining how, to protect our ailing friends, our brothers in arms, we would pretend the war was still being fought. To give them purpose, we would start manning the listening room again, searching for signals that did not — could not — exist, since there was no one left alive to send them.

According to the captain, this is how we saved our men, how we kept them safe long enough for our beards to gray, for our bodies to grow stooped and fat.

Still the dim turned increasingly dangerous, first to themselves and then to the rest of us. We waited until they began threatening murder and mutiny, then the captain had them shot and stacked one by one in the courtyard or else pushed them out across the ice to seek the meaningless shore, the phantom promise of the waiting transport ship, a ship that existed only in the stories I told the men. That existed only to give them purpose, to give them hope they might yet be saved.

The captain says, At first, you chose who would stay and who I would force from the tower. You were still the major, even if no one remembered. You said it was my duty to give them someone to hate, if that was what it took to hold them together, to unite them in this new life they had no choice but to live.

Later, after you dimmed too, I had to decide myself when it was time to use the pistol or to drive a man out of the tower and onto the ice.

I have done my best, he tells me, but I am not you. I have had to be cruel. I have had to become a monster. All these decisions, I have had to make alone. The captain stops speaking, turns his face toward the wall. There is only the sound of his breathing, of mine in turn, until he says, I wish you could remember for yourself.

He says, It's not as if this is the only time I've told you.

Now it is my turn to look away, ashamed, for him and for myself. For what we did together.

I say, You have done your duty well.

And you yours, he says. Better than you hoped, even.

But why switch places? How did we know? That you would remember, and I wouldn't?

He shakes his head. You've had your three questions, and now you must go.

No, I say. Tell me. How did we know?

We didn't, he says. We guessed.

The captain says nothing more. Eventually, he falls asleep in his chair, resuming his quiet snoring, his hands folded over the ampleness of his belly. I try to stay awake, to hold on to what he has told me, to try to see how these newly remembered truths might save our men, but they cannot, or perhaps they already have. Exhausted, I doze myself, and when I wake I can recall only this little of what was said between us. Maybe it is for the best. Maybe whatever he remembered is an illusion, another hallucinated landscape we dreamed up together to replace what we have lost. Perhaps all there has ever been is this receiving tower and the others like it, separated by ice and snow and mountains, and then, somewhere else, some lost continent, shapeless in my mind, where some interminable war cost us everything.

I leave the captain alive, not because I have promised to, but because I am afraid that, at the end of my journey, it will be proven that he has always been right, that there is no ship waiting, that to lead these men out across the tundra would be to lead them to their deaths. I walk the halls of the receiving tower one more time, making one last effort to remember, to hold on to what is left of the captain's words. I meet some of the dim going about their duties, each of them following my commands to leave me alone, obeying me as they would the captain. I take my time, knowing they will not remember seeing me, will not report my small betrayal. Eventually, I find myself wandering the rows of empty bunks at the far end of the barracks, too many beds for the number of men I can remember being lost. I try to remember who these others were, but I cannot. Their bunks are covered in dust, their bedding stripped to replace our own threadbare blankets and pillows. These bunks must belong to the dead stacked in the courtyard, but perhaps also to others like me, men who took it upon themselves to reach the sea long ago, further back than I can remember.

There must have been so many men here, and now they are nearly all dead and forgotten by us, the very men they'd meant to rescue.

As a final act of defiance, I climb the tower to the listening room, where I make one last attempt to hear something, anything. I put on my headphones and slowly move the dials through the full spectrum of frequencies. I hear nothing but the hum and hiss of the omnipresent static, a blizzard of meaningless sound falling unceasingly upon my ears.

There was a time when I knew over one hundred words for static, but now there is only the one, so insufficient for the complexity of what splendor it describes.

I take off my headphones, then log out of my console. Before I do, I change the password to some new word, some gibberish, something I would never have been able to remember, even in the prime of my life, all those long decades ago.

I do not look back as I cross the threshold of the receiving tower, nor when I open the gate at the far end of the courtyard, but I can feel the captain watching me from atop the parapets. I wonder if he has kept vigil for all the others who began this exodus, the lost men who once slept in those bunks. I wonder if, like now, he kept quiet, hurling neither threats nor warnings against the piercing wind, leaving those brave men to question and to doubt, to wonder if it truly was the captain who was wrong, or only themselves.

I wonder how long he waits for me before going back inside; I wonder when I will no longer be able to sense his heavy eyes darkening my every step. And then I know.

I discover Onchu—who I had forgotten, who I beg forgiveness of now that he is found again—while the aurora shimmers overhead on the first night of my journey. I scrape at the snow and ice around his face, revealing the black frostbitten skin which will never decay, this place too cold and removed from the earth even for maggots or worms. After I have stared as long as I dare, I use my pick to dig his body from the ice, desperate for the backpack clenched in his arms, immobile with frost. I have no choice but to snap the bones with my pick, then peel his limbs away from the bag's canvas.

I open the pack's drawstrings to find fistfuls of photographs, frozen into unidentifiable clumps, then bundles of wrecked letters, misshapen ice balls of trinkets. At the bottom of the pack is a threadbare dress uniform, rolled tightly and creased with frost, unmarked except for its insignia declaring a major's rank, some higher-ranking officer I can no longer remember. All these artifacts might once have told me who I was, who we all were, but not now. If I reach the coast, I will have to become some new Maon, a man who remembers nothing, who did not see his only friends frozen to the earth, who did not see his compatriots gunned down by their captain, the man who once swore to keep them all safe.

I leave these relics behind, scattered around Onchu's frigid form. Let our memories keep him company, if they can.

Once injured it is so easy to forget the sudden shift of the ice, the fall into the crevasse that followed. To forget the snapping of bones, sounding so much like the cracking of the centuries-old ice beneath my feet. Eventually, I reach down to find again the ruin of my shattered shin, and then I scream until I black out, unable to remember enough to keep from shocking myself all over again once I wake.

In my few lucid moments, I stare up through the cracked ice, out of this cave and into the air beyond. I want to survive at least until the aurora blooms one last time, until the falling ruins of space streak across the sky again, but I have no way of telling which direction I'm facing, which slivered shard of sky I might be able to see.

Rather than risk dying in the wrong place, I decide that I might be able to splint the bone with the frame of my backpack, if I am brave and if I hurry.

I can at least hurry.

Twisting painfully, I open my pack to find all the chemical torches broken open and mixed together, so that all my meager possessions glow a ghastly shade of yellow, barely enough to work by. I cry out more than once, but eventually I manage to set the bone, binding it with the wrenched steel of my pack frame and torn strips of blanket. After that, there is only the climb, only the hard chill of ice cutting through my belly and thighs as I drag myself up the frozen incline, each inch a mile's worth of struggle, all to return to a surface as inhospitable as the underworld I am leaving.

Out here, away from the illumination of the receiving tower, night on the ice is an even-blacker shade of dark. I crave a new word for it, crave to expand a vocabulary I have mostly forgotten, words that could have described more than simplest night, snow, ice, failure, all of which have more than one degree. I have to keep walking, one crooked step at a time, or else I will freeze. Everything I have left encircles me: my death, the aurora, and there, beyond it, the veil which obscures this life from the next.

When I cannot will myself to try again to stand, I struggle instead from my back to a seated position and retrieve my pistol from its holster. It glows yellow where I've touched it, smeared with some chemical I no longer recognize. I pull back the slide, then put the muzzle to the fleshy muscle beneath my jaw. There is a tenderness there already, but I push hard anyway, feel the pain ignite my frozen nerves. I close my eyes, take a breath, and squeeze the trigger, howling as loud as the wind when the pistol produces only a dry, useless click.

I return my pistol to its holster, force myself to my feet. I start walking, leaning heavily on my one good leg, dragging the other behind, until a stumbling collapse delivers me to the ice. I struggle to sit, surrounded by the loud creak of my frozen muscles, of tendons contracting away from bone.

Then the pistol, then the confusion of the muzzle-press bruise, then the frustration of the empty chamber. Then the struggle to my feet, the few awkward steps, the next painful crash to this ice.

I drop the pistol, fail to find it in the blowing powder.

I try to draw the pistol, only to find it missing, lost somewhere behind me.

Lying on the ice in the darkness, I hear a bird cry far above me, riding the currents of rising, warmer air that must flow even here. I cannot recognize its speech, cannot remember how to differentiate between the ravens and owls who hunt the tundra and the gulls and terns found only near the shore. As useful as that information might be, I know it doesn't matter. I do not open my eyes to look or even strain to hear the bird again. I am sure I have dreamed it, as I am dreaming all the other, older things I see flashing behind the closed curtains of my eyelids. And then the rest of me breaks free, flies away, rises above, taking the words that tied these dreams to me, and afterward there are no ships, no shores, no signals, no static, then no towers, no captains. Then there is no Maon, and then I run out of words, and then I

Inheritance

The generation and nourishment of proper soul takes place in the heart; it resides in the heart and arteries, and is transmitted from the heart to the organs through the arteries. At first, it enters the master organs such as the brain, liver or reproductive organs; from there it goes to other organs, while the nature of the soul is being modified in each of them.
— Avicenna, *The Canon of Medicine*

1]

After he died Gaab took apart a goat with a letter opener and a switchblade.

The goat was fat and Gaab was not and Gaab worked his sharpnesses within the bound of its screaming. Against and then under its seams.

Gaab believed if he could get the goat open and take what pumped inside, then he might think as the goat did, so content in its little pen. Might see as it saw, might taste what it tasted, might survive better than he had before.

He had only one heart then. Only one pair of eyes, one pair of ears. Just one tongue and one stomach, its greedy hungering set deep in his workings.

And after he removed some of those organs? Then the goat's eyes gooping his sockets; then its ears and tongue, staining his screws.

Gaab shook in the torn dirt of the well-gored pen, amid all that fur and matting, and as the red sun rose over the sand he held the goat's heart in his hands, he clutched the sticky weight until it dried. Despite his want he lacked the courage to try his other mechanism after the bloody mess he'd made of his face had failed: To first spin wide his chest-crank. To unclasp his remade organ from its chest-hatch. To replace what he'd been given with what he'd taken.

When Brother found Gaab in that pen, then Gaab must have looked to Brother like a barbarian of the old world, of that storied age when men were still filled with blood, just like the goats and the horses and the other beasts.

It was only sometime after Brother found him that Gaab felt what queer pumpings he'd desired: the dull delay of a second heart, the angry thud of a third — and then he better understood the other way he might live.

It was with Brother that he stole his fourth from the gasping chest of another, and then from other bodies other tongues and stomachs, other eyes and ears.

The dark-cassocked priests had told Gaab nothing of this, of what next he could be. Because mostly the priests had not cared how Gaab lived. Only that he did.

2]

Remember how the company of riders numbered thirteen then, thirteen for now.

Remember their brokebacked bentkneed mounts, all the horses they could find along the rim road, its long curve flung far from the main spokes of the highway, farthest from the city, the glassed towers that none in the company had ever seen: the towers belonging to whomever the priests belonged to, to whom the priests said the dead belonged too.

The company belonged to no one, Brother said, or else only Brother.

Remember how at his command the company rode their horses through forests of stony trees and across hillocks scorched free of their scrub, with faces haggard and uniforms filthy and reeking and their gunlocks gleaming dully at their hips and their saber blades the only part of them wiped clean. All that world buzzing and aglow and blunted by sand everywhere and in everything. And while worry creased the faces of some of the riders, it never crossed the angles of Brother's, his face instead lit always with a scheming smirk, some unkillable smile.

Remember how only Brother determined that dread company's direction. How only he set its heading and mood. How only he could recruit a new rider, saying this man should be spared the shot and the blade, be taken in instead.

Gaab was the first, but even Gaab did not know the men Brother would choose, some dragged from hovels or dry shallow plots barely marked; some discovered exiled from their living homes, thieves with chests burst, limbs staked in the sand; some killers with empty eyes runny with sloshed preservative, ear-sockets burned shut by scars; and then some others with tendencies made worse by bodies not needing to ejaculate, by the swelled flesh hung between their dead legs, a rough rubber doomed to be cut off for what they'd done—unless they joined up, rode on. And then still others with other crimes, until there were for a time these thirteen riders and these thirteen horses, the beasts alive in a fashion their riders weren't. And so always the animals wary and nervous and snorting and stamping at this inauspicious and unlucky and matching number, the largest the company had grown. And if their riders went hungry and thirsty for great lengths, the horses could not. Together they were pushed into banditry and raiding the rim road, riding onward beneath the thundering sun, the shelterless sky.

The company rode across the sand and they rode into the dusty dead streets of the trembling villages, and above those streets sometimes there might appear one face or two faces in the highest windows.

Remember how the company mostly left those faces unmolested because Brother would punish any man who fired his weapon without leave. But how sometimes it was Brother who started the shooting. How he would haul his carbine from its sheath and in a single motion put a bullet through a high-hung window. How sometimes the shot figure fell back into its room and sometimes it fell forward, down and out and thudding to the street, the mess of cracked pavement hard beneath the endless sand.

Remember how sometimes the body stood and clutched its face or chest and put its fingers into its newest hole while Brother reloaded with movements calm and careful and unbothered by worry. How the figure shot would cry out with pain and anger and injustice but how that hardly helped. Or how, if it did bring help, the company cut down all comers.

Feel your memory-heart squeezing in your chest and remember: How more often the shot man or woman or deathless child merely covered its new wound with terrified hands and cowered on its knees or else ran off down the street. How sometimes the company later passed in silence that unbleeding shape sitting on the shoulder of the road, the snuffling breath of the company horses the only comment filling the expanding echo of the gunshot. But how other times they passed in laughter. Or at least those among the company who were that day possessed of the right hearts for mirth and merrymaking.

3]

What did Gaab remember from his life before?

Some folk he had lived with before he lived with Brother remembered everything: the names of their parents, the ages of their siblings the day the sky split, subjects they had learned in buildings that now sat empty, for any children that yet lived were too old for school, and there were no more come to take their seats.

Most of those buildings were fallen down anyway,

for they hadn't been built for this much wind and sand and sun.

But Gaab remembered less, found little inside the pumpings of his self-heart. The goat was not his first memory but it was close. Before that, only some fragments, hard to reach: A house with three or four rooms. A mother and a father, perhaps. A den set half beneath the earth with a fireplace and one wall on which a picture hung, of some phantasmagoric heaven: a rush of water cascading between the wrong-colored trees, all their shades of green flung across that wall by some artist's dishonest hand.

There were other memories too, but they were as hard to claim as dreams and came less often, only slowly, slowly.

After the goat, what Gaab remembered was Brother's big body and his big head and his small hands. He remembered injuries that would have scarred had blood pumped them closed, that were instead stitched shut, sealed with plastinate and other priestly humors. He remembered how Brother had buried those stitchings beneath layers of wound cloth. To keep the sun away. From skin that burned but never paled, no matter in what darkness he slunk. From eyes that wept even behind goggles or mesh.

What good was it to have a death that lasted forever if for eternity you could only diminish.

Remember how Brother carried the brightest blade and the longest-barreled carbine. How his far eye saw the best of any upon the rim, how no one escaped his gaze. How his rage-heart pumped the angriest thoughts, his torture-heart the most sick. How the pockets of his wrap contained more variety than any other's, a heart and a tongue and a stomach and eyes and ears for every possible moment, every desirable action. How he could change them faster than any of the rest of the company and how even without his heart he could cross a room without stumbling, without falling gasping to the floor, something no other rider would attempt.

How he was the only one among them who no longer had his self-set, so that he was not ever exactly himself, however infinitely changeable whoever he was might be.

How no matter how much he took there was still this that he did not possess and it was this lack he could not abide.

Remember how sometimes at night he walked in through the wavery edge of the campfire's penumbra, then out past its shimmering reach. Out into the darkness and back into the light and farther out of that light and into the outer dark. His footsteps silent, his boots as small as his gloves, his gait wide, and how long had he been bow-legged? Not forever but a long time now, and maybe he'd never ridden before he died but now always the smell of horse in his nostrils, now always the saber still at his belt, the pistol hung off the opposite hip and the carbine slung sheathed, a slash across his back, its strap bisecting his ill-fitted chest, that fatted flesh pressing his fell uniform tight, the buttons straining—and whose name was written on the breast? He owned the tongue of the man who'd worn it last but it told him nothing, the tongue of a mute such a useless muscle.

Sometimes Brother polished the uniform's straining brass until it sparked a mile off. Sometimes he stuck the mute-tongue in Gaab's mouth. Remember Brother laughing at Gaab's protests: a big sound from a body so shot and stabbed and slashed and burned. Staked and arrowriddled and leadblasted. Speared with hooked barbs that tugged hard, peeled back what they sliced open. And inside that faststitched flesh a clockwork man, a machine never exhausted, built to last and to last forever, a final trick of the late magic, the same magic all the rest of the dead received — except in Brother Gaab thought no man alive or dead could end it.

4]

Gaab, the other, known only by the sound that came from his mouth at their first meeting: a bleating, a greeting from the goat pen.

Brother naming Gaab before Gaab might better name himself. But then *brother* also a state defined only by relation. And so afterward those were their names, known first only to each other.

Gaab, Brother had said, I am to be like a brother to you.

He'd said, You're not the best brother but you're the brother that's mine.

Remember how for Gaab it never stopped hurting him to remove his own eyes but how it was sometimes worth the pain. Ditto ears and tongue and stomach, and doubly his heart.

But then how he was improved: how with his farseeing-eyes he might see a horizon placed half again as far.

How with his deaf-ears he might turn unflinching toward the screams of those the company's sabers pierced.

How with his scribe-heart he might be able to remember the recent past; how with his sorrow-heart he might mourn what he remembered.

How with his dumb-heart he might make himself numb, so that he might live with what he had done, would do.

And tucked between them all, in the leather scroll within which he kept his treasures: the letter opener; the switch-blade. To remind him even when his heart might not.

5]

Not every hovel was left unlawed. Krum, where Brother had found Gaab and where he had given Gaab his name, was still governed by the priests, and there were others too, villages both named and nameless where the company rode up to the gates and wheeled their horses neighing before the walls until the gatemen appeared to meet their holler. Remember how, at one such place, Brother entreated the gatemen to grant the company entry, for the company's horses needed to be fed and to be reshod and one horse was sick or else lame and might need shooting if there was no good doctor taking residence in that town.

Remember how the gatemen agreed to open the village to the company but only after some delay. How nervous the gatemen appeared as they swung back the panels of high wood, revealing the rotted backs that would surely have given way had they instead barred Brother's entry. But by then the streets were emptied of horses and mules and goats, all hidden now in cellars and bedrooms where perhaps the company would not bother to look, to look and then to covet. As in those days there was nothing that was not irreplaceable.

The company bedded their horses except for the ones that were to be shod and the one lamed up and the riders of those beasts went to begin their barter with the blacksmith, a man dead as all the others but otherwise unlike the men of the company: for the villagers lived their death with only one heart, one set of ears and eyes and one tongue, given to them by the priests, made from their own flesh and returned to work within it. Anything else was forbidden, and the villagers feared the priests' birdmasks and their black cassocks above all else, for their power was that of life over death, over the deaths they were living. And if they were caught defying the terms of their making, then what happened next, and was it worse than this death everlasting.

6]

The company rested in the village square and the villagers kept their distance. Sometimes one scurried through the alleys around them, and the company men yelled out jeers at her disappearance. But mostly the riders kept to the shaded parts of the square, and there was so much less threat from the company then, less than when those men had been filled with blood and bile and jizzum: now there was only the violence and violence alone was generative of only so much fear. And even what pain did come might be made more temporary—for the village folk could be resewn and rewound and restrung—and it was said on the rim that it took a thousand cuts to put something so asunder that the priests would recognize its dissolution.

In that emptied square the company provoked no threats nor made any of their own and they made no unmet demands. The riders with the needy horses paid in fair trade for the work they wanted and out of old courtesies the villagers brought the rest some small meal of hard bread and water even though it was not necessary for them to eat or drink and in return those irregulars asked for nothing else except the dust and air they inhabited. But after Brother's company had occupied the square for an afternoon and most of an evening a boy with a burned face stepped out of the village's largest house and into the descending dusk and Gaab saw that the boy was not afraid of the company of riders and their gruesome gear: the dried blood on their uniforms; the knotted locks of hair stuffed under short-brimmed hats or else escaped from those confines; the stitchscars across their cheeks and brows and necks where amateur surgeons or else each other had put their flesh back to its right shape after the sharp passing of broadhead or lance or blade or bullet. And in some of those nameless low men there was even some of that flesh missing and even those gross displays did not stop the boy's advance.

7]

Remember now the burned boy, the little chief of that little village, half his face a long open mess, crawled with sand; his chest shirtless and Y scarred; his chest-hatch stuck, its seams faded from lack of use, its crank still buried in the stopped flesh; buttonless pants belted with rope made of hemp or hair; baby teeth still rotting in his head, visible when he spoke, asking the riders where they were from and where they were going and why they were camped in his village.

Remember how in any way but shape he was not what was previously called *boy*, was instead only some stalled dwarf. How there had not been true boys among the rim-folk in that time but he looked like nothing else and so what else to call him. No adolescence had ever come upon his frame, but inside his skull rode an ancient mind, a brain first meant for no more than eighty or a hundred years, and who could tell how long it had been. And if there was eternity outside the bounds of the world, then it was never meant for the earthly kingdom and yet how eternity was all this longfailing world had left, for those there stranded.

The boy wore no shirt to hide the pistol scabbard draped around his body, slid upon a belt cut for the waist of a grown man, now falling down the boy-chief's skinny bones from right shoulder to left hip, made with an old-world craft long forgotten, so that any replacement would be cruder made, if better fit. The revolver held at that hip was bar-reled as long as the boy's forearm, and Gaab startled at the sight of its grip, wondered how a body so small could fire a cannon of such girth. But the burned boy wouldn't have it if he couldn't.

And in the boy's other hand, outstretched toward the company: a small wetness, wrapped in cloth.

8]

At last Brother rising. His own body shorter than some other of the riders' but bigger than all. Only his hands diminutive by comparison. As they wiped the dusk and dust from the epaulets of his uniform. As they rubbed themselves together before him and his speech.

Brother saying, We want feed for our horses, to take with us when we leave.

Only feed, the burned boy said. That's all?

The feed is where we want to start.

The boy looked down at his own feet, shoeless since for ever. Then back up at Brother: Are you trading or taking?

Trading, Brother said.

To start, the boy said.

To start, agreed Brother.

The boy's hand sprawled on his cannon—the hand open, fingers splayed so only the boy's palm fell alight on the wooden grip. We've seen such a company before, he said. Burned faces and blue uniforms, come to trade—and yet afterward only new begging and theft for my people.

Brother knelt down and picked his cap up out of the street and shook it clean and placed it back on his head. Hid that big baldness from the burned boy.

What happened to your last chief, Brother said. And remember how Brother's questions were never questions.

And then the boy speaking again, saying: He was my father. But that sadness is long gone.

Remember the boy's hand floating, unsure, then tapping hesitant his chest-hatch, that heart-cover. A space for him never opened. The boy always only himself, limited by the bounds laid down at his birth, both his birthings.

Liar, said Brother.

Brother unfastened the flap of his uniform, let the button-bearing left fall away, then the claspholed right. His chest flabby and shaking beneath a stained undershirt cut to the belly button to afford easy access. Then putting that access to use: spinning free the crank, swinging open the hatch. And inside, the beating of something monstrous. A mechanical pumping that moved no blood but thrummed with what blood had once signified. Back in the first of these days, before the last books, and in older times too, when books were scrolls and tablets and carvings in the caves. Those unreasoned ages, epochs ruled by nature and not by priests, their years long but maybe not longer than these.

Once Brother saw the burned boy had seen his offer, then Brother closed his hatch and shut his crank and buttoned back his shirt.

Liar, said Brother, again. Liar.

Remember that smile upon Brother's face, remember his shifting his weight leg to leg, remember his words: If you want to remember your father, then best to see the world he saw. The memories of the missing.

9]

The boy's eyes gleaming. Almost wet. But what moisture could they make.

And in his hand the small bundle, the biggest of its contents only the size of an apple, a fist held within a fist. And then some other miscellanea surrounding.

What remained: an inheritance.

10]

Gaab and two of the others held the boy down in the moony street and when he was mostly still then Brother set to digging with the point of his knife to expose the crank in the boy's chest, hidden near one clavicle or the other. The plastinated flesh flaked at the knife's touch but even as the boy screamed he did not bleed anything thinner than sap and when the hole was dug then Brother's fingers pushed into the hole to turn the crank, to unlatch the chest-hatch—and still that movement would not come free until Brother further perforated its seams, an additional bit of knifework.

Remember the boy's heart-hole open to the night air for the first time, and how it was too dark in that square for the boy to see down into himself from his angle and how for that he should have been thankful.

The machinery of the boy's body and also the machine it had been made to be: a dry mechanism, without even the wash of blood to hide its working. And still the boy released an animal of noise when Brother broke the priestlaid fleshbonds that prevented his work, when he unplaced the boy's self-heart and laid it upon the wrap, when he pushed the older other into its space, and then again as he plucked out the boy's eyes and unsocketed his ears and his tongue and replaced them with what did not belong to him, this mismatched set of old-world biology.

11]

When Gaab stood he found his body shaken by the boy's kicking and while that motion continued before him on the ground he watched as some number of the other villagers crowded near, circling the company in the fallen dark. A rough scatter of pale faces hidden behind veils and wide-brimmed hats, coverings meant to slow the sun's decaying rays, and also those reflung by the moon's reflecting, and among the villagers were men armed with some small weaponry and also women who shook with tearless weeping. Then the rending of their clothes, the wailing at what they had witnessed, until into their sound the boy stood up upon his old bones, himself still but in a new way: Remember a slight cock of the wrong hip. Eyes bulging and hue-shifted, ears misfit upon his head. Gaab saw perhaps the boy was no longer left-handed, that his hands fluttered in the wrong portion of the air, that he would have to switch his weapon over or else learn his other hand to hold it.

12]

The boy spoke.

I had forgotten, he said. Just a boy when the sky last burst. How bright that last sun was. And how that day my father was a man and I was a boy and so it was as a boy that I woke to the priests.

Their faces masked and beaked as eagles. Their hands holding angled steel like borrowed claws. The carvings they made, the clucking sounds of their tongues.

How little I understood afterward. How not even my parents would explain what I did not. How the words it would have taken were forbidden by the priests, who in those days still lived among us, instructing us how they wished us most to be.

What great meeknesses they asked of us. And then the world passed on, then the years passed.

I aged without getting older. How much worse it was to be this way. How much worse it was for my father and my mother to watch.

And yet how long they each did watch. And what quiet grief we made each night.

And then suddenly my father was dead, decades later, dead again by hands like yours, his body scattered so that he could not be restored.

And then my mother walking into the desert because she would not live here without him, not even after we found these few parts of who he was.

Since that day I have been chief instead. And now how many indistinguishable days has it been?

13]

Remember the other words of the boy, the way he could not stop his speaking of the world before this, until all the company was aflame with passion for what had been lost, but see also Brother in that moment as Gaab saw him: His master. His leader. His brother, so named. Remember how Brother's lips moved in time with the boy's. Perhaps he had tasted the heart's memories already, before. Perhaps it was not one like Brother who had ended the boy's father but one exactly Brother. Because there was nothing that Brother could not know or do. Because he had turned upon the rim since the beginning of this long end. Because Brother could not be killed again, because always he would remain unpunished. But even if Brother did know the words that the boy spoke, still they were not his own words. For of all the riders in the company it was only Brother who had no self-heart, and with no self-heart of his own no words he spoke were ever wholly his, not any combination of syllables Gaab had ever heard him speak.

14]

The crowd moved closer through the moonlight, an entire village closing around the company enclosed around their chief. Men and women and children moved together, and despite the spectrum of the shapes of their deaths all now roughly the same age: for what difference did the small fractions make, the few years of the last age they'd shared before this new one began. The priests had woken them as one body and now they moved in the same way against the new transgressor and against the company, and if Brother did not yet break the boy's stare, then still his riders were not ignorant of the village's progress, the loop drawing tight.

It wasn't only violence that the riders could make but it was at violence that they were their most capable. A sword or a saber, a pistol or carbine loaded with powder and shot: these were the dictions of their best language. And some days only their loudest threat was speech enough. But the villagers knew that if the boy was allowed to stay, then the next priest who visited would see he was not who he had been, for the dead did not so quickly change. And then what hard hell to pay. The priests' books said that under the sky upon the earth every man was already judged but that it was not the place of man to know his own judgment. Yet sometimes the evil man revealed himself to his brothers and his sisters and then it was their station to cast him from their midst. And anyway the boy-chief was no longer who he had been. For their chief had had eyes of brown and this other had eyes of green and even if they had not seen the surgery there in the darkness still they were not ignorant of what this change evidenced.

15]

The company put their backs to Brother and the burned boy and when the circle was complete it was Gaab who stood closest to his master, his own chest already full of shield-heart, his wary-eyes installed since the moment the riders had sat down in the dusty village square. And when the villagers fell upon them it was Gaab who fired the first shot and he watched his bullet clear some portion of the skull from a grayskin woman, the back of her skull-shape flapping away, made a new and bloody bird taking wing.

Remember how nothing flowed from Gaab's shield-heart except satisfaction that his charge remained safe, that Brother went untouched. And then how his saber pushed into the belly of a man and then another man and then some false child armed with a club studded with nails lifted too high, exposing a span of unprotected fat that flopped open at Gaab's suggestion. How Gaab stepped around those dropping weights to prick another as the villagers set upon the company with their amateur applications of sticks and stones and the repurposed instruments of their agriculture. In return that irregular company responded with musket and pistol and hatchet and mattock and machete—but despite those many bullets and blades there was no blood spilled between the dead, who could not bleed: only the parting of skin and plastinate. And until it was over there sounded only the clash of steel and the boom of powder and here and there some sudden surprise, voiced at the results of the dull blasts of the company's firearms, the grunting work of ax and sword through already stopped flesh.

16]

Afterward, the villagers who could scattered to the holes of their homes and then the company stepped back too, widening their circle. Some among the company were sent to fetch the horses and to take what feed and tackle they had already bargained for and others were set to preparing their departure. One of the riders switched in his lust-heart and dragged the woman Gaab had made headless behind the deadened tree of the square and there he rode her bones until some of their number came unseamed, and though in his disgust Gaab turned away, still he heard the act's grunting echo reverberate across the square, until at last he pocketed his ears.

17]

Remember what else Gaab saw, when he joined Brother standing watch over the sitting chief. How the boy sat slumped in dirt, his chin nodded onto his chest. How Gaab looked first at Brother, whose face declared no emotion, or else only the beginnings of a smile.

Remember your own such thought-relics, like a joke recalled.

Gaab saw the boy's revolver in Brother's hand but that didn't mean Brother had fired it. He knelt before the boy, lifted the boy's cheeks with his hands.

How the boy's right eye was shot through. How despite its large caliber the bullet had made no backdoor exit, instead lodged somewhere in the putty of the brain.

How that boy's smallest glimpse of the old world was either over or else inside his skull it would be everlasting and either way there was then no way to retrieve it, to make him speak again its visions, for no matter what tongue they next put in his head he would speak no story. And perhaps he would never be fixed. For even the priests did not waste their efforts rebuilding what was only partway broken. But the boy could stand and he could walk even if he could not shut the slackness of his empty mouth and so Brother strapped the boy's cannon to his own belt and then he tied a lead around the boy's neck and he fastened its end to his saddle and for some time after they left that village the boy would run after Brother wherever Brother went, his shut memories of the past trailing behind the company as the wedge of their horses carved slowly forward, into the long stall of future still ahead.

18]

Some nights later they camped in a ruin surrounded by other ruins, the older culture of that land emerged from the sands for some temporary span, jutted out from some former landscape revealed by the shifting of the new one. At the front of the hill a rolling door slid upward, grinding in its tracks to give entry to a stonefloored room, hung with the heads of tools topping wallstuck hooks, the wood of their shafts long rotted above partmelted plastic bins full of ransacked rubbage from that other age, its rummage and its waste.

The riders broke through the locked front door to find the main room of the house sunk, shifted down. Cracks in the carpet made way for rot in the wood and below that rot there plunged a darkness filled with chitter and crawl and around its perimeter the company laid down their blankets and took up their tin plates. They didn't need to eat every day but that basement was still full of scrawned-out desert rats and with the tips of their sabers the company men pried them from between the floorboards, slicing or kicking them until they halted, their bodies deflated but still offering some small squirt, bursting between fingers like giant unripe mosquitoes. The men carved a fire into the low point of the depression, let the flick and the spit and the sputter form in that house, its smoke hanging in the rafters until after false stomachs had been filled and emptied, until want and conversation were exhausted. And in the middle hours of the night the weakest part of the floor collapsed as they slept, carrying the flames down into the dark, while around that pit the company dreamed on, and in Gaab's dream-heart there was but one dream borne through the heat and the flames, a repeated vision of a thousand skulls, a thousand thousand: Skulls bleached white and bigger than a man's. Horns curved out from their heads long as a giant's forearm and blacker than the most petrified wood. Fallen ribs like beams to build a house, so that even the highway's largest stalled metal husks might have shivered in that field. Everywhere everything mossed the texture of death. And what calamity had struck, long before the one that sundered the sky from the earth, that left it cracked naked before the sun?

Walking among those dream-bones there was a terror in Gaab he had never known, and he had no heart that knew how to give it a name. And if the dead could pray he would have prayed for wind and for sand, to wash those skulls away, to bury them below. Brother had told Gaab that this world had once been covered in tall grass, green and yellow, in thin stalks making long waves undulating in the wind, and those waves had sung a song that would never be heard again, so that when the last multitudes of the living came down the old rim road they never suspected what surrounded them on every side, these skulls, these deaths their fathers' fathers had dealt. But how always the skulls had been there waiting. And how now in the last desert that death had come again revealed. And if ever Gaab ventured that prairie, then perhaps he would see for himself.

Remember Gaab's relief upon waking that the dreams in the dream-heart were not his own, belonging only to another gone, gone to the same place as the beast of a thousand thousand skulls, all they ever were carried away by the chattering creeping classes of creatures, all of them except their bones, too heavy with history to move, and by the fire, which when he awoke he saw burning upward from below the fallen earth.

19]

Later the ruined bodies left in the dust of the village were found in their stillness, and in pairs the black-cassocked priests loaded the emptied forms into the wagon. Each of the dead was laid arms and legs straight, three lengths laid three wide and each set of heels touching the crown of the head below. Between loads the sun shimmered and sang in the sky and those left baked atop the dust. Skin dried and blistered and splitting. The smell of scorch. And no matter the stench the birdmasked priests did not quit their task. After the streets were emptied the priests went door-to-door in their pairs. Without knocking, because the dead could not have granted their entry. And in each house they searched each room. They searched inside each closet and cabinet and beneath each table and above each ceiling for often the dead were hidden in the attics so that the priests might not find them. But the priests always found the dead and they always marked their stilled chests with the forked sign of their knives and they always removed the organs and eyes and ears and tongues and when the bodies were empty the priests repaired what they could, filled the hollows back up—and then the priests set their meat machines to motion, to motion and to marching. Marching back the way they came, or else according to new orders, a migration of the village's dead begun at last, a new life beginning in the absence of their chief: into the stillness of the sunstruck past, preserved forever by new memories inserted into old shells. But when they awoke the dead did not always understand the memories they saw, because how long it was then since waving grass, how long since the bright lands cataloged in the old books. How late the birds now, never returning; how once more the sky blotted with butterflies and then they were gone forever. And so to the coyote would go the earth, and to the cockroaches the kingdom.

20]

In the season of migration that followed, the marching dead saw a world moving on. As they walked their long walk they saw once a thousand sheep burning in the fields with their flesh stripped and the fat left on their bones providing fuel for the blaze, and all around the shepherds of that flock arrayed in wailing tearless grief at the ruin of their charges.

They saw other priests in their birdmasks riding high white horses and they saw the blackguard soldiers the priests had made from more loyal flesh and they saw the hounds that accompanied them, the leapings of their gray bodies, the bounding after.

They saw vultures circling adrift on the high air and they saw other scavengers below upon the crests of the ridges and the lips of cliffs of sand. From roach to beetle to hyena and coyote, and what new order these creatures might make, what evolved fraternity.

They saw dogs that had become wolves again; and also what wolves had become.

They saw the other dead in clothes sewn from the skins of their animals or woven from the cotton and flax of their fields, all abandoned or burned, dug up. They saw their bellies bulged useless with meals they could not stop wanting and yet could not digest. They saw in every face one dark eye but in the other eye a manufactured light.

They saw the red sun roiling in the sky and they saw the cracked atmosphere shimmer and buzz with its heat that crossed the void between the sun and the sky in just eight seconds, come to disperse the cool of night, to blast back the shadows, until the sun traded realms with the moon, and then how the umbric creep covered the land—and even in shadow there were in some pockets deeper shadows still.

The roving dead sometimes saw Gaab on his horse but they did not know his name and they saw Brother riding before him and they did not know his either, nor any of those who rode in their company, who fell under them or against them. But so much else in those renewed but deathless years went unnamed too, or else named but unknown. And so what was it to the roving dead that this pair led their company of horses and riders around that circled road, the rim at the end of the world.

They saw the other dead moving in droves between other villages and in that season of migration it was at the priests' command that they moved. But the priests' rhyme or reason was kept from their charges so that none knew why this village should be emptied or that one filled.

The priests saw in those patched refugees no ambition or will to escape what fate they had been given. Only desert lives for desert dwellers. Only acceptance and acquiescence and struggle against everything but their chains. And how the dead might never be sure where was the darkest dark, how deep within the earth might such a place soar its hidden towers. And how once the people of this world had begged to live forever.

VI

Cataclysm Baby

ABELARD, ABRAHAM, ABSALOM

This smoldered cigar, last of a box of twenty, bought to celebrate happier times, now smoked to keep away the smell of our unwashed skin, of our slipping flesh, of our baby grown in my wife's belly, the submerged sign of a prophecy burning, stretching taut her hard bulge: all hair, just like the others, gone wrong again.

Fists of black hail fall from the cloudless sky and spatter the house, streak the skin of our walls, break windows above broken beds. The birth room fills with air the texture of mud, with black birds forgetting how to fly, these crows and vultures waiting to make a nest of our child, and still I focus, keep my eyes on shattered glass, on my wife's pelvis tilting toward sunlight, toward sun turned the color of baby's first stool, then the color of blood.

Then the blood, flowing between my wife's legs.

Hopeful cigar smoked, held between loose teeth, I say, Push. I say, Push right now.

And then it comes, becomes: a baby boy, hair on cheeks, on forehead, on lips and tongue. Inverse of our own nakedness. Shame in an equal and opposite amount.

For our baby, a name chosen from a book of names. Each name exhausted one after another, a sequenced failure. I hook a finger into our baby's tiny mouth and pull out hair, hair ball. From furred windpipe. From matted esophagus.

Only my wife cries. Only the birds caw, flap their wings. Only again a howl of spoor, cigar sputter.

Pull, my wife says. *Pull.*

As if I could ever pull enough. As if I could ever clear the lungs of this fur. As if I could clear the stomach. As if I could clear the heart, its chambers full, clenched, wrong for what harrowed world awaits. Pull, she says. Pull. Pull. Pull. And what coward I would be to stop.

BEATRICE, BELLA, BLAISE

The older was the first to show us the scars, the archaeology of her sister-scribed history, hard-written by their cutting, their stabbing, their sawing. The younger better hid her sister's handiwork, bore well the bands of reddened flesh and puckered scars beneath shirt, beneath sleeve, beneath shorts and underwear.

Even in the bath we barely noticed.

Even when the younger found trouble standing, even then we refused to believe.

Always the younger had limped, we argued. Always she had struggled to balance. Always her ears had been notched, her fingers a crooked nine.

What trust we had in the older then, what light touch

she had, what blinding perfect smile made to answer our questions.

It had taken the younger's retribution to reveal the older's now-avenged crime, took the continuing destruction of that first body for us to discover the slower attrition of the second, and so afterward what right to anger did we have toward the younger, even at the shocking sight of the diminished older, our beloved eldest?

Perhaps none, we decided. Perhaps girls will be girls, no matter what we parents say.

And what else to do next, but let them work this out themselves?

To support their interests, we buy stocks of whetstones, of wood blocks filled with meat knives, of blister-packaged scissors, until at last our house is pregnant with the voices of children playing, craving only to get nearer each other, to have the other close at hand: *Tag, you're it,* then *Duck, duck, goose!* The older leads these games, a born teacher, but it is the younger who best exploits their rules. Every evening their screaming laughter cuts through our locked bedroom door, until one night we hear only the voice of the younger, playing all alone.

Ring around the rosie, she sings, skipping through the house, calling out our names, our titles — yelling *Mother* up the stairs, shouting *Father* outside our door.

We all fall down, she sings, throwing her skinny bones against the bolts. *We all fall down together!*

And then: the creak of the doorframe, the give of the lock, the tenuous grace of a chain, pulled short.

CAIN, CALEB, CAMERON

The doctors promised twins but delivered only one baby from my wife's pummeled womb, her troubled cavity. First the push, push, then the blood, then my mistake-toothed firstborn gnashing in the nurse's arms: chubby, too chubby, too covered in mother's gore.

And then my wife continuing to scream.

And then the doctors begging her to stop.

And then what came next, what loose hair, what loose skin, what loose son or daughter, what delta of destruction flowing: my eyes, my wife's nose, swimming small and recognizable in the flotsam, and then what once-plump arms, what legs covered in bite marks, such expired flesh taken clean off soft baby bones.

In the nursery, our son cried sleepless, sucked frozen pacifiers, pulled at his ears with his fingers, and from behind the glass between us I watched helpless as he chewed his blanket, as he choked past his pillow's stuffing, unsatisfied.

At home, it is my wife who cries, while our firstborn sucks her tit dry, while his rows of teeth puncture her skin, pockmark her areola. And how to respond when she complains of his always-hunger, when in an empty voice she begs me to allow the bottle instead?

But look at our son, I say.

Look how tall he's grown. Look how strong.

Look how he walks, only a month old.

Look how he lifts the icebox lid, how he opens the packaging with his teeth.

Look at his mouth, stained again a ring of red, just like the day he was born.

DOMINA, DOREEN, DORMA

What month of dark mornings followed? What spring or fall, what remade season of locusts and blackflies besetting our town, flown in on thickening air and sickening smell? And there, in the middle of its days, appears this chrysalis, this cocoon, this child-shaped bundle found wrapped in our morning sheets, tangled in the space where our toddling daughter once slept, dream thrashed and nightmare ridden as she clung to our skin, our heat.

A chrysalis? I ask my wife. A cocoon?

What's the difference, she says, when it's your child inside, when it's your caterpillar?

We vow to keep it close, to sleep beside it until it ruptures, until what cocoons are for: until she emerges, no longer a child.

To cradle my pupa in my arms. To rock it in the rocking chair. To wait and hope, and at last to see the new shape pressed urgent against the inner skin of the chitin, to crack wide the chrysalis with one hand, to with the other force my daughter free.

To behold the dripping wings, the glistening thorax, the changed head, the new mouth.

I open the nursery window and let the room fill with locusts and flies, those other black wings, other black legs, other black mouths bent on devouring all they can catch: Only me, only what flaking skin I have left. Only my daughter's fresh wings, her span of translucent amber flapping free the scent of molt dust, of moth smoke.

And then the hairy touch of her legs on my legs, on my hips, on my chest, then the click of her mandibles, clipping locusts from my ears, knocking flies from my lips and eyes.

And then my wife and I at the nursery window, watching her leave. Watching her join the town's other golden children, together flying a sky clouded shut. Keeping us safe, at least until the locusts run out. Until the flies are gone. Until the trees and grass and shrubs are empty of leaf and branch.

Until all the rest the creeping thing stops.

Until my grief-stung wife disappears, first into herself, a body spun inside a heartache, and then again outside our home, into the cloud of children blacking our sky.

The rest of us shut our hungry bodies away, whisper through glass pane, through locked door: You can't ever come home, we say, but no words can stop the knocking against our lit windows, our delicate houses.

The next time I see her, how big she's gotten: My only daughter, all grown up.

And now her string of milky eggs across the window.

Now her own caterpillars, hungry for what world remains.

EDGAR, EDRIC, EDUARDO

My wife and I are too bloated to climb by the time the vines reach the floor of this spoiled forest, our bodies too quaking with fat to grasp even the lowest of their fruits. We call for our son, that skinny boy sunburned from his scavenging, and then we teach him to climb, to imitate the monkeys that screech from the branches. From our backs, we holler how best to shimmy the twenty-story vines of this new jungle, this eruption of trunk and thorn and branch and thistle rising from where our concrete once strangled the earth: all that old life gone now, replaced by towering trees, by mud made anew, by daily wallows and failed waddles, by the deforestation diet of my hungry wife and my own hearty appetite.

To our son: Climb, we cry. Climb, and bring us back what there is to find.

For some while it works. He returns with bony arms full of guavas, peaches, papayas, descends the vines with breeches torn and stained, his pockets stuffed with bananas, other fruits dropped whole into my gulping gullet, into the strained esophagus of his mother.

Our baby boy, our darling son, born into this lonely forest, made for this world to which we cannot adapt: without him we would be lost, would surely starve and waste away.

For a month he brings such quantities of fruit, until our cheeks bulge with the feasts of his foraging, and after each feeding we bid him stay close, bid him to sit beside us while we question him about the treetops. We ask, Have you seen anyone else above, in the sway and the swing? Are there others still left? Other boys and girls feeding other parents trapped below?

Our boy shakes his head in feigned loneliness, but each passing day reveals the length of his lie: first a bracelet of flowering vines, knit by another, then a pox of hickeys, a necklace of bruises. *Suck marks,* my wife sneers, driving our son back into the high trees, where he leaps easy from vine to branch to trunk. Her disapproval follows him, pushes him higher and higher, until there is nothing to see, until the forest is silent around us.

Then our breakfast arriving slow, our lunch late.

Then our dinners not coming at all.

Then our guts aching, desperate for what grows above.

We gather our quivering bodies, release our screamed demands into the canopy, but still no son appears. Still no meal follows. To keep us company there is only the squawk of the monkeys descending lower by the day, growing braver on the vines in the absence of our son. There are only their toothy muzzles, stained with the fruits of the hunt, and then, from far above, the airy laughter of our child, of all our children who have ascended into the bowers, into the verdant newness suspended above this fallen earth, this last of all the muck and mud we've known.

FAWN, FIONA, FJOLA

They take our daughter and in return they grant us eight hours of light a day, plus nutrient-enriched air pumped thick and cool through the vents in the concrete ceilings, the nonslip floors. The mother and I alternate days washing in the extra fifteen minutes of water we're rationed, but this cleanliness does not lead us to renewed conversation, to revigored copulation.

Before the makings of our daughter I did not know this woman, and now that our daughter is gone we rarely speak, barely look at each other even when the thrumming lights permit.

Instead, our eyes swivel toward the silver screens set into the walls, into every tight-cornered wall. Working silently, the mother and I move all our furniture: In the living room, we discard tables and ottomans, push the couch so near we have to climb over the arms to sit cross-legged before the flicker, and then in the bedroom we shift our mattress into the cleared space below the largest screen, beneath the silver stretch of video as long as our once-used bed.

On our knees, we press our faces to the screen, put our ears to speakers making only soothing static, the swooping sound of television dreams: this is where they promised we'd see our daughter again, where they said she'd return beautiful and whole, not womb-thrashed and gene-short, not malnourished and depressed.

Not like her parents, they promised.

The mother and I waste our brightest hours peering into the static, but no matter how many channels we check, we find no daughter, and also no other programming, as there was the last cycle of abundant light, of quick electricity.

Each day that passes, we breathe deeper of the processed air, let its engineered taste force us into health, into some state we're told feels like happiness.

Each day, we wash in our daily bucket of water, perfume ourselves before showing off our broadening faces, our fresh flesh plump with improved circumstance.

For one minute we tell each other our trade was worth it, because only then can we bring ourselves to gaze again into the daughterless static, to stare until our eyes ache, until we cannot resist calling the talent scouts who took from us our only child.

Into the phone, we say, Where is her better life you promised? Where is her bright and shining future? What a channel you guaranteed, what better reality captured beneath lights and microphones—where can it be found?

All they say is, Keep watching.

All they say is, Trust us—and what other choice do we have?

How healthy the mother appears, how fat my face reflected in her worried eyes, until the day the power whirs off, the lights go dark, the fans stop blowing.

The television's dwindling dim casts us into silence, leaving only our still-stinking breath to fill the air once stubborn with its sound. With hands held between us for the first time since the daughter-making, the mother and I kneel upon the bed, press our bodies to the screen. Racked with rediscovered heat and hunger, we beg for a glimpse, any single sign of our mistake-given daughter, but the screen offers only glassy potential, only what might still be, if we watch, if we believe.

I have forgotten our daughter's face, the mother says, her deflating cheeks pressed against the screen, her tears streaming its stale dark, washing the dust from its silence.

She says, Please. Please describe her, remind me, tell me what I cannot see so that I might recognize her when she comes: her new hair, her new face, her new body.

I tell the mother again what the scout promised, what he told us our daughter would have because of our sacrifice, because of our willingness to go without.

I tell her how our daughter resides now on the surface, under the sun we have not seen in years except on this still-dark screen.

I tell her about the shining mane that surely grows from our daughter's once-shorn scalp, the teeth that must sprout white from her once-unsocketed gums.

I tell her about our daughter's rebuilt mind, her promised ability to sound whole words, to speak in fullest sentences, her voice made so different from when she lived with us.

I tell her how I see our once-daughter hugged by new parents.

I tell her how this girl has probably forgotten all about us.

How she's never coming back. How that's a kindness.

I tell her, The power will be restored any minute. They promised us.

This for that, I tell her. This for that is what they promised us.

I tell her, Stop crying.

I tell her, Stop crying right now.

GREYSON, GRIFFIN, GUILLERMO

Perhaps only their mother could distinguish between the boys, could reckon their slight variations in weight, the distinct cervix bends of their skulls. I never could, not when they appeared as three redheaded infants and not when they were toddlers, all dressed alike in the preference of my good and then gone wife.

As teenagers they each ate the same amount of porridge each morning, the same third of a meat can at dusk, and even the first time I caught one masturbating, I caught all three, circled between their bunks, each mimicking the motion of another's hands. Ditto drinking, ditto the glass pipes, ditto the new milk-drawn drugs I'd never known before their schoolmaster called.

When the boys had their mandatory facemasks and goggles affixed, no one could tell them apart, but then no one could recognize anyone else either, not after the baggy state-issued jumpsuits, the preventative head shavings.

Even after this handicapping, some people remained more charming than others, and if there was an attribute each of my sons possessed equally, it was charm.

All these excuses and more were given by the women in town after every wife and daughter and matron and maiden from fourteen to forty-five swelled with my sons' oft-spilled spunk, with the fruits of their inseparable loins. Later it grew difficult to prove whose child each mother carried, amid whole seasons of confused houses packed with breaking bellies, those quick-sequenced summer and fall and winter months filled with spread legs, with the emptying of wombs, with new mothers seeking out my sons for shotgun weddings and promises of child support.

Hidden away in my house, my sons now celebrate their success: This is how you start a dynasty, one says over family dinner, a meal eaten behind blackout curtains, barricaded doors.

A kingdom, says the next, then corrects himself. A franchise.

In a world that's dying, says the third, isn't this all sort of beautiful?

I ask you: What possible solution to these childbirths overpopulating this town with more redheaded babies, with fiery scalps awaiting the state razor, whole streets lined with my sons' progeny, with their strong genes wiping out the faces of their children's mothers in deference to their own perfect jawlines?

How many babies are born before we realize that all their children are boys? That our town's women are the past, thanks to my one-note issue, to their deadly sperm making deathly pregnancies, taking each of their partners the way of their own mother: blood-wet, breath-gasped, split-wombed, at best to linger, never to recover from the makings of their children?

Now these babies left behind. Now only me and my three sons, only us four shut-ins against a town full of adulterated widowers, of shamed cuckolds and seething fathers, all parading our yard, my many grandsons in tow.

Now the first babies being left on our doorstep. Now the rest, following soon after.

Now my walking out onto the front porch to see the rows and rows of abandoned twins and triplets, the exponential crop of my line.

What loud reverberations their hunger cries make! What diaper complaints, what pain, what suffering, and amid it always my boys, unfeeling for what they have done, and so what else to do but discipline again these three failed fathers, these three no-use sons of mine?

What next but to make them take up the scythe and the shovel, if they will not take up their right roles instead?

What point in anything else? What good fathering could boys as bad as these possibly do?

So at last their lesson in how to reap. And how to sow. And how, when there is nothing better, to plow the world back under.

HALI, HALLE, HAMAKO

The day came when we could no longer hide the glistening sight of our daughter's flippers, nor the secret of her skin, its oils and fur.

Like the other parents afflicted before us, we took her to the lonely end of the island, to the cliffs hung high above the breaking surf. There my wife kissed our daughter's wet nose, after which I bound tight her swaddling, stilling her wide limbs to her sleek middle, and then together we let our baby tumble from our hands, through the tall air, into the swallowing sea.

Afterward, what endeavors we undertook to forget, even as our guilty bodies tried again for some more right-birthed baby, even as our bodies proved unable to produce another—as we entered this famished sea, this season of nets cast and collected empty, until throughout our village every stomach was as hollowed as our crib.

And now these legs, walking me back to the cliff, my guilt-path worn through the jungle.

Now these eyes, watching the ocean crash its anger-fist upon the shore, a parade of knuckles on top of knuckles on top of knuckles; watching how other times the ocean is flat like so much glass, like the unwalked beach below, its sand stormed upon, lightning-fused and mirror-smooth.

Those waveless days, I see my face or a face like my face staring back from the water beyond, but not the faces of the fish that once swam in those depths.

Our fish are gone, and our daughter too, and together her mother and I pray for some rewinding of waves, so that our daughter might one day find her way to the flatter side of the island, to the yellow beaches, to the path leading to our small hut, our home meant once to be her home.

And if it happens? If our pup returns?

Then what?

Then how: With anger? With forgiveness? With love?

Or with what we deserve instead, a new mood from our new daughter, dredged deep from the dark, rising slow and sure, purposed only to take us back down.

ISAAC, ISAIAH, ISHMAEL

Even at birth they were already damaged, their brittle bones opened and crushed, powdered by their mother's powerful organs, her pressing canal: All those thin ribs snapped and splintered upon the stainless steel of the operating room. All those skulls crooked and cracked, all those twisted greenstick limbs. We lifted each child out from the mother's body and into surgeries of its own, did our best to splint and screw our prides together.

So few survived, and for what next chance? On what legs would they stand, with no milk to grow them strong except from the body that had already failed to make them so?

If only there were some other mother, some second receptacle for the babies we want so badly to make. But no, there is only me and my brothers, only this last-caught woman between us.

To quell my brothers' anger, to beg their patience, I say, This woman may not be capable of producing what heir we need, but perhaps she may yet birth the one who might, if only one of her daughters lives.

I say, The end isn't short, but long. And so always we must not rush, must be in no hurry.

And so we fill the mother with powdered milk, with canned peaches, with vitamin paste squeezed from nearly empty tubes. And so we fill her with meat.

Every new wish is followed by another waiting, followed by another failure: Push, we say, our voices speaking in unison, our wants aligned after a lifetime of bitterest division, of brotherly strife. Together, we make what we can make, and we save what we can save. Push, we say, and then comes this next baby born just as broken, its first cries already choked with the chalk of its bones. Its newborn everything else shattering into dust. This daughterlike reminder that not all birthed into this world shall see it reborn—and then again our determination, our willingness to try once more.

And then, Lie still, I say, and then, Hold her, brothers, hold her, and then, I will plant again in her this seed, until at last we grow the world we desire.

JUSTINA, JUSTINE, JUSTISE

For the first crime my daughters took only my thumb. They refused to apologize for their aggression, even after I confronted them, after I tossed their bedroom and confiscated the hatchet hidden in their toy box, beneath their miniature gavel. When lined up and accused beside her sisters, all the oldest would say was that my trial had been fair, their court complete even without my presence. One daughter for a judge, one for the prosecution, one for the defense.

My middle daughter, she spit onto what was left of our thread-worn carpet, said my defense had been particularly difficult, considering my obvious guilt.

She said, Perhaps you should tell our mother you cut your thumb at work, so that she will not have to know why we took it.

She said, Your records are sealed until you unseal them, and then she made the locking motion over her lips that I taught her when she was my baby, when she first needed to know what secrets were.

What milky-stern eyes the youngest had too, set in her pale face, floating above the high collar of her blackest dress: blinded as both her sisters, still her blank eyes accused, threatened, made me sorry for what I was.

This youngest daughter, she walked me back to my

room, her hand folded small in my uninjured one as she explained that she and the others hoped I had learned my lesson, because they did not want to hear my sorry case again.

Then the key turning in the lock, jailing me for my wife to rescue, to admonish for leaving the girls alone, because who knew what trouble they might make when no one was watching.

How I tried to be sneakier: To send messages only at work. To go out after they were already in bed. To change my clothes away from home, so that they might not smell the other upon me.

And then waking with my hand gone, divorced from my wrist, a tourniquet tightened around my stump, and my mouth cottoned with morphine. And then wondering where my beautiful daughters could have gotten their tools, their skillful medicines.

And then not knowing what to tell my wife or my mistress, each curious about my wounds, and also still being unable to choose, to pick one woman over the other.

How now the gavel sounds in my sleep, how I hear my oldest pounding its loud weight against the surface of her child-sized desk, bringing into line the pointless arguing of the middle daughter, of the youngest — because in my defense, what could the middle daughter say? What judicious lies could she tell that the others might believe? When all she wanted was for me to see the wrong of my ways, to repent so her mother and I might remain married forever?

In the last days of my affair, I lift my middle daughter

into my arms, feel how much weight she's lost, how her hair has wisped beneath its ribbons.

She meets my apologies with a slap, squirms free. She says, Don't think I'm still Daddy's little girl.

She says, I only defended you because no one else would.

She says, In justice, we are divided, but in punishment, we are one.

The lullaby she sings as she walks away, I am the one who taught it to her. I am the one who sat beside her crib and held her hand when she could not sleep. I am the one who rocked her and fed her when her mother could not, exhausted as she was by her difficult pregnancies and the changing of the air.

I want this good behavior to matter, but I know it does not.

Some weeks later, I awake restrained to my now-half-empty bed, nothing visible in the darkness except the silhouettes of my blind daughters in their black dresses, their white blindfolds wrapped tight round empty eyes.

And then it comes, and then they come with it: the children I deserve, if never the children I wanted, my three furious daughters.

KIDD, KIER, KIMBALL

Another new rain falls, dumped from the complicated sky, its acid-heavy droplets pelting our shoulders as we run from awning to awning, from collapsing home porch to crumbling chapel steps. Along our way, we see every kind of bird upon the ground, all heavy with forgotten flying, and around them their mud-left eggs, as thin walled as my wife's uterus, that tender space slung inside her unsteady body.

Within it, within us both, sound always these trapped prayers, necessary to be loosed.

Inside the church, that last dry place, we give them voice from our lungs, beg them from our knees, clasp them between hands wrapped in rosaries gathered from this dead town, this plague-slapped village. Above our heads, stained glass strains against the wind, refracts the last minutes of dusk-light wrong and weird upon our faces, reduces our speech to mumbles. Exhausted of words, we move together to light a candle for each baby lost, each fetus formed but not right-birthed.

By now, this takes us all night long. This takes every minute of every night.

At dawn, we extinguish the flames so the candles will be there to relight tomorrow, and then again we pray: Oh Lord, just once. Just once, deliver us a child not wrecked from the beginning. Grant us a son not lousy with fur, not ruined with scales or feathers. Give us a daughter made for the old world instead of this new one, this waste of weather and wild.

And what we would do.

And how we would do anything.

Our only answers are the church's silent histories, those sequenced promises written in terrible stone, decorating each circling step from the vestibule to the altar, from the sacristy to the last unburned pews. Each station a horrid hope too unbearable to believe, this world made only the end of mystery, only the opposite of miracles.

Inside my wife, perhaps there is only the same, only these doubling doubts, these many questions that fill my own still-beating heart: Oh Lord, for who else might be promised the inheritance of the earth? For who else is meant the receiving of the kingdom? If not our impossible, short-lived children, then what new race still to come, undreamed in our present darkness? Who are these next babes about to be poured down upon the earth, come at last to wash us from off its tear-soaked face?

LAKIN, LAKSHMI, LAMIA

Remember the difficulty of your labor, and how at first the doctors mistook our daughter for a breech birth, but then came no foot, no other hard limb or promontory leading the way?

What was stuck instead: Only plump flesh, only greased rolls of fat. Only flush skin in handfuls, leaving nothing for the doctors to do but tug the mess free—and what a baby they found within, what gigantic girth of daughter, her face hung with meat, her fingers barely able to poke free from the folds of her wrists.

Remember how afterward you were too weak to hold her weight, how for the first months of her life the only way to feed her was to bring your breast to her buried mouth, those lips moving within the pancake of her face? How at bath time you would stretch her skin tight so I might wash within her creases, so that together we could clear the lint-slop between, scrub free the mold grown in every hanging crevice?

Remember the surgeons advising operations to remove that excess, to suck the fat from around her eyes so she might be able to see? From around her ears, so she might be able to hear?

How you hated the doctors then: for trying to decide in what ways our daughter could be beautiful, how she should see the world, and how the world should see her.

No, you said. She will eat what she wants to eat, until she fills out that great skin, until she stretches it taut, until jagged lines of purpled flesh mark new territories upon the body of her person.

My daughter could fill a room, you said, and still I would think her perfect.

Remember saying these words?

Tell me you remember. Turn around from the stove, from the meat-stink you're making, and tell me.

Remember how she grew, how she continued to grow? How her head sagged so she needed a brace to support it, and yet there was no device that could fit the trunk of her neck? How she toddled, now a worm the size of a bulldog, buried in rolls of flesh that restricted her movement, that reduced her to a slither, to lunging and dragging across the carpet?

Blind and deaf, mumbling behind the smothering weight of her face, she cried for help, but all we heard was a muffle, a moan, and still you refused your pretty darling, your shining star.

Remember how you buried your face in her belly, laughing and tickling her with your lips? How you said she was so delicious you wanted to eat her? Or how the salt-shame of her tears collected in the shelves of her face, left their etchings for us to find with the washcloth?

When the doctors finally cut our skin-gorged daughter free, when they returned her wrapped in bandages, mutilated of face, but escaped from the flapping weight of her birth, how bad was it for her then, because we'd pretended for so long?

How much worse when the bandages came off, and we saw what skinny creature your honest love had hid?

How hungry she was then, how little food there was left in the stores, the depleted and shuttered supermarkets, and how dry your breasts were, empty as our larder —

And then what? How to feed our daughter, who you loved, whose forgiveness you wished to earn?

Remember how once, long before this gristle-spat daughter now munching and chewing in her high chair, you said my legs were my best attribute, that you fell in love starting from my toes and working your way up?

Remember how thick the muscle of my thighs, how fine the curve of my calves?

Say you remember, then look again upon our daughter's refleshed face: as awful as it was to make her a monster before, how much worse to have made her so again?

Remember how once I claimed I would stop this, but how you believed me wrong, because who am I, without those legs?

Who am I, without those hands, offered in the absence of better gifts?

Who I am: I am still her father. I am still your husband, your partner, a half wedded to match your half, and even if you have made me less of a man to make her more of a daughter, still I mean to retake the whole of what is mine.

Come close, my onetime love. Come closer and find out our ravening daughter is not the only one with teeth, nor the only one who hungers.

Closer now. Closer.

Closer: Taste what's happened to me, to you, to our daughter, this fat wedge shoved between us until we splintered. Open your mouth as we have opened ours, and taste how soon I will tear you both free, how I will wrench our daughter from you, from where you are together wrapped tight, trapped, floating mad within the weight of all she once was.

MESHACH, MESHACH, MESHACH

We knew our firstborn might not last, his weak constitution revealed even before he could walk, signaled by his crinkled little fingers, his wet coughs full of sputum and phlegm. Still my wife nursed him, still I wiped the sweat off his sallow face and his caved chest. At night, we let him sleep between our bodies, even though his raucous breathing often woke us, even though there was no need to keep warm his small shape, not in the furnace of our bedchamber, our tiny hole of a home.

Each morning, we awoke from our dreams covered in the night's soot, the expectorate that blew upward from the vents in the floor, the ash and worse that could not escape through the clogged height of the chimney above.

Once our boy could walk, once his toddler arms were thick enough to lift himself, then we wrapped his mouth and nose with breathable cloth and set him at the ledge of the chimney, at the bottom rung of the skinny ladder leading up into the narrow smokestack.

Up, we cried. Up, and loose what there is to be loosed.

Oh, and what a baby he was then! What cries and wails at being separated from us, at being alone in the dark of the stack. But still he climbed, did his best to keep the air flowing, to keep what came from below ascending to wherever it floated above.

By the time he was old enough to talk, his voice was already strained with the black glass the heat made of his lungs.

By then, his brother baked in my wife's womb, growing to replace him when he inevitably tumbled loose, plummeting from the chimney's great heights.

When we heard the thump of his crash, we set aside our brooms, left the newest ash where it lay, so that we might hold him as he went.

We cried for him as best we could, but those years the furnaces were so hot that no moisture lasted: not our tears, not the milk of my wife's breast. Our second boy never had enough to eat, and when his growth halted I put another in his mother's belly, even though there was no room for the three of us then birthed, even though we could barely stand the sight of one another in the heat-stunk cramp of our chamber.

Our second boy climbs as his brother once did, and when he descends to see us he is black skinned, slick with wide burns shut tight by soot. His only words are cries for mercy, entreaties against going back up the chimney, but of course he must go.

When he refuses, I tell him about the good of the many. About the good of my wife, about the good of myself, about the good of his baby brother, coming soon. I take him bodily and I force him into the chimney, push with my hands until he is above the damper, the trapdoor between our world and his, and then I hold the damper shut while I tell him the truth I have never wanted to tell.

I tell him I can make more of him, but there is only one of me, only one of his mother.

I tell him that when he is gone, I will still love him as much as I loved the brother before, as much as I will love the brother who comes after.

I tell him, This is why we gave you all the same name, so that you might be equals in our hearts.

This conversation, it is an understanding I began with one son long ago and will end with another, perhaps here in this hot room built between the furnace below and the floor above or perhaps somewhere new, some earned place cool and starstruck, or else some other kind of heaven I have not yet imagined, set aside as reward for our long hot labors, our series of sacrifices.

I do not know. I have only been in this one room, and I cannot guess what others the world might yet contain.

I know only this: Myself, the father. Her, the mother. Them, the son. And between us all, this hot hell to be shared, and the crematorium chimney above to be kept clean no matter what the cost, lest all below choke on the ashes of our ashes.

NESSA, NEVE, NEVINA

We watch our kids scatter through the fields, lowing and bleating, until what storm they smell in the air chases them back to us, to the fence line that separates pasture from village. They put their hoofed hands upon the rungs of our fences, then resume their sad noises, the warning signs our village long ago learned to heed.

Within an hour we are gathered in the meeting hall, where, one after another, we men say what we always say first: What bad timing our children have, when all around us grow these fields of barely-hay, of almost-wheat, our first true harvest in a decade, more precious than anything else we've grown on this blasted plain.

Still, if it comes down to our children or our crops, then for once we must pick our children.

We say this, and we do our best to mean every word, but without our crops, we will starve.

Without our children, without their wool-covered skins so easily sheared, we may be cold, but we will not be hungry.

I am not the richest man in the village, nor the tallest nor the strongest nor the smartest, but I am a married man with my own farm, and so in the meeting hall my voice is the equal of any other. Once everyone has spoken, I stand again and say what must be said next, what has always been called out whenever wild weather waits on the horizon, whenever our children have warned of some dust storm or sod twister threatening our homes and our fields.

What I say is this: It is not all of our children who have to go.

One will be enough, I say.

I say, One has always been enough before, and then my neighbors clamor to their feet, clapping their hands and stomping the wooden floorboards in assent, praising me for my bravery.

I have seen this praise given but have never received it, and so I beam as I organize the writing of our children's names on slips of paper, then the mixing of the slips into my hat.

All that's left is for someone to pick a name, knowing that for the next year he'll be the most reviled person in town, hated for singling out someone's son or daughter for what must be done to save the rest.

When no one steps forward, I volunteer myself, because my wife and I only have one child, and out of all the other possibilities what is the chance of her name being the one I choose?

And then reaching into the hat.

And then pulling one slip out.

And then reading my daughter's name, first to myself, then slowly to the others assembled, who again chant my name, applaud my ability to save their families.

While my wife wails, I go with the other men to lift my daughter over the fence line and into the town square, the open butcher block of this shared abattoir. I stroke her head, her long ears. With my nose to her muzzle, I tell her I love her, that her mother loves her, that what happens next is not her fault.

I say, You're just a little girl—all child-fur and finger-hooves—and so how could it be?

Even though this is her eighth season, still she bawls when we shear her, and even after, when she is naked of wool, folded and trembling in my arms. By dusk light I hold her quiet so each husband and wife can lay a hand on her forehead, so all that we have done wrong—our petty crimes, our coveting and untruths, our backward parenting, inadequate for these new children—all can be placed upon my daughter.

As I walk her out of the village with my wife and our neighbors trailing behind, I try not to look at the empty sky, at the lack of storm our children's crying prophesied. At the lack of obvious reason for what we are about to do.

I try not to think about how we haven't had a plains storm in years.

Not since I was a boy, maybe.

Thanks to this ritual, I tell myself. Thanks to these sacrifices.

Past the far limit of our fences, at the crossroads between our village and the wilderness, there I set down my daughter.

I step back, and from the distance between us I take a stone.

While she quivers, cold on skinny legs, I choose another.

It is enough to simply drive her off, so to the others I say,

I do not wish to see my daughter hurt—but as all around me the rocks fly, what hurt there is, what whimper in her throat, what storm in her eyes!

And in return her herd sounds from beyond the fences, adding their voices to her crying, her begging caught beneath our hail of scape-stones that must continue until she is gone away. The other children bang their bodies against the slats, bleat with their mouths so different from ours, enough to distract us, to give us pause.

To give us pause, but not to make us stop.

ONEIDA, OPHELIA, ORNELLA

My siren-daughters, my sweet-singing beauties: Whose songs pierced the thickest of our soundproofed buildings, even the home where once they lived inside, when they were last part of my fractured family, children under my care. Who, long before the floods began, once lined up beside their mother upon her piano bench, each daughter differing only in age and size, otherwise blessed with the same white-blonde hair, the same eyes so green they glittered even after we extinguished the lamplight.

While their mother pressed each key in turn, these three daughters hummed along, matching their voices to the piano's percussion, to the tones that escaped its upright body. One by one they captured its voice, contained it in their chests until soon we heard the piano even when no one was playing, its notes coming from our white-fenced

yard, from their playroom, from the tight porcelain confines of their shared bath times.

It wasn't until the rains started that the oldest learned to
mimic her mother's mouth-noises, and so it was she who
first licked her lips at the dinner table and then repeated
every sonorous syllable of my wife's speech, the description of her day at the dikes, binding dams with all the other
mothers recently pressed into service, no longer allowed
to stay home with their children. Soon the younger two
could do as well as the oldest, all of them speaking in their
mother's many voices, matching the pitch and timbre that
accompanied each shift of mood and mannerism.

How soon after did they learn to throw their own voices,
to call out from places they could not possibly be? When
did I first hear my wife's words from every room, calling
me to dinner, calling me to work, calling me to bed to make
another daughter, so the song might swell?

What choir of sisters my daughters wanted, and what
chorus they were denied, for my wife had already shut her
womb to me and to the wet world around us, saying that if
we could not ensure the future of the children we already
had, then what point was there in bringing more into our
flooding home?

Still our daughters pestered. Still they mimicked. Still I
fell for their many tricks, because I too wanted the next
child they wished my wife to make.

With their changeable voices, they lured me out of the
study, out of the house, and into the drowned neighborhood
left behind by the breaching of the levees, those imperfect
barriers giving way to the rush of rainwater, to the floating

freeze of recent hail. And if I never caught my daughters, I at least found what they wanted to show me, the new landmarks of our remade neighborhood: first, a dog floating short leashed and bloated, then the submerged beauty of our once-dry library. Other things they'd wanted, and by our failing world were denied.

What family meeting we had then, each daughter throwing out her mother's speech and then mine too, until all our parentage was lost to their same-enunciated disavowals, on and on until my lungs hung empty against my sorrowed heart, until I could no longer give voice to the word *no*, to the word *stop*, to the words *no please stop*.

And what then? What could we do to these daughters after we were forced to move onto the second floor, those cramped rooms stuck atop our submerged stairs? Or even later, when our neighbors rowed over to bring us news about the first of the drowned, victims rushing out into the water to save some loved one screaming for help but finding only undertows thick with brambles and water snakes?

To pretend it wasn't happening. To go to rooftop funerals and say nothing. To stand with my hand in my wife's or some daughter's while widows and widowers lamented that they'd never hear their loved ones again, and then to say, Well, perhaps not, but perhaps yes too.

And then my wife being lured out. My wife who should have known better being trapped in water over her head, treading for hours in the river that used to be our tree-lined street.

And then my not going to help her, my believing her dying words only the voices of our missing daughters, another of their tricks: that it was me they were trying to kill, and their mother's voice the bait.

And then those daughters returned to my side, mock crying into one another's mourning dresses, each bedecked with my wife's pearls, her costume brooches and rings. Long after her funeral barge had been pushed away, still I heard my wife begging me to save her from the steep waters beyond the bounds of our town, swirling beneath the all-day and all-night pitch of our cloud-darked world.

When my rowboat left again and did not come back, when my daughters who took it did not come back either, even then I did not fear for their safety, because still at night I could stand on my roof and listen to my wife crying out in the downpour, accompanied only by the frog song and wind roar that replaced all the other sounds I once heard upon our submerged street.

And now? How many wet years has it been? How long since I last saw land, since I knew the smell of grass or tree or rock or dirt?

How far removed those things seem, despite their voices still out there, somewhere upon the surface of the water, remembered only by my daughters who cry out in the yip of the coyote, the slither of the snake, the rustle of oak and fern.

Now there is only me, floating after them in the dark.

Now only me and also this barge, built from the flotsam and jetsam that bumped into my sunken home, and above me only these clouds, and around me only this rain, which I must bail every second I am not steering, not sinking my pole toward some hopeful bottom.

All this, so someday I might walk again on dry land, so I might stand before my three wife-voiced daughters, so I might tell them that I am not mad anymore.

That although they have cost me everything, I will not punish them.

That because everything they took from me was all they had themselves, they have already been punished enough.

PRESCOTT, PRESLEY, PRESTON

Know how we once believed our coming children would surprise us. And how we were wrong.

Know how as soon as he can speak our oldest tells us the day and date his first brother will be born, and then together they apprise us of the youngest's coming, disclosing the hour of my wife's water breaking, the length of her labor, the exact moment of the crowning of their brother's head.

Know that by the end of each family breakfast they predict the rest of our day: What hour it will rain. What my wife will cook for lunch and dinner. What horrible words I will say when my sons will not stop talking, and also how I will try to force them into saying anything that is not a prediction, that is not the certainty-cursed future coming our way.

Before my wife can send them to their shared bedroom, my sons have already told her she will, and it's there that our oldest starts his book, the book he calls his diary even though its every word is the future, some event coming later, some doom to fear, to be traumatized by both before and after.

The day he turns thirteen, he tells me I will wait three more months before I sneak into his room and read this diary, and that by then it will be too late.

He says, You could save us if you read it today, but I know you won't.

Know it's a lie, another adolescent taunt, a poke at what he knows has already happened, because I have read his diary, including the early entry predicting I would: at the end of the summer, our house will burn, and all my boys will burn too, caught in their shared bedroom because their mother cannot stand anymore to always be told what will happen next, cannot bear her life being scripted by her oldest son, appended and corrected in the margins by his younger brothers.

Know I could stop her. Know my sons knowing I could.

Know how when the day comes they bang their fists against the locked and nailed door, the thick-boarded windows. Know how they curse and accuse and scream for mercy when the house begins to collapse, and even after it crumbles, while still they struggle beneath its weight of wood and stone.

My wife and I hold hands in the street, at the end of our yard, safely past the widening circle of heat-blackened, smoke-wilted grass, and what joy crosses her face then, despite the last screams of our sons: To again have a world unknown, beset with unexpected joys, unplanned tribulations. To again live our lives with doubt and hope.

Know how she says, Will you ever forgive me?

And how I say, Not yet. But soon.

My wife stares at my face, wondering but not knowing whether I have stolen the diary she believed still hidden in the boy's room, secreted under their bunks. And also not knowing that our eldest told me I would take it. That I wouldn't be able to give up possessing the future just because he was gone.

What else she doesn't know: that there are only a few pages past today's date, and on each page only a single day.

Know there is not much else to know.

Know there is a finite amount of everything remaining.

Know this future is almost over, know we will live to see it end.

And afterward: whatever cataclysm follows, at last a surprise.

QUELLA, QUERIDA, QUINTESSA

How beautiful our daughter is in her white Tethering dress, dancing her younger cousins across the decorated length of our yard: first the waltz, then the cha-cha, then the tango. At eleven she called them old-people dances, but now, twelve years old, feet shod for the final time in bobby socks and dress flats, she can't wait to teach the others every step and turn and twirl, every last aching contact of foot upon grass.

The band plays on while my wife cuts the cake, while she passes out thick frosting-dripped slices of vanilla to everyone present, whether they want cake or not. Only afterward is our flush-faced daughter allowed to open her presents, her gifts from her many aunts and uncles, this family extending to include our entire community, all us lonely adults closer now than when we were kids, when there were no Tethering parties to bring us together.

My daughter is all teeth and dimples as she says thank you to each gift giver, to each sad-eyed parent in the crowd, and as she lifts her ankle to show off the present her mother and I gave her, opened during the Tethering itself: a steel cuff, clasped around her ankle, concealed by the fanciest lace and pearls we could afford.

After the party ends, I help her pack, placing each gift — each sealed bottle of water, each nonperishable food item, each oversize cable-knit sweater — into her tether-bags, attached to the braided-steel cord already fed through the carabiners and guide loops, already secured to the clasp on her tether, that anklet which will for a time keep her life close to ours.

And then me hugging her goodbye. And then her mother doing the same, refusing to let go.

And then pulling mother from daughter so that our child might climb the ladder to the platform.

How great our sorrow is during the first few months, when she is still close enough that we can climb the ladder ourselves to hold her floating hands, to bring her food and drink so that she might not consume the supplies meant for the trip ahead. Already she longs to be farther away, to be up in the air with the other sons and daughters drifting in the wind, her cousins ballooned with this adolescent gas that fills their bodies and never filled ours.

Together, my wife and I wait until our daughter is ten or

twelve feet above the platform, her belly bloating until she floats out of reach, then out of yelling distance, then too far away to see with the naked eye.

Only then do we host this second party, the one where everyone brings binoculars and spyglasses instead of presents and a dish to pass.

The Untethering, it is more a party for us than for our daughter, but it doesn't feel like a celebration, not with everyone dressed all in black.

Midway through the dancing, I remind my wife that she's the one who must release our daughter.

I say, If our daughter was a son, then I would do it, because it is what has to be done, what has always been done since the time of the first rising.

I say, We don't know where she will float to, but if you do not let her go, then she will starve to death upon her tether. Together, we will have to watch her deflate, then float back to the earth, our own lifeless feather.

Our hushed guests wait while my wife looks through her spyglass at our daughter, that fat far-off speck caught in an updraft, spinning uncomfortably at the end of her line. They watch through their binoculars, struggling to read my daughter's lips, the last message of our only child, only half mouthed when my wife, already turning away, finally pulls the release lever.

How quick the rest of the cord shoots up and out through the guide loops, speeding into the air behind my daughter, and how fast our baby girl disappears, off for whatever world awaits her up there in the atmosphere, among all the other children this town has released.

And who can imagine what far-off countries they might settle, what new families they might next inhabit?

All we know is how sad our landlocked bodies are, comforted only by one another's flightless, balloonless limbs. Her mother and I, we weep, black clad, while our neighbors sing the Untethering song and cut our Untethering cake: chocolate, my wife's favorite, the one she hasn't had since the day our allergic daughter was born, when we traded its pleasure for some other flavor, some taste thought even sweeter.

ROHAN, ROHIT, ROHO

Sod furrows behind the plow, behind our slow son tacked to its traces, his shoulders and thighs bulging as he scratches the blade across the earth, sundering scars to be scabbed over by his mother's following hand. All day she walks behind the hulk of him, doing the work I used to do. With her slender fingers she pushes the seeds carefully into the dank dirt, into soil exposed only briefly to this uncertain sun, this angry air, this quavering question posed as perhaps unreasonable hope: Because even though what grows from the world's womb might be no better than what grew from my wife's, what other choice do we have but to try again?

There are some who say it's the earth that's gone wrong, and some that say the seed, and it is this my wife and I debate after she pushes my wheelchair up to the dining table, after she sets the brakes my fumbling fingers are too weak to work.

While we fight, our son takes more than his share of our food, offers less than his fair part to the conversation. Everything about him is retarded except his appetite, the cost of his too-big body, his still-nameless face, left so because what right name was there? What title for a child best loved as a beast of burden, best desired for the plow he can drag, for the twisted tree trunks he pulls from the ground to make more farm?

What do you call an animal that eats more than it helps grow, until crop after crop yields less, until soon there won't be enough feed for the three of you?

What do you even say to a son like that?

What you say is, Come here, boy.

In the middle of the night, you say this.

You say, Carry me, and then he carries you.

With your crippled body in his arms, he chases your pointing finger out of the bedroom, out of the house, out into the field still flipped fresh by the plowing.

Right here, you say. Do it right here.

You say, Hug me the way you hugged me last.

You say, This time, away from the house, there'll be no mother to stop us.

And then you give thanks for a boy too stupid to know his own strength, too broken to understand the patricide carried latent within his thick fingers, his ox-stunk palms that close over your skull, that crack those flat bones loose from their jagged moorings.

And what then? What's this?

Already a world where nothing grows right, and now a world where nothing dies?

More, you beg, more: Son, tear me from the earth like a

trunk! Husk me like the corn! Scatter me into seed again, plant me in the earth, let grow what grows! Feed your mother my share, or else plant her too—

And then your bored son dropping you unfinished to the dirt, then you watching as he bounds away, his big idiot-happy body receding, leaving you broken in the fields, screaming hoarsely for morning, for the sharp edge of the approaching plow.

SVARA, SVETA, SYLVANA

See now our subterranean daughters, our dark-eyed beauties so impossible to keep in their wicker cribs, to keep inside our rude-made gravedigger's hut, perched at the rent edge of this barren plot.

See them squirm free of their cribs, their new and segmented bodies falling to the packed-dirt floor, down and out of this home I built for them and their mother.

See me with shovel and mattock, tearing up the flooring, uncovering tunnels, chambers, new and deeper rooms.

See them tangled in one another's sleeping bodies, keeping each other warm in the dampness of the earth, their spade-thumbs sucked and suckled in the absence of us, their parents.

See what watch I keep, what eyes I fix on their cribs, but see also how it is never enough, how all day there are piles of the plagued to heap into graves, how all night there is their sick mother, bedridden, her vulgar pains leaving her no chance of sleep.

See me feed their mother through her stomach tube. See me soak her sore skin. See her tears at the rub of the sponge, the touch of the soap.

See our daughters taking advantage of my absence to again escape the confines of their cribs.

See me waking to their three tiny gowns beside three tiny holes, three petite piles of spent dirt, then to their wailing mother in the next room.

See me digging up the floor to find their burrows empty.

See me on my knees, reaching into the dirt, feeling their new passages, exit vectors from the confines of our home, our yard: three tunnels for three baby girls, each in a direction of its own.

See my wife, their mother, my fading light. See me cutting her screaming hair while she cries for her children to return.

See also what I do not do: see me not covering the burrows, not filling in the caved pit of our kitchen floor, the room where I fed our daughters porridge after prying free the grubs and beetles they held stubborn in their hands and mouths.

See the day my wife loses her last voice, the day she sends me from the room with weak flurries of spotted hands, because if she cannot have her daughters she does not want me instead.

See how I crawl down into the dirt, into the sunken ruins of our home. See me whisper into the center of the earth, see me beg them to come back, to visit their mother once more before she is gone.

See the day they emerge together, clothed only in gravedirt.

See how they've grown, how their toddling days have ended, how some new age is upon them.

See next their fists clenched around ginger and burdock, around echinacea, around licorice and marshmallow.

See me gather them up onto my chest. See me carry all three at once in my arms. See me take them into our bedchamber, their hands stuffed with the medicine they traveled so far to find.

See until you cannot see anymore.

Listen: their first words in turn, three broken intonations of *cure* and *mother* and *save her, save her*. What stories they tell then, of places they have gone, of the things they have seen! What hard hurt of my heart follows, what ungrantable wish shaping this trembling flesh, this poor gravedigger again made quaking father!

Listen: the sound of herbs hitting the floor is a whisper, then a word. Roots collapse, tubers tumble, and what sentence can follow? What good noise can I make for my daughters then, clinging reluctant to my body, this earth they no longer love?

TRAVIS, TRAVON, TREMAINE

Only when we are sure the hospital is empty do we leave the youngest to hold the mother's hand, to stroke the clammy baldness of her head while the rest of us search and scavenge, bulge backpacks with clean gauze, ample medicines, new needles for her drips and fresh inserts for her catheters, everything else we will need for her care.

For ourselves, we take what last food remains in the commissary, what few blankets we cannot go without.

We take as little as possible, because their mother is already so much to carry.

At the top of the spiral stairs we collapse her gurney, fold its wheels beneath its chassis, and then we lift, each as much as he can: myself at the bottom, walking the heavy end backward into the decline, and then my small sons at the head of the bed, doing the best their little bodies can do.

At each landing, I bark orders, beg my boys to lift, lift higher, over the railing and around the corner, and then again we descend. For twenty floors, we do this. We do this for two hundred vertical feet, and then we are in the lobby, then across the paper-strewn reception, then through the handprint-smeared glass doors and out onto the street.

What destruction greets us, surrounds us, hangs above us: The high-rises swaying in their foundations. The towers towering. The diseased dead crashed everywhere, up and over and around all the abandoned cars and trucks, the overturned carts and stalls.

And then the sky spitting black rain, and then my boys each opening his umbrella, crowding in close to keep their sick mother dry.

I drag their mother. I drag their mother's gurney. I drag the gurney flat like a sledge, with their mother atop it, with the boys and their umbrellas huddled close because the rain never stops.

At every rest, we do what the doctors once did, what they taught us to do before they fled: My boys know the names of their mother's medicines, have learned every sequenced step involved in her care. Beneath their umbrellas they change her dressings, inject appropriate doses into her ports, pour cans of gray formula into her feeding tube until her belly bloats, until her waste bag is ready for the emptying.

One after the other, they pump her legs to keep the muscles straight, flex her arms to do the same, because still they believe she might one day need them, because on our long walk I tell the boys that when I am gone she might once again carry them, as we have carried her so far.

We make weeks of slow progress across the city, until one morning I awake fevered, the sound of my new cough setting my youngest to bawling, to clutching at my pant leg. By the next morning, my muscles have already begun to tighten, as the boy's mother complained hers did, back when no doctor knew what these signs portended.

I look around at my three boys, my exhausted sons arrayed, each smaller than the next, each spaced too far apart to fill another's shoes, let alone mine, and then I do what I can: I take my oldest son aside, and I tell him that I will go on alone, that alone I will enter the rumble and ramble to prepare the way for their passage.

Through my coughing, I tell him that I love him, and that I love his brothers, and that he is the one who must watch over the others from now on.

Don't go, he says. We need you yet.

No, I say. He has his mother, still alive, still sleeping. He has his brothers.

He has enough, I tell him. What he has, it will have to be enough.

And then he is the man of the family, and then I tell him so: two separate events, happening so close that I can barely separate them afterward, when I am crawling alone through streets of panic-crushed cars, disease-fat corpses, caught up in the tight spaces the mother-laden gurney would never have fit, no matter how hard I tugged.

And then the sins of the spirit, punished upon the flesh; until I cannot move, until my muscles clutch into paralysis.

How much later is it when I hear their voices following, coming behind me through the dark, shouting my name, my title, reminders of my renounced fatherhood?

And then their little hands lifting me onto the empty gurney.

And then their ignoring me when I ask or try to ask, Where is your mother?

In silence the younger two move my joints, bend my elbows and shoulders and knees to busy me while the oldest wipes clean a used needle on his stained trousers, then seeks its entrance to my veins. As they prepare me for transit, all I see are their determined faces, foreheads bent with their decision to trade one near-dead parent for the other by this mistake they have made, leaving behind the only person they were ever tasked with caring for, all so that they might preserve what's left of me, this shell of an undeserving father, who tried so hard to abandon them first.

ULMER, ULRIC, URSA

I wait until the winter moon peeks from behind its shadow, and then I call to the harrow-hunt this pack, these sons and cousins and half brothers and grandsons, all these evolutions of my own beast-headed form, an overlapping of altered progenies, some mimicking my own shape and some their mothers', so that we are become a family united by blood but not body, our forms as far-ranging as our hunting grounds, as the sprawl of forest we've claimed for ourselves, where despite our differing shapes we live together by the same rules:

That each kill we make is shared between the pack.

That each wound incurred in the hunt is licked clean by a brother.

That after we hunt we eat. And after we eat we howl. And after we howl we run.

The moon waxes wider each night, and soon there is little time to pause, no matter how empty our bellies or how tired our legs. In single file, we cross forest floor and snow-clenched clearing, each pack mate putting his paws in the unshared footprints of a father or brother, until together we reach the high rock, the place of decision agreed upon a year ago, when last the forest tribes met.

What spectacle there is to see upon our arrival, what new variety of form only a year past our last meeting: what bear-bodies, what cougar-hearts, what boar-teeth, and among them all the other wolf-head packs, flush with brothers despite the endless snow, the failing prey.

When all are assembled and greeted — when we have

each sniffed and nuzzled and marked each other as friends, as temporary extended family — then each father alpha relates his tale in turn, some with words, some with beast-noise, some with both at once. We speak loudly and at great length, give speeches that consume many nights, that take the whole fullness of the moon to complete.

We speak these many words as if we have to, as if the limitations of syllables could somehow mask the truer language of our shifted bodies.

The failure of our great hunt, the one each tribe is engaged in for the good of all others, it has already been communicated by our lowered heads, our tucked tails. Even before our speeches all our boys know what we fathers know too: it has been years since any of us has seen a human woman, and the beast-heads make no daughters.

The wives we share our dens with welcome us gladly because they too are short of number, their own males scarce even before the dwindling of the world, but they cannot give us human children, cannot keep our lines from drifting toward wildness.

They cannot, and if we complain they cry bitterly, for they do not see why our children should look only like us, why they should not also take after their mothers.

They say this, but it is not their race that is disappeared, and so our sorrow is not theirs to share. They do not mind their children who are only wolves, only cougars, only bears and boars, because what else should they desire but more of themselves, new packs made stronger by our mingled blood and seed?

When the meeting is over—when the moon enters the waning that awaits it on the other side of our words—only then do we give up one language for another, to come together as one people, one troubled nation of tribes. As one mouth we combine our voices, a cacophony rising as if to crack the earth, as if to shake the heavens, as if to loose the turning moon from its mount and bring it crashing down upon us, the only mass heavy enough to bury our giant grief.

There is this big noise, and then afterward there is my prone form, whole of body but spirit-quaked, hope-bloodied.

My wolf-children gather around me, licking my face and chest, pulling loose what matter they find fouled upon my fur, while beside them my beast-headed boys stroke my coat with clawed fingers, speak the few words their dumb tongues can make.

All these children, these many pups, and yet gathered to me are no true sons, no sons I wanted, in their place rise only these altered generations, these boys who will not grow up to be their father, not without the mothers I wanted them to have.

And if I refuse to stand? If, like the other alphas, I demand to be left here at the meeting place, the high rock of the woods? If I tell my sons and grandsons that I have failed, that I am no longer worthy to lead their pack, what then follows my quitting them, their family?

Then the song of farewell.

Then the song of forgiveness.

Then the song of funeral.

Then the song of their teeth upon my throat, upon my

haunch and perineum and tendons, the soft spots of the easy kill.

Then in my mind only the face of my own father, the last human visage I saw, which I never again brought forth upon this wilding world, despite all my efforts to prevent his line's extinction, despite all my attempts to raise these lost boys in his image.

VIRGIL, VIROTTE, VITALIS

From the middle of the country we follow the rumors, the talk that there are no more mothers or daughters, none remaining to bear our future forth except those afloat beyond the last lands of the West, collected aboard a ship, some tanker meant to carry them away, to keep them safe.

What I know, despite those rumors: there are no women left except the one beside me, this daughter disguised as a son, who I must somehow see aboard that ship.

On our way west, I cull her hair every few days, steal her layers of clothing from abandoned storefronts, thick shirts and thermal underwear and patterned button-ups distracting enough so that what lies beneath might be harder to see, to suss out and desire. As we walk, I tell her that once this sandy stretch of waste was a plains state, was all fields of waving wheat and corn. Mile after mile, I offer her some bit of this world I've known, some memory of what once lay on either side of the wide freeways littered with abandoned cars. For a thousand footsore miles I do this, not running out of stories until we cross the last state line, the last desert. Until we enter the last city, perched at the far end of the earth, where we climb down to the shore, our descent cut with broken roads providing unsure passage, switchbacking to the crowded docks leading out above the tossing water.

And there in the distance: the tanker we'd hoped to catch, too quickly departed, left without my daughter.

What choice do we have? No other option but to go out onto the docks anyway, to push through this great crowd of men, only and always men, all armed, all fat with fury, all crowding the shore or else wading out into the oil-black of the water, its brackish thickness, their voices begging, cajoling, demanding the ship to turn back, to return to them these last few mothers and daughters, these final receptacles for the making of legacy, a continuation of our failure.

We push through, my daughter's hand in my hand, in the one not clutched around my revolver, my own six chances to clear the way. I pull my daughter close, wrap her tight in the leather of my duster, and in the distance the tanker taunts us with its purpose, its promise to stay afloat until all us men are gone, until at least the worst of us have passed, leaving the world for those more deserving of its inheritance—

And then my daughter saying, Look.

Then her eyes peeking out from the blanket of my coat, her hand pointing over the water, and her saying, Look, Daddy.

There, Daddy. *There.*

How few they are: all the good women of the world. All

gathered except for my daughter, who should be among their number.

How few, and how far, but perhaps still close enough.

I nod, open my duster, tell her to get ready.

I tell her, When I start shooting, you run for the end of the dock, and no matter what, you keep running.

I tell her, You swim as fast as you can and pray they rescue you.

She sobs once as I raise the heavy hammer of my revolver, but there is no time for goodbye, and no other word I wish to say that our thousand shared miles did not already allow. I push her out of my duster, follow her into the space my bullets tear free from the men blocking her way, and with each shot I get her one falling body closer to the end of the dock, our escape hung out over the water.

And then my hand scrabbling fresh shells from my pocket, then after I reload six more shots making six holes in six men, making ten feet of running space.

And then my daughter, covered in the blood of those who would want only what she is, never *who*, men waiting to mar her, to rip her away, to hold back her body they desire.

And then reload and fire, reload and fire, and then we run until there are no more men ahead, until we tumble off the edge of the dock, fall far into the cold waves, where the ocean fills my mouth and nostrils, drenches my heavy clothes so tight I can barely kick to get my head above the surface, to suck again the sickened air.

What I know: my daughter is no longer nearby, no longer close at hand, but surely she can't be lost.

As I am dragged ashore by the kin of the men I have struck down, as they beat the angry butts of their rifles against my face and chest, as they take from me what satisfaction they could not take from my daughter, I tell myself that I know she swims on unmolested, that without us men to hold her back she kicks by the buoys that mark the end of this world's dominion, makes what powerful strokes she needs to take her out past the breakwater, toward the waiting tanker and then into the future, that far flatness beyond.

WALKER, WALLACE, WARREN

Now to make a memorial, a memory meant to outlast those recently gone from my head, lost through the holes eaten by this new wind blowing across my farm, bleached blank by the cloudy water that climbs thick and sluggish from my well. In goggles and duster, I gather my tools, go out of the house and into the ashy remains of the yard, this family orchard once lush and full of apples.

And all around me: Only stilled wood, dead branches over dirty ground. Only this lonely world grown atop my buried children, my planted wife.

With awl and adze, with hammer and chisel, I carve my oldest out of the first tree. I remake him as best I remember, shaping the roundness of his cheeks, grooving out the spaces between his teeth and toes.

When I am done, I fill my ears with my fingers to hold in the sound of his voice, the last words he said to me before we lost him. I clench my eyes so his image might not get diffused by the weak sunlight poking through my goggles, a dimness forever threatening to steal him from behind my lids.

Across the orchard, it takes weeks to rough in his sister and his sister and his brother and his brother. Upon a lightning-split husk, I stencil the twins that followed, then whittle out the other babies impossible to call boys or girls, their flesh too bent and broken upon their bones to name.

Our last child, the one birthed runny as yolk, I do not carve it at all. I haven't the talent to make its nothing form out of wood, haven't the strength to try.

On the first day of fall, I cut my wife's body free of the centermost trunk, using my tools to re-create the inverted ribs of her diseased chest, the long-ago smoothness of her oft-emptied belly. With every skill I've learned, I remember her upon the wood: Her eyes exactly the proper shape and size, exactly the right tilt to complement the laughing smile last heard too long ago. Her nose alone I work on for days, slicing curl after curl off the bridge until it is the same nose whose tip I kissed goodbye every night, even at the end, when there was so little of it left. I spend a week curving bark into hair, and then a month carving her favorite blouse, the many folds of its matching skirt, both worn the sun-drenched day we were wed.

And then believing myself done, every cut and carved son as partially complete as he was in life, every doomed daughter dancing in wood around the figure of my long-missed wife.

And then waking to forgetting her name. And then forgetting all their names. And then wishing I had carved those syllables into the trees, so I might know which child is which.

And then telling myself it doesn't matter, that their names are not important.

It was not their names I loved. It is not their names I miss.

Another weird wind blows, and then it is winter. And then there is me, no longer remembering any day when it was not winter. And still this project, seemingly unfinished: Always some new detail for me to add, some torso to reshape or dimple to correct. Some finger needing a nail, some foot needing the rest of its toes—because surely a child would have ten toes, ten fingers? Surely every child would have hair and eyes and ears and a nose?

Surely no child could be as incomplete as these?

And then one day berating myself for the lack of skill that left them ugly and warped, rent and ruined.

And then who are these people.

And then who am I to them, these ten perfect children made of trees, this one woman grown out of the apple-wood to raise them.

And how I wish I could join her. And how I wish I could be the father and she the mother and all these our children, so that none of us would be lonely again.

And how sure I am that whoever made them is not the good one who made me, because who would be so cruel as to keep us apart, with this unbearable distance between wood and flesh, this unchangeable differential of atoms.

All winter long I brush the snow from off their faces, so

that I might study each one in turn, so that I might practice falling in love with them, as some father must have done, so long ago.

When the snow finally melts, see then this improbable sight, sprung forth from the palm of some unrecognizable child: some new leaf, some green branchlet blooming.

See now how I hold it in my fingers. And how I let it lay its buds across my palm. And how every day I think again I might pluck its growth free of the trunk, so that its fresh promise might tease me no more.

XARLES, XAVIER, XENOS

And all around me, only disappointment: Only my house, slowly sinking into the ever-muddying earth. Only my horses and my one remaining milk cow, lying together upon their sides, moaning in the swamp of our fields. Only my crops, the husk-barren corn plants unable to grow past my kneecaps.

Only my son, with his gray skin and strange skull, his cleft-lisped voice, his useless hands making the arts and crafts his mother taught him, as all around our world shifts, less solid, less able to keep us above its porous skin.

While I spend my days adding hopeful supports to our house, burying beams in search of denser ground, this son—this boy I no longer wish to claim—he makes portraits of his mother with the cheap watercolors we bought him as a child. He paints her eyes wrong, colors her hair black instead of blonde, and so every night I take away his papers and throw them into the puddle of our yard.

Every night, I tell him, Again you didn't paint her right.

I say, Nothing better to do, and still you can't remember your mother's face.

I say, All our house surrounded by this new swamp, this mad earth that swallowed our neighbors, that sucked deep your mother, when you would not set down your dolls to save her —

This world has taken everything from me, and still there is my boy, sitting here doing nothing, while I have to farm, to herd, to build the struts and floats keeping our house atop this shivering earth.

I say, What good use is a son, if he is a son like you?

So unfair he thinks me, so cruel! Perhaps so, but in no less measure than he deserves, when even after this speech he only puts away his paints to pick up his clay, ready to begin another set of misshapen family figurines, another pairing of plump mothers and dwarfed crack-chested fathers.

What tears when I smash them with my fist, when I crush their bodies upon our food-bare table!

What good tears, so that he might get them out, so that without them he might become the man I want him to be.

For another week, I come in from the fields each night to pull down his construction-paper mobiles, to crumble his finger paintings, his collages cut from our family photo albums.

For another week, I indulge his teenage wastefulness, and then I say, No more.

Then I say, Follow me.

With my rifle in my hands, I say this.

On our porch—warped atop this land of mud-paths and quick-muck—I put my hand on his shoulder.

I put my hand on his shoulder, and then I take it off.

I say, I have decided I would rather have no son than have you.

I say, I will give you a fifty-yard head start, and then I will shoot just once.

If you aren't killed, then good luck to you.

My sensitive son, always he cries! So unfair, he says. So wrong to do this to my own child, no matter what our differences, sending him out into a world unstable and wet, where who knows which paths might lead to safety, and which to sinking death.

I say, Yes, only I know which paths, because I have tread them every day, growing what crops might grow, caring for what horse and cow might scrape through even now.

You have done none of these things, even when asked, even when I wished to teach you to be the man that I am, and so you know nothing of the world outside our walls, outside the confines of your stupid and strange head.

I say, I have never liked you. Not when you were a baby, and not now, when you are less than a man.

I say, I do not know I want to kill you, but I suppose I want a chance. Just to see how this thing might feel that I have daydreamed for so long.

And then I kick him off the porch, and then I tell him to run.

I wait until he reaches the sycamore slanted at the far border of my yard, slanted as crooked as his limping run, his trunk pulled this way and that by his heavy head, and then I raise the rifle.

I pull the trigger, squeeze its weight made glorious, and then for an instant I am no longer disappointed, despite all this awful world: the short blaze of a muzzle flash, the uncertain flight of a bullet, the razor edge of chance between one bad outcome and another, worse.

YARETZI, YASMINA, YATIMA

From between my wife's legs quickened only this puff of womb-air, this gasp of baby-breath trapped for months inside her, followed by no body, no afterbirth, no cord to cut or miscarriage to scrape away. Afterward, my wife insisted she heard the sound of our baby girl crying, but what was I to say in the absence of that child's shape? How was I to call her anything other than mad, when my wife insisted our baby was near, that she could hear her every move?

If only my wife had lasted longer! If only she could have made it through the too many years of try, try again, through the eventual barrenness that followed all those pregnancies producing only air, only wet sound, then together we might have enjoyed what I first heard only in the weeks and months after her passing: a voice, tinkling from beside my bed, from near my right ear whenever I sat in the rocking chair bought to rock the many daughters I did not believe had lived.

And what words this daughter-voice says! What new machines she gives to me, filling this old tinker's mind with complex combinations of horns and needles, with great spoolings of copper wire meant to circle the spindle of our house, reaching higher and higher—

It takes time to build what she first tells me to build, but with the closing of the factories I have nothing but time.

With the departure of every neighbor for miles around, it's just me and the daughter-voice, together day after day, conversing in whispers while I rig new antennas atop the roof of our house, welding them from the left-behinds of those fled for more hopeful havens.

When she tells me the house isn't tall enough to reach the signal she's promised, then I take her advice and abandon the low roof, begin my first true tower in the rock-stubbed field behind our home.

When the tower is finished, the daughter-voice says, Close, but not quite.

She says, Try again, Pa, try again.

And then erecting a second tower taller than the first.

And then a third taller than the second. And then a fourth and a fifth.

Then a whole array of towers, of scavenged wood and steel hung up toward the heavens, an entire village rubbled so I might build the monoliths the daughter-voice commands.

By the time there are a dozen towers dotting the field, it already takes a whole day to climb the tallest, to wrap bundles of wire around some new hanging dongle, some better apparatus designed with her help.

By the time there is a score of towers, my back is stooped, my fingers arthritic. The daughter-voice is older too, her speech husky like mine.

You take after me, I tell her.

Upon the scaffolding of my newest height, I say, Your mother's voice was softer, sweeter.

With my wet face freezing in the high wind, I say, She never once raised her tone in anger. Not even when I didn't believe you were real, when she was the only one who could hear you speak.

And the daughter-voice says, Build.

She says, Build so that you might climb, then climb so you might speak to her again.

She says, All the world below is death, but above it other lands still float.

By twenty stories there are no buildings below to go home to, everything scavenged for tower after tower, and so I build bunks in the sky. When the earth below is so wasted nothing will grow, then at twenty-five stories I plant a garden, lifting the last good sod with rope and pulley, hauling questionable seeds up ladders in satchels and packs.

At thirty stories I realize I'm going blind.

At forty, I lose control of my bowels for the first time.

At sixty, I fall deaf in my right ear, and when I scream I hear only half the fear I feel.

When the daughter-voice returns, I refuse to build another inch until she reassures me, and so she tells me to sit still until she teaches me to put my good ear to the final horn I installed, to listen for what I can.

At last! At last I think I'm going to hear my wife, but no, I do not.

What I hear are several voices just like hers.

Voices as similar to my wife's as the daughter-voice is to mine.

Other daughters, born of other pregnancies, other once-thought failures, now flying at this height, this six-hundredth foot of up-stretched steel. All these voices raised without me because I could not see them, could not touch them, because without sight and without touch I would not believe they were real.

How sad they must have been as they drifted upward, floating frightened in the drafts until they caught here in the first rung of clouds, with all the rest of their sisters.

My daughter-voice says, Pa, you have to build.

She says, You're so old now.

She says, I'm so old now too.

Please, she says. How long before your other ear goes? Then what good are these towers? What good is it to reach mother's voice, still shrieking in the heights, and you with no ear to hear her?

Build, my daughter says, and for the rest of my life I build and I climb, and at each new story I strain to hear the first voice I ever loved, the only one I still wish added to the crowded air around me, the dozen daughters singing static from every earpiece and speaker and receiver and crank-powered radio installed along the way.

Their voices lift me, and upon them I climb until below me are only clouds, and below them some lost world I need never see again, because what I want most is already up here with me or else waiting above. I climb until all I am is wind-carved wrinkles, sun-bleached whiskers, until my hands are crippled by the hammer and the saw and the wire snips, by the frost that dusts my knuckles every morning.

I climb until my eyes are as empty and useless as the clouds, and always my first daughter teases me with her mother, keeps me chasing my wife, this sky-flung memory she promises still floats.

Higher, the daughter-voice says, her voice crone rasped, cough hacked.

Higher, until the sun burns you free of your weak meat. Until you are nothing but voice too. Until you are the same as we, the last loves you have left.

A life is not too much to give, my daughter says.

After how you tortured our mother, a life is hardly anything at all.

ZACHARY, ZAHIR, ZEDEKIAH

And then the last crib combusting. And then the wallpaper smoking and the carpets melting. And then the hallways coursing fire room to room, the master bedroom, the master bath. And then the whole house engulfed. And then the timbers splintering, shattering, crashing against the foundations. And then the chimney crumbling. And then the roof tar slopping across the yard. And then the yard catching. And then the fence, the long-dry grass beyond. And then this great conflagration burning bright, hungry for wood and plain and village. And then all these recently emerged landscapes, ruined first with failure and now with flame. And then the cities blazing. And then the skyscrapers swaying unsteady upon their supports. And then the bridges tipping into their rivers, the overpasses falling onto overpasses. And then whole cities buckling into the dirt. And then the collapse of everything between making sudden highways to nowhere. And then the satellites all falling voiceless and empty from the sky. And then the rain. And then the hail. And then the sleet. And then this pyre taking unmarked decades to smolder out.

And then ashes to ashes. And then maggots in the ash.

And then for a time no more centuries, no more millennia.

And then for a time no more time.

And then only ages: The age of bones. The age of worms. The age of flies. The age of locusts. The age of devouring. The age of dust. The age of sand. The age of flooding. The age of earthquakes and mud. The age of clouds. The age of waterspouts and tornadoes. The age of snow and ice. The age of melting. The age of new stone, new clay, new soil.

And then at last, at last, the age of seeds.

And then. And then. And then.

And then every morning, some new and constant sun, born upon the horizon.

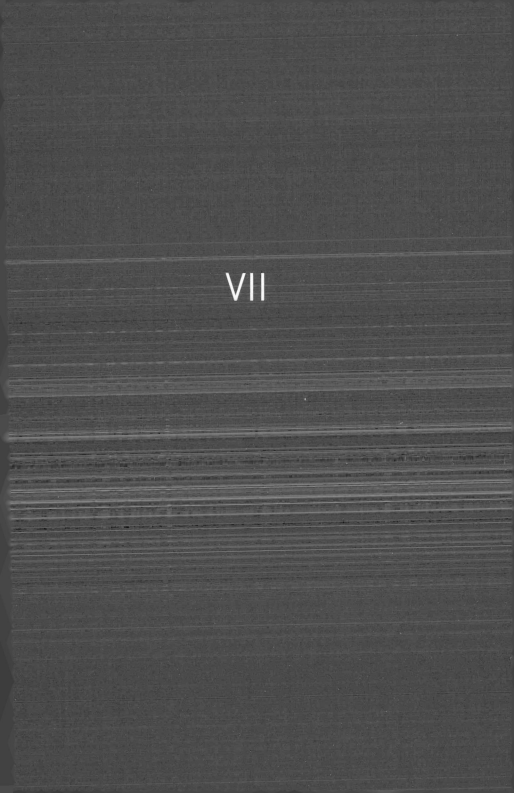

VII

A Long Walk With Only Chalk to Mark the Way

L ATER, THE FATHER AND THE boy were separated, the boy taken deeper inside the hospital and the father told to wait while the doctors ran their tests. Somewhere, the doctors in their white coats passed the boy through their white machines, made him wait too, in countless white rooms tucked at the end of long white-walled hallways. In one room, uniformed nurses pulled on white latex gloves and then drew the boy's red blood, collected his dark yellow urine. In another, they held him down while the doctors tapped his spine, made it weep into the cylinders of their syringes.

As for the father, he did not want to stay all in one place, even though wandering meant he might get lost in the hospital's blank halls, its confusing passageways and staircases. The father climbed down to the first floor and walked outside, back into the courtyard full of patients taking in the morning sun, some standing on their own two legs and some crashed into wheelchairs. He watched them move their sicknesses around the yard as if they did not know what else to do with them, then reentered the hospital through the emergency entrance, the entrance he'd used years before. This time the father and the boy had come in through general admissions, because the doctors said that what was happening to the boy was not an emergency.

It wasn't routine, they said, not exactly, but certainly it was not an emergency.

The hospital was a maze the father believed he could navigate. There were signs that pointed this way to the elevators, that way to the restrooms, and between every set of restrooms was a water fountain. It was possible to stay hydrated, if only he followed the signs. Others pointed to the cafeteria, where he could find food, and to the chapel, where he could try again to find something else. The hospital was a place the father thought he could live a long time, if he had to.

On the eleventh floor of the hospital was the pediatrics ward, where some children were learning how to die and some were learning how to live again. This was where the father found out on which side of that divide his own boy would have to stay from now on.

What the doctors told the father was that the boy was going to grow old and then he was going to die. It was what happened to everyone, but it was going to happen so much faster to the boy. The doctors gave the boy's disease a name, and then they gave that name to the father, who said nothing in return, only shook his head when the doctors asked if he had any questions. He did not. There was their truth and there was his truth, and never again would they be the same.

The book the father and the boy would soon read together in the boy's hospital room had once been the mother's, her favorite, and the father had been waiting for the boy to be old enough to read it himself, so that he might love what the mother had once loved. The book was thick, black skinned, filled with many pages of tight-spaced text, all still too hard for the boy to decipher on his own, and so the father decided he couldn't wait any longer. He would read the book to the boy, as much as he could in the time they had left together.

The book was many things, although even the father did not know this at first. The book was a story and a guide and a map, one that pointed the way through a maze, with sentences and paragraphs instead of symbols and lines, so that even before the father told the boy there was a maze to be solved, the book was already teaching him how he might do such a thing, if only he paid attention, if only he were careful.

The story in the book was simple: it was about another boy—a young boy, thirteen or fourteen, older than the father's boy but a boy nonetheless—who went into a maze to save his own life, aided by a girl who loved him.

The father's own boy did not have a girl who loved him, not yet, but he had a father, and it would have to be enough.

The boy asked, What was he looking for in the maze?

The father said, Nothing. He only wanted to find his way back out, so he could be with the girl.

But then why did he have to go into the maze in the first place?

Okay, the father said. There was something else.

He said, There was something in the maze that wanted to hurt the boy, but the boy planned to hurt it first.

A monster?

Yes, said the father. Yes, in the maze, there was a monster.

The boy loved the book, listened rapt while the father read. The boy told the father he wished he could go on his own adventure, that anything would be better than lying in his hospital bed all day. And so the father, who no longer denied the boy anything, promised he would.

For the last time, the father left the boy alone. He went to their home, where he boarded the windows, as if for a storm. He walked once more from room to room, cataloging their contents, then he stepped out the front door and locked the house tight. Afterward, he shopped, gathered supplies. At one store, he found himself a good backpack, bought a smaller but otherwise identical one for the boy. At another, he bought a dozen pounds of dehydrated food, then went back for another dozen. He didn't know how much he needed of anything. He selected two sleeping bags, then a tent a salesman guaranteed him could be put up in the dark by a single person. He bought flashlights, to light their way, and also thick sticks of glow-in-the-dark chalk, to mark their passage. He chose new boots for the long walk ahead, size elevens for himself and size twos for the boy. When he held up the boy's boots, the father felt as he always did when he bought the boy clothes: how could the boy be this small and still always be in so much danger?

The father waited until his hands stopped shaking, and then he took the boots to the hospital and put them on the boy's feet.

—

The father showed the boy the pack, taught him how to adjust the shoulder straps, how to fasten the load-bearing belt so that it rested above his jutting hip bones. The father explained that the backpack wasn't like the one the boy had worn to school, that other he would never wear again. There would be no more school, no more books except for the last.

The father told the boy that the hospital was like the maze in the book, that the boy was like the hero of that story. He said that like the hero, the boy already knew the way out, but that it wasn't enough to know how to escape. There was something the boy needed to find first. Only once he found it would he be allowed to leave.

The boy asked, Is it a monster? Like in the book?

No, the father said. There's no monster, not for you. For you, there is a way to get better. To leave what's wrong with you here in this place, where it might never be able to escape.

A lie, yes, but a necessary one.

Or not a lie, but a story.

The father told the boy a story, and the boy believed, and once the boy believed he was ready to walk.

The first day, the father and the boy worked their way through the pediatric wing, marking their passage with discreet chalk marks beside doorways, under the lips of desktops, and on top of tables. Awkward in their new gear, they talked to no one, ignored the queries of confused nurses. At every turn, the father asked the boy which way they should go. Only after the boy pointed out his decision would the father make his small chalk mark, an arrow pointing the way forward.

When they came again to their arrows, the boy would look up at the father, his brow furrowed, and he would say, This maze is so hard, and we barely even know what we're looking for.

But also the boy would smile, and then he would take the father's hand, and then the father would know that at least today the boy would not die.

Another thing that happened in the hospital was that the father sometimes saw the mother there. He saw her only in doorways, but he saw her in many of them, in many different parts of the hospital. He saw her in the doorway to the boy's room, and also in the doorways to other wings, other examination rooms, other chambers full of testing equipment which the doctors still required the boy to visit over and over, even though they had already pronounced him dying, even though the father believed they had already given up any hope of saving his life.

The mother never said anything to the father, merely stood silent, stared, and waited. He didn't know what she waited for, didn't know what he was supposed to do.

The mother had died and the father had not, and afterward the father had done his best. He had tried to do better, to be better, but it had taken him too long, and now the boy was fading too. In the coming months, a year or two at most, the father would see the boy's puberty and then his teenage years, his twenties and thirties and forties. He would see the boy's hair gray and his face wrinkle and his limbs atrophy. He would watch the boy's memory go, watch him forget the little bit of learning he'd done.

According to the doctors, it would not take more than a few years. The boy might not celebrate his tenth birthday, much less his eighteenth, his twenty-fifth. With so little time left, the boy would never do any of the things the father had done with his own life.

The boy would never even fall in love, and perhaps that was for the best, because then he would never have to live through the agony of a wife dying, of her tumbling away from him, and then, too soon, of a son falling after.

Soon the father realizes he must force himself to wake before the boy. While the boy sleeps, the father loosens the ties that hold down the upper flap of the boy's pack, then removes some of the weight, secretly lightening the load the boy will carry. Still the boy struggles, exhausted by noon or else what passes for noon in hallways lit with fluorescence twenty-four hours a day. The boy's thin veins strain against his pale temples, his body shakes, threatens to seizure. The next morning, the father removes the boy's spare pair of boots, secures them to the frame of his own pack, and then the morning after he takes one of the boy's blankets and rolls it inside his own.

In his bed, the boy coughs and coughs. The father wants to go to him until the fit passes, but he does not. Instead, he opens the book and reads the next few pages by flashlight. It is a book of great sorrow, but also it is a book of triumph through perseverance, through wit and wisdom, through greatness of spirit. There is sadness, but after the sadness there is laughter. It takes the grace of the gods to escape the maze, but the father does not believe in gods. Eventually, the boy climbs out of the bed and touches the father's face with his small hand, bringing the father back to the world they both share, this world made now of mazes, of stretched well-lit corridors, of spiraling staircases, all separate from the similar constructs of the book's world, where only the father can go alone.

Only the father, reading, and also one other, one who has always been there, who the father has already sensed lurking, waiting to be discovered in the middle of the book's pages. All the father hopes is that he and the boy reach those pages together, that whatever lies past the terrible middle is somehow better than what came before.

The father feeds the boy breakfast, gives him pills to swallow. The boy's coughing is worst in the morning and in the evening, after the boy awakens and right before he falls asleep, but during the day, the boy can walk, and so they walk.

The book claims that its maze was carved out of rock, buried beneath an island kingdom ruled by a cruel king, its walls chipped from limestone and shale and polished smooth so that they might offer no landmarks for the hero to recognize as he walked in the dark. The father overlays this description onto the hospital as he feels his way forward, keeping his left hand on the wall and his right hand on the boy. They walk for hours, ignoring the other patients — those poor pale shades, the father tells the boy — and when the wall turns or gives way to a crossroads, the father always lets the boy make the choice, offering advice only when solicited. Otherwise they rarely speak, relying instead upon other forms of communication, on the tactile telling that happens through the constant contact of the father's right hand holding the boy's left. The boy is so much quieter than before, and it is this quietness which pushes the father farthest, extending their search past the sterile operating theaters, the sick-crowded wards, all the way into the true depths of the hospital.

Only occasionally does the boy's curiosity return, and it is then that he asks questions the father is not prepared to answer.

The son asks, How much longer will we have to walk?

Or, How will we know when we find what we are looking for?

Or, How did the hero know, if he couldn't see through the dark?

The father answers these questions the best he can, because he long ago promised the boy that he would never lie to him, that he would always try to tell him the truth. He made both of these promises, but he knows he did not mean exactly the same by each one, knows that to keep one promise he might have to break the other.

What the father doesn't tell the boy is what he knows already, without ever having finished the book: the hero never found what he was looking for, but let it find him instead. That is the reason to keep moving. They must make it easy for what trails the boy to track them, so that they might face it together.

Sometimes, while they are camped in his room, the boy crawls out of his bed and into the tent the father sleeps in, pitched upon the linoleum. Curling into his father's arms, the boy says, Tell me again what my mother was like.

The father says, She was very beautiful. She was tall and strong and brave and she loved you very much.

He says, Your mother was everything that was good in this world. Before you were born, she was the reason I existed.

The boy says, And now you're the reason for me. You and mom.

Every time the boy says this, the father takes the boy's hands in his, then brings the boy's hands to his mouth, so that even in the dark the boy can touch his thin smile, can feel how happy his words make the father. He moves the boy's hands to his eyes, so the boy can feel how sad the idea of the boy dying makes the father.

Word of the father and the boy spreads fast until the doctors and nurses learn to leave them alone, to allow the father and the boy their private fantasy by ignoring their too-warm dress, their backpacks and compasses. The patients take longer to adjust, plus new ones are always coming in. The boy obeys the father's commands to ignore these others, no matter how strongly they try to make themselves known. The father knows it is hardest for the boy when the curious party is a child, when the future ghost is a little boy or girl of the same age. This is when the father must be like steel, must speak sharp as a blade. He will protect the boy from those who would love him only to leave him again. The other children in the ward have come to die. The boy does not need to know their names, does not need to join them in play before they go. It would only make it worse when he later recognizes their failed immune systems, their lowered blood-cell counts, their assembled tumors arrayed in their too-small chests like trapped treasures.

It's in this hall that the father first smells the beast, as he watches the orderlies roll a sheet-covered gurney down into the chambers below the hospital, the cold steel rooms where the dead are kept waiting in the dark until they can be claimed.

The mother had not died right away, despite what the father had told the boy.

What the father had told the boy was that the mother had fallen down, that after she fell the father drove her to the hospital, where she passed away. But she hadn't, at least not right then.

The doctors explained that a blood vessel had burst in her head, that it could have happened anytime. That probably the problem had been there since she was a little girl, waiting to end her.

The doctors told the father they could keep her alive, but she would never wake up again.

The father considered the doctors' speeches imploring him to let her go, and then he refused their advice. He didn't care how many machines it took or how many tubes had to run in and out of her body. He wanted her to live and live and live, no matter what.

While the mother was in the hospital, the father sometimes left the boy at home by himself, crying in his crib, so that he could be with the mother a little longer. It was wrong, he knew, but his wife was dying and the boy was not, and in those days the father loved the mother more than the boy, who was still an infant.

It wasn't even a choice between them, not then, when he had just met the boy.

The nurses taught the father how to help care for the mother, how to work her arms and legs and neck so that her muscles would not atrophy. Moving her body because she could not do it herself, it was a way to stay close to her, to touch her in a way that others would understand. They did not like the way he had touched her when he first came to the hospital, like she was still his wife, like she was still a living person who might one day again return his affections.

Sometimes he had put his fingers in her mouth and made her face look at him in ways he recognized, made her lips and teeth and tongue say the last words he wished she would say.

Afterward, when the father returned home, he would always find the boy wrapped in his blankets, sound asleep in his crib, as if the boy didn't need him. He knew it wasn't true—knew that a baby needed to be touched and loved and cared for—but watching the boy sleep so contentedly made it easy for the father to lie to himself, at least until after the mother was gone.

The father and the boy discover a room where men and women in white coats take tubes of blood and spin them in centrifuges to find out what is wrong with their patients' bodies, to discover what kind of dying the blood has in it. They watch these technicians use small plastic containers of urine and feces to separate the patients into those who are going to die now and those who won't die until later.

While they watch, the father wonders what is done with the spent samples, wonders how long they are stored after the tests are run. Is there still blood from the mother there? Samples of her tissues? Is there still a vial full of whatever they took from the boy's spine, whatever it was that might have told the doctors how he is going to die?

What the father wonders is if he could save the boy by putting all of it back inside him.

Before the doctors ran their tests, the boy had been sick. Now they have his blood and tissue and spinal fluid, and now he is going to die.

The father and the boy stare through the windows into the lab until the boy grows bored. The boy asks, What we're looking for, it's not in there, is it?

The father shakes his head. No. There are pieces of it there, but then there are pieces of it everywhere. He bends down and puts a big chalk x on the floor. He knows it won't remain when they return, that it will be wiped clean by the hospital's frustratingly thorough janitorial staff. He hopes just making it will be enough to remind him that they should never come this way again.

The father's watch doesn't break, not exactly, but it no longer tells any kind of time the father knows. Dates flicker across the digital display, offering days that have long passed, days that have never come. The father unsnaps it, shoves it into his pocket. The father's compass fails next, its needle claiming every point as north, every path as equally right or wrong.

At night, the father reads by flashlight until the batteries die, until the flashlight itself stops working no matter how many times the batteries are replaced.

As his instruments cease functioning, the father leaves them behind, hides them on the lips of lounge windows or underneath waiting-room tables, a trail of failed technology leading nowhere, marking neither the way forward nor the way back, offering only the fact that once he and the boy had been there.

When they again cross over the path, the father tries not to let the boy see, but of course the boy is close to him and knows what he knows.

The father leads the boy down more hallways, up more stairs, around more corners. Every day they walk as far as they're able, with the father keeping to the wall and the boy keeping to the father. Outside the hospital it is winter now. The temperature inside the hospital remains unchanged, but the boy complains he can't stay warm. The father dresses himself and the boy in more layers, each of them walking in coat and gloves. At night they sleep in their clothes, curled together in the bed or in the tent, depending on who joins who in the darkness.

Sometimes, the father has to help the boy when he goes

to the bathroom. The boy is not that young anymore, but sometimes he is still that little. They're both going bald together, both wrinkling around the mouth and eyes. For a little longer, the father and the boy will appear the same age, a man and his homunculus, and then the balance will shift and the boy will start to fail faster than the father. The father already feels his own creaks, fits of arthritis and shortness of breath. He doesn't want to see the same in the boy, but he knows he will, and soon.

Soon, he thinks, and then, now, here it is.

The next part of the book is occasionally annotated in the mother's thin handwriting. In the margins, the father finds her comments on the follies of the girl, on the heroics of the boy. On the nature of what awaited them both.

She wrote, *But* labyrinth *and* maze *are not synonyms. A maze is something you can get lost in, full of turns and dead ends, while a labyrinth will always lead you to the center, if only you walk far enough.*

She wrote, *At the center of the labyrinth is the beast, and if the beast does not devour you, then all it takes to return home is a decisive turn: back, away, upward.*

At breakfast and lunch and dinner, the father and the boy eat the jerky and then the dehydrated soup and then the granola. They eat the dried apricots and banana chips and the whole box of raisins. They eat the trail mix and the thin chocolate bars the father has been saving for something special. They eat until the father's teeth begin to feel loose in his mouth, his skin achy and sore. Scurvy, he thinks, or some other sort of malnutrition. He checks the boy for similar signs while he sleeps, but the boy's skin is harder to inspect. The boy is pocked with liver spots and varicose veins, his hairline receding, leaving a horseshoe of brittle white hair.

One morning, the boy stops walking and says, I think it's my birthday.

The boy says, I'm ten years old now, and the father nods without speaking, without meeting the boy's eyes.

The boy says, We don't even know where we are or where we're going. Every night we end up in the same stupid place, no matter how far we walk.

He says, Shouldn't you take me to a hospital already?

The father is alarmed but says nothing, just keeps pulling the boy forward along the wall. They're both too tired to talk more, too cold or too hungry to argue. When the boy stops eating, then the father stops too, and still they do not die. The boy takes his pills, and the father takes nothing. They go on, and they go through, and they go up, up every staircase they can find.

The next morning, the father, continuing to read past the pages he has given the boy to know, reaches the middle of the book, the chamber of words waiting there.

The father reads the words within, and then the father turns the page.

And then the father turns the next page.

And then the father turns another and another and another another another.

And then what? What can the father do, what can he possibly think to do, if there is nothing else written, if the rest of the book is just blank, hundreds of empty pages stretching from the center to the back cover, to the far edge of all the story he meant to tell the boy? What then?

That night the father awakens to the sound of the boy moving around the room. By the time he gets out of his tent, the boy has made it to the window, where he stands hunched over, one hand pressed to the small of his back, the other parting the blinds to reveal the parking lot lights, glowing below the window's height, and then the pouring rain. The father moves to the boy slowly. It has been a long time since they have seen outside the hospital, since the father has allowed their wanderings to take them to the outer walls of the building, where the boy might see for himself.

The father puts his hands on the boy's tiny shoulders, feels bones meeting skin without the interference of muscle or fat. He wants to turn the boy, to see the expression on his face, but instead he watches the window, as rapt with wonder as the boy.

The father has heard rain in the past few months but not seen it.

He has forgotten how beautiful the weather can be, falling in shattered sheets against thick panes of glass.

While they watch together, lightning flashes, and then the parking lot lamps snap off, all at once. Seconds later, the lights inside the room go as well.

Now there is only the rain and the darkness and the boy and the father.

Now there is only the boy turning, trying to say

something, but unable at first to produce the words, to find the voice to bring them to air.

Eventually the boy wheezes, says, I'm so cold.

And scared. I'm cold and scared.

The father says, We have to go. We have to go right now.

Outside the boy's room, the father finds the darkness disorienting, despite months of treating the hospital's fluorescent halls as the pitched passageways of a labyrinth. He puts his hand to the wall like before, but this time it is out of necessity rather than imagination. It is dark now, darker than anywhere either the father or the boy have been in months, and yet not as dark as it might have been: Everywhere he looks he sees the glowing chalk marks of their long passages, xs everywhere, and it is only with all other light sources extinguished that the father begins to see— begins to imagine, he tries to tell himself—that the boy himself glows, his bones alight beneath his skin.

The boy touches his hands to each other, covering up the glow of one with the glow of the other. He touches his face and his eyes and his nose, all his features flickering in the dark, and then he sits down on the floor of the hallway. He slips his backpack off his shoulders and lets it fall beside him.

The boy says, I'm too tired to go walking.

He says, Dad, I think I'm ready, and then the father feels it, coming fast now, charging down the empty hallway toward them.

The thing comes not for him but for the boy.

The father says, Stand, and when the boy cannot, the

father steps forward on his own, into the way of this thing rushing forward, intent on hurting all that is his to protect.

Even through the black, the father can smell it coming.

The smell, it is worse than what the father expected, because it is not death.

Not death at all but great vibrant life, the thing's belly gorged with everything that the father and the boy have already lost together, everything they still stand to lose.

The smell is enough to cause the father to falter. His heart seizes in his chest, numbs his left arm, the left side of his face, then restarts. The father's vision swims and when it clears there is only the darkened hallway stretching in front and behind. There is only the boy, still sitting at the father's feet. The boy's glimmer streams from him now, smokes bright from his mouth and nose. It fills the father's vision, all sparks.

The father says, Get up.

He says, Please. Please get up.

The boy tries, but he is too weak to stand without the father's help. When the father lifts the boy into his arms, he feels how terribly light his body is now, how the boy's body is almost nothing but light.

The boy opens his mouth to speak, but all the father hears is the glimmer, and the father thinks, What am I possibly supposed to say to that? What words for when there are no words?

Back, away, or else upward, he tells the boy.

Back, away, or else upward, the best part of a book where the boy never heard the end.

The father carries the boy down the hall, toward the

door marked EXIT, marked STAIRS. He climbs the spiral of the stairs one slow step at a time, trying not to look down, not to see the end of the world trapped in the boy's eyes.

The father lifts his boy up and up and up, and then his boy dies in his arms, and then the father lifts him still.

The father opens the door onto the rooftop, carries the boy out into the rain, into the vastness of the outside world they'd once known. At the center of the roof, the father lays the boy down, then arranges his arms and legs against his lean body, shutters his tiny eyelids over his tiny eyes. The father looks to the sky, then to the falling water washing the boy's face clean, then to the open doorway leading back to the staircase, where again he sees the mother.

The father says, Please. Tell me what to do.

He says, Help me, but the mother only shakes her head, toes the threshold of the door. Whatever is left of her is still caught up in the hospital, trapped in the wasted vials, in the hallways the father knows he made too much of because he did not know what else to do.

To the mother, the father says, I loved you too. More than him, for too long.

It was a mistake, he says, but I can't pay for it, not again.

I can't let him be trapped here too.

The mother looks behind her, into the spiral of stairs, then back at the father. She opens her mouth and says to the father the words he put there with his own fingers, all those years ago, the words he most needed to hear the day he last made her mouth move, the last day he visited her, words that could bring to an end any good story, no matter how many blank pages remain.

With her permission, it is easy to do what he has to do, to hold on by letting go.

The father takes the boy's shirt in his fists, tears it to expose the thin chest, the hollowed skin. He spreads his own fingers across the boy's sternum, he closes his eyes.

He thinks: How a hospital can be a labyrinth if only you look at it right. How he looked at it right. How he and his son, they looked at it right together.

A labyrinth can be solved, but afterward there's nothing to do but walk back out again, nothing to gain but whatever treasure you had when you began.

With his fingertips digging into the boy's flesh, the father pushes until the skin opens like parchment, giving way to the hidden body within—but he exposes no dead machinery, no ribs and lungs, no liver or stomach, no heart, as much as he knows there must have been a heart.

All there is inside the boy is light, all hot and bright and white, thick and wet where he scoops it with his hands.

The father hurries now. Time is short and he knows he must get all of it out. He lifts up whole handfuls of light, the heat blistering his fingers and palms, and then he throws each handful into the air, each new clump floating, spiraling upward to follow the last.

When the father finishes, he turns back to the doorway, to the stairway. The mother is gone. Soon some doctor or nurse or security guard will appear in her place, having seen the father carrying the boy through the dark confusion of the hospital. Alone still, the father stands and waits, puts his burned left fist over his shattering chest. The pain radiates farther now, numbing half his body. He stumbles, then regains his feet, stands his ground. Overhead, the lights he took from within the boy lift and swirl and coalesce in the dark, become great globes, glassy spheres floating higher, refracting the falling rain. As he raises his head to watch them dance across the sky, defying the storm, he feels his own heart beat, then blare, then blast open, he imagines his shell emptying of the story he told the boy, losing the pages he memorized from the book the mother left him to read, forgetting the way out of the maze it trapped them all in together.

Without the mother and the boy, eventually the father's real life must resume, and what story will he tell then about who he is?

The name *father* taken from him. The name *husband* longer gone.

The man he is instead wants to ask, *What next*, but there is no one to ask, not until the doctors and the nurses arrive. Alone on the rooftop, he remembers his home, the home where he and the boy lived after his wife, where he and his wife lived before the boy. When the doctors and nurses are done with him, he leaves the hospital, goes there again. *What next*. Alone he unlocks the doors, alone he unboards the windows, alone he knows will live every inch of his remaining life in these silent rooms where he's already lived so many other louder days. He is quiet in the empty house, but often he feels he wants to speak, that he would speak if only there was someone to speak to. *What next*. Sometimes he thinks he is dying too, but he knows he is not. *What next*. He will live, *what next*, he will live — and this is what this man's selfish heart has always feared most of all, not the loss but the life after, the future outside the maze, the forever of *what next*, the terrible freedom of the last survivor.

Acknowledgments

A number of the stories in *A Tree or a Person or a Wall* were first collected in slightly different form in two earlier volumes, *How They Were Found* from Keyhole Press and *Cataclysm Baby* from Mud Luscious Press, thanks to publishers Peter Cole and J.A. Tyler. Thanks also to the many editors who first published these stories in their magazines, at *Alice Blue, American Short Fiction, Annalemma, Anthillo, Artvoice, Caketrain, Conjunctions, Everyday Genius, FANZINE, Gargoyle, Guernica, Gulf Coast, Hayden's Ferry Review, JMWW, Keyhole, kill author, Knee-Jerk, The Literary Review, The Lifted Brow, Meridian, Ninth Letter, No Colony, PANK, Poor Claudia, Puerto del Sol, Redivider, Sleepingfish, Storyglossia, TripleQuick Fiction, Unstuck, Wigleaf, Willow Springs*, and *Wrong Tree Review*.

My continued gratitude goes to my amazing team at Soho Press: Janine Agro, Meredith Barnes, Juliet Grames, Amara Hoshijo, Abby Koski, Rachel Kowal, Rudy Martinez, Kevin Murphy, and Paul Oliver, and especially my editor Mark Doten and my publisher Bronwen Hruska. It's a rare pleasure to have published multiple books with such talented and enthusiastic people, and I'm grateful as always for their unceasing championing of my fiction.

Thank you also to my agent Kirby Kim, for his invaluable advice and advocacy; to my copyeditor Susan Bradanini Betz; to cover designer Kapo Ng; to my friends at Bowling Green State University, who years ago read many of these stories in their first drafts; and to Northern Michigan University and Arizona State University, for the time and resources I received to finish the most recent stories collected here.

As always, I owe so much to my wife and partner Jessica, for her talent and her wit, for her love and her friendship, which together make every good thing possible.